SUITCASE BOOKS

The Curry Mile

A novel by Zahid Hussain

ISBN 1-905778-00-7

Suitcase books are published by
Shorelines: info@shorelines.org.uk

Suitcase books are distributed by Turnaround Publisher Services Ltd,
Unit 3, Olympia Trading Estate, Coburg Rd, Wood Green, London N22
6TZ.

Cover design by Ian Bobb (07799137492)
Printed by LPPS Ltd, 128 Northampton Rd, Wellingborough, NN8 3PJ

British Library Cataloguing in Publication Data. A catalogue record for
this book is available from the British Library.

To My Mother

Early Reviews of The Curry Mile

Desi-culture Manc-style: Zahid Hussain's The Curry Mile is a fascinating glimpse into life in Bombay mix Britain.
Mark Sullivan, award winning playwright, author

A fresh and lively account of contemporary British Asian life which lifts the lid on the fierce rivalry and fiery family sagas behind Manchester's beloved Curry Mile.
Cath Staincliffe, author, Blue Murder TV series originator

Revealing and quirky. A chick flick cum chappati thriller: worth reading if only for the outrageous *jalfrezi* of Asian and English phrases.
Shamshad Khan, international poet

This is a revealing 'behind the scenes' look at living in the restaurant trade written with soul, exuberance and pathos. The Curry Mile tackles the issues of living in a multi religious, multi generational, materialistic society with singular panache and candour.
Qaisra Shahraz, author of *The Holy Woman* and *Typhoon*

The Curry Mile reminded me of Nobel Laureate Naguib Mahfouz's Cairo Trilogy: family feuds, infuriating fathers and a strong sense of place. Manchester: along the roads through the rain to the heart of the city.

Tom Palmer, author, literature activist

The depiction of the restaurant trade rings true - amidst the spicy emotions and boiling passions, it's a world viewed with tenderness and an eye for detail.

Dinesh Allirajah, poet and short story specialist, member, Asian Voices, Asian Lives

This novel offers something more than a comic take on restauranteurs vying for business and scrapping over the National Curry Awards. It's a shrewd study of cultural shape-shifters and their responses to the conflicting demands of age, faith and materialism. Essential reading.

Dr Corinne Fowler, Lancaster University, UK

1

Red lipstick on the coach window was the first thing Sorayah saw when she awoke. Fleetingly disoriented, she pulled out her headphones, rubbed her eyes and craned her neck. *Are we any closer to Manchester?* The M6 kept the remaining distance locked inside its tarmac heart. Vehicles flicked past. *Heading nowhere. Is this what it means to be coming home? Going from nowhere to nowhere?* She retrieved a tissue paper from her black leather jacket and wiped off the lipstick.

The coach was full of students returning home, faded women, old jangling men with their heads nodding like demented rocking chairs, burnt out mothers, fleeced out fathers and squealing, psyched-up children, high on food stimulants and confinement. Sourceless conversations mingled with tinny music rising from CD players, MP3 blasters and Walkmans.

Her gaze slipped back to the blurring motorway, searching for a light at the end of the tunnel of grey. *I should have stayed in London. Damn him, damn the bastard.*

She rummaged in her Gucci handbag and brought out her Nokia. Its envelope icon was flashing. *Another text from him.* She ignored it, returning the mobile to her tiny bag. She whispered a curse. It could only be from Ravinder. *Rav bloody cheating Rav.* There it was, a tight wedge of hatred so pure and hard you could build a city on it. She felt the tears clawing up through her throat, but they'd never reach the surface, never erupt. She possessed only ugly pitted memories.

A road sign appeared. MANCHESTER 26.

Two seats ahead she caught an Asian man turning around, trying to catch her eye. She turned back to the road, pulled on the headphones, and thumbed her Ipod to release the fusion synthetic tones of Rishi Rich. Then she closed her eyes, her long dark hair fell across her face and she expertly feigned sleep.

Imran saved me. Kept me sane. Sorayah still couldn't admit to Imran she'd been so deeply pagal in love with Ravinder she'd been blind to his blemishes. "My Dr Hrithik was a Mister Hyde," she'd confessed to her friends. *I owe Immy big time.*

She moved in with Imran a few days after leaving Ravinder. Imran insisted she take his bedroom. "I'll take the spare room, it's not as if I'm here anyway," he said. *The world wouldn't be the same without big brothers.* Guiltily, she took his room, promising herself it wasn't for keeps. The weeks became months, the months became her own private no-man's-land. Ravinder had soaked into her heart and she couldn't wring him out.

She had a deep jealous streak, and perhaps the relationship was doomed from their first kiss, with Ravinder being such a flirt. He was tall and slim and had muscles in all the right places. "Oh, they can't help themselves," he'd often say to her. "But it's you I love. Come on Sorayah, stop sulking." She'd fallen for him hook, line and stinker. *Why do I always go for the same flipping type? Why can't I just be a normal apnee and do the normal apna thing?*

She met Ravinder at Bombay Rouge, an Asian nightclub. He was dancing with his mates to a desi beat and she was mesmerised. She was drunk on Baccardi and Coke, new to London, trying to forget Manchester and never clearly remembered how they got talking, but two dates later she'd moved in with him. Her visits home became less frequent as their love blossomed. When holidays came she lied to her family that she had too much studying to do, and when the academic year ended she claimed she'd got a job.

"But you can come and work for me," suggested her father.

"I'm not into restaurants, Dad."

"But…"

"Abbu, I want to do something with my degree."

"Are you sure, my sweet?" her father pressed. Guilt marinated in her heart, but she closed her eyes and repeated the lie. *I'm not into restaurants.* She'd made up her mind: Ravinder was her future and the past didn't matter. She lied from day one that there was no phone in the flat to avoid Ravinder answering it. Her mum, dad and the rest of the family could contact her by mobile phone and the one occasion both parents were in London for a wedding, she'd had ample time to hide Ravinder's countless Manchester United T-shirts and other paraphernalia that patterned their shared lives.

In those days Imran was still studying medicine at the Royal Free. He always covered for her. "What am I gonna do?" Imran asked her. "Tell Mum and Dad about stuff that doesn't concern 'em? Nope, little sis, I've got better things to do. They'd probably blame me anyway – everyone shoots the messenger, you know. Bang bang – no thank you, ma'am!"

Sorayah's blissful subterfuge ended the day her dad met her boyfriend.

Once the shock of discovery had faded, Sorayah and Ravinder continued living a life close to perfect in modern multicultural Bombay-mix Britain. That he was a Hindu and she was a Muslim was irrelevant. The issue raised its head only when she daydreamed about how they'd bring up their children (she'd planned the number and the names and even the careers they'd have). She believed their love would conquer any divide.

Her favourite memory was the three weeks they spent on the Greek island of Lefkus at the end of her second year at North London University where she was reading Sociology. She remembered when Ravinder had eaten crayfish too quickly and almost choked to death. She'd laughed all the way to the hospital, winning puzzled glances from the paramedic and driver. Later, she'd regretted not snapping a picture of him stretched out in the rickety Greek ambulance.

During their second year together, their relationship had matured. They'd become a live-in couple and it was nirvana; watching 'Friends' with Ravinder, shopping with Ravinder, clubbing with Ravinder, walking in the local park with Ravinder…Ravinder was everywhere.

They had planned to go to the United States on holiday after she'd completed her degree, but she'd started a new job. The money her dad deposited in her bank account had dwindled and her absence from Manchester and the growing distance between herself and the family had made her a poor little rich girl for the first time in her life. Her heart was set on a life in academia. She wanted to save up for her Masters so began working for a small charity.

"I can't go with you. I've only just started working here. I'm on probation," she tried explaining to Ravinder.

"You did this on purpose, init, you didn't want to go with me, did you?"

"Honest, Rav. I didn't realise I wouldn't be able to

take any holidays. I can't go. We'll go later in the year."

"I fuckin' planned for this. Why don't you throw a bloody sicky?"

"What? For three weeks? Don't be ridiculous!"

"Why'd you bloody want to work anyway? Phone your old man and get him to send you some dosh. He's bloody rich enough."

"Don't talk about my dad like that. I want to earn the money myself. Don't you get it?"

"If you don't bloody want to go with me, somebody fuckin' else will!"

They'd broken up and two weeks later Ravinder went to the States with his best friend, Bobby. *That's when he probably started cheating on me. Maybe he'd always been cheating.*

While he was away she changed the locks. On his return Ravinder came round with flowers, fell on his knees and refused to leave until she opened the door and forgave him. She did. They picked up their relationship almost from where they'd left off, but it wasn't the same. She convinced herself the high of the early days had become the plateau of maturity, but in her heart of hearts she didn't believe it.

Nazia, an old friend from undergraduate days, informed her of Ravinder's treachery. Sorayah was at home watching 'Friends' Series Four while painting her nails black.

"He's with *her*," Nazia began.

"Who? What do you mean?"

"Rav's with that cow, Vinny." Vinny was a girl from Ravinder's Business Studies course. Vinny was Bollywood beautiful. Sorayah loathed being told by friends that she looked like Vinny. She'd often seen Vinny at parties and at friends' places over the years. She hated the way Vinny's eyes lingered on Ravinder, a little too long, a little too hard. Ravinder accused her of jealousy and she'd let it go. *I was jealous.*

"You still there?" Nazia asked.

"Yes. Maybe they're revising." *What a stupid thing to say!* "He's got his exams coming up," she heard herself say. *His finals for the third time.*

Sorayah heard Nazia sigh. She imagined her plump friend, mobile against her ear, making exasperated faces. Sorayah heard the sound of music in the background and guessed Nazia was in Rhubarb, a glitzy bar-cum-cabaret in Covent Garden, a favourite haunt of theirs famed for its coterie of jet-setting celebrities who rubbed shoulders with the natives before shooting off to exotic locations.

"I shouldn't tell you this, but…" Nazia paused, "…they're at the Bollywood Brasserie."

"He's meant to be revising." Her words sounded hollow even to herself. Warm tears fell down her face and she wiped them away angrily. *I'm going to tear that kutti's eyes out!*

"He's so bad to you, Sorayah, why can't you see it? You're beautiful, you can do better than him." And then the classic Nazia line. "There are tonnes of fish out there, why do you need a shark?" *There isn't anyone better than Rav. He loves me.* And there it was, the awful truth, the reality she'd been aware of, but had carefully avoided. Ravinderitis.

She simply had to know if Nazia was telling the truth, witness the truth even if it shattered her.

She cut the conversation short and raced to the nearest Tube station not caring to check her appearance. She took London's underground to Covent Garden from Holloway Tube Station changing once at King's Cross. She strode to the Bollywood Brasserie, an expensive Indian restaurant she'd visited once with Ravinder. She hadn't been impressed with the gaudy pink decoration and overdone karahis, but the chicken tikka was aromatic, sweet and tender. She remembered Ravinder saying he detested the place and never wanted to return. *He pretended he hated it so I'd never go there and discover him smooching with some time-pass.* She smiled grimly.

Was it chance that brought Vinny and Ravinder immediately into view through the windows of the Bollywood Brasserie, oblivious to everything around them? *It was kismet. I was meant to see them.* Ravinder was holding Vinny's hand across the table. They were laughing, sitting opposite each other. Ravinder was facing in Sorayah's direction, and she saw his eyes were filled with emotions that once belonged to her alone. Ravinder moved forward to kiss Vinny. Sorayah's stomach lurched. She yearned to claw out Ravinder's eyes, but she was powerless. As Ravinder's lips pressed down on Vinny's, Sorayah's hands clenched in fury. She hated Ravinder with a fierceness that took her by surprise and brought tears to her eyes. "But he loved me," she whispered. Her gaze was glued to the two lovers. It took a brutal blink to tear herself away.

The journey back was a blur. Later, she remembered stifling her tears as she approached Covent Garden Tube Station and roughly pushing through Japanese tourists, ignoring their smiling disapproval. She ran sobbing out of Holloway Road Tube Station. When she arrived at the flat, her fingers fumbled to get the key into the lock. It stubbornly refused to fit. She banged the door in helplessness and hit her head against it. The pain calmed her and steadied her hand. She inserted the key, turned the lock and threw open the door to a flat that reminded her of stagnation, death and betrayal. Something inside her broke.

Her mind swung into survival mode.

She washed her face in the bathroom sink and blew her nose. She dried her face. She phoned Nazia who sounded as if she was still in Rhubarb, but now the music was louder.

"Nazia," she said, "can I stay with you for a couple of days?" Her voice was a croak. Sorayah knew the word would be out within seconds of the phone call ending that she and Ravinder were history.

"Of course you can, darling. Did you see Rav and… ?"

"Yes. I saw him – I saw *them*," she paused. "Thanks Naz."

"You OK, sweetie?"

"I just need to pack some stuff and then I'll call a taxi. It'll take me a couple of hours."

"We can come over and pick you up if you like."

"No. I'll be alright. Honest."

"OK, we'll be home in about an hour. Come over when you're ready. If there's no answer when you ring the bell then call me on the mobi. Don't worry Sorayah, there's plenty more fish in the sea." *It's like she's happy she was right about Rav being a shark.*

After packing her bags, Sorayah felt an emptiness like she had vomited her guts out. *How long is this hangover going to last?*

She carefully cut up the holiday pictures of the three weeks they'd spent in Greece, in Ibiza, in Paris and the countless other places they'd visited. She ended with the photos she'd so lovingly kept in her purse. They were the hardest ones to cut. She gritted her teeth, pressed her lips tightly together and cut through the image of Ravinder, his arm draped around her shoulders.

She wrote the goodbye letter to him while sitting cross-legged on the bed. She didn't feel anything when she'd finished. She held the brown envelope in her hand; it was the only one in the drawer they'd kept for bills, a discarded Housing Benefit envelope. Then she ripped up the letter. *Why do I have to explain anything to him?* She put the pieces in her purse in case he unearthed them and pieced them together.

When she'd brought everything down to the entrance hall, she scanned her belongings. Three suitcases, a cardboard box filled with sociology textbooks and chick lit paperbacks. She clutched her Gucci bag like a talisman. She sat there, on the second step of the stairs and waited forever for the cab on that hot June night. It was a long wait. All her memories of Ravinder came to visit and they left scars. *It was meant to last forever.*

Ravinder had spoilt all her plans and now she was adrift, rudderless, lost.

When the taxi arrived, she quickly opened the door and pulled the suitcases out, anxious Ravinder might return at any moment. The cabby helped her with her luggage. It took both of them to get the cardboard box into the taxi boot. "Opening a library, sweetheart?" the cabbie quipped. She answered with silence. They drove off and Sorayah looked back at the flat which had been her London home for so long. *Don't think about him, don't think about him.* The cabby nattered on about meeting George Best, Gerry Halliwell, Madonna, Jose Mourinho and Mr Blobby. "Listen," she finally snapped, "I've just broken up with my boyfriend and I'd like some peace!"

"Oh. Right. Didn't know that. No." the cabby said.

They drove in silence for the rest of the journey.

The cabby helped her with the suitcases and cardboard box when she arrived at Nazia's. "Well, good luck," he said to her and she nodded. She stood looking up at the terraced house Nazia was sharing with friends. She wondered if she should have left her flat keys. She'd never need them again. *Why make life easier for Rav?* she smiled. That made her feel much better. She rang the doorbell.

She stayed two nights at Nazia's and then moved in with Imran.

It was hard to swallow her pride and Sorayah was choking. She'd made a solemn promise never to return to Manchester. *This wasn't meant to happen. I wasn't meant to come back.* Five long years in virtual exile, away from the place that was more home and haven than anyone could ever have wished and she'd left it. Even two days ago she'd been dithering.

She cursed herself for breaking her own promises.

Imran changed her mind. They were having breakfast: she was munching tasteless supermarket branded cornflakes and Imran was pottering about the flat getting ready for work.

"What you gonna do? I don't get you, little sister, Manchester's just bricks and mortar, how could it possibly bite you? My mate's got a cobra that'll bite you if you like. I know it's strange having a pet cobra, but it keeps him out of trouble. Anyway, it's your mate's wedding, right?"

"Get lost, freak," she'd replied.

"You're pouting again! You always do that when you

know you're wrong." He'd been saying that for years. She glared at Imran. She knew she couldn't miss her best friend's wedding, even if it complicated her life.

"OK. Maybe you're right."

"Maybe? Where's the maybe? I'm always right – even when I'm wrong!"

After she'd made up her mind to return to Manchester, she'd phoned the moneylender.

"I'll be arriving in Manchester later this week," she'd told him, speaking in Urdu.

"I knew you'd come."

"Our agreement still stands?" she'd pressed, loathing herself for begging.

"Of course. I don't break my promises."

The RDB rap Bhangra fusion tunes rocked Sorayah out of her daydreaming, reminding her of her urban desi roots. *Going home is like admitting you couldn't do it: live your own way, apna gora stylee.* She wondered if the bitterness she tasted was a symptom of failure in life, or the residue of lost love. She only had to close her eyes and everything would contract into a moment and she'd sense Ravinder's warmth next to her, hear the softness in his voice and if she turned she'd look into his eyes and she'd melt like a snowflake.

She blinked and the motorway winked back at her. She squinted. *I shouldn't have listened to Immy. What a fool I was. I'll make sure it's a hit and run.* Her mobile beeped twice. She didn't look. She knew the text message would be from Ravinder. *Rav flippin' Rav.* It amazed her that a year had already passed and he hadn't stopped chasing, trying to make it up to her like he did after returning from the United States. *Not this time, Rav. Not ever.*

2

Mere yaar, Killer Instinct, where are you? Ajmal Butt ground his teeth, furrowed his brow and straightened his red silk tie in the bathroom mirror. He stuck his tongue out. It looked pale in the sickly electric light. He thrust his tongue back with an audible click and clinically contemplated his reflection. These moments in front of the mirror laid the day's foundation. Ajmal Butt had calculated in his youth that the veneer of success was the most important thing for a businesswala. Come rain or thup, he would be ready to seize any opportunity. When he was a new entrepreneur, his Greek tailor advised him: "Never wear the same suit two days in a row; they lasting longer that way." Fourteen clones of the same black suit were stored in his large bedroom wardrobe. The current batch had endured more than five years. Soon, he would revisit his tailor to order the next batch. *One more year.*

He patted down his oiled hair and made a rapid prayer in his native Punjabi, "My Lord, keep my heart strong and make my enemies wither. And make me more successful today than yesterday. Ameen." He couldn't afford failure today, he'd arranged a crucial meeting with an old business associate and friend. Looking spotless could be the difference between victory, the realisation of the Holy Man's prophecy, or a return to the plague of nightmares.

He blinked his eyes forcefully in quick succession, but they remained groggy. With thick brown fingers he tried to pry the tiredness from his eyes. Fatigue clung like poultry dyed with haldi.

Last night had left him exhausted. Sleepless and restless, thoughts circled: slip, gully and point ready to catch him out. The impending business meeting fused with Sorayah's return from the dirty bowels of London. He'd always despised the capital, not least because his youngest brother settled there and established a successful hosiery business, a slap in Ajmal's face.

"Sorayah will be coming tomorrow," his wife informed him yesterday evening.

Ajmal had returned home to touch base before the evening shift, as per his normal routine. Often, his wife would be entertaining friends and relatives, but yesterday the house was silent as a mute. He'd already been informed that Sorayah was coming by Shazia, Shokat and Imran, who were concerned he might create a scene. *Why would I do that? She hasn't been back to her rightful home for years, why wouldn't I be happy to see her?* He feigned surprised when Mumtaz raised the issue of their daughter's arrival.

"Is she?" Ajmal pursed his lips. He hadn't seen his daughter for two long years, not since he'd met her boyfriend. *I should have snapped his legs off, but how could I? My little Sorayah.* The day he'd uncovered Sorayah's secret life he'd decided, while walking back to his car from his daughter's flat, that he'd never tell Mumtaz. He'd come close over the last two years, but he'd resisted. It didn't matter anyway as Mumtaz had always considered Sorayah to be a goree, the blame placed squarely at Ajmal's feet.

Months after Sorayah had gone bad, Mumtaz had resurrected her old complaint as anticipated. She moaned how Ajmal had brought dishonour onto the family by letting Sorayah do whatever she'd wanted. *Just like you spoiled our idiot son, Basharat.* Ajmal ignored her despite the guilt gnawing at his stomach, because he needed his food freshly cooked in the morning. *Besti is only besti if others know.* He'd finally tired of his wife's complaints and told her it was pointless staying in touch with a daughter who was too busy ignoring her family. To his surprise the complaints had stopped.

Yesterday evening as Mumtaz poured tea into his favourite porcelain cup Ajmal had been lost in a thoughtful silence. The cup had jarred a memory. It had been part of a set brought over by his eldest sister when she was visiting Manchester from Pakistan. The blue and white cup reminded him of a time before his children became rebellious.

"If you don't want her to stay here she can use the spare bedroom in Shazia's house. Ajmal?"

"No, it's okay," Ajmal replied. "She can stay here. Her room's still free, isn't it? Unless you've moved it when I wasn't here?" Mumtaz didn't respond to his jibe. She was always moving things around the house. Only his bedroom was spared her random obsession with home improvement.

Ajmal sipped the perfectly brewed Pakistani tea. "The Pir did a special prayer for Sorayah. He said she'd return and she has! You said to me that she was kharab and she'd brought besti on us, but look, she's coming home. What more do you want?"

His wife stared at him expressionlessly and slipped noiselessly back into the kitchen to get his pills.

Pir Syed Ismaeel Barakullah was the local Holy Man. He was the pulsating heart of a brand of Islam radiating peace and stability. Two years previously, Ajmal had rushed to Pir Barakullah on returning from the trip that had broken his heart. He'd gone to London to give his daughter a belated birthday present and offer her the opportunity to set up his first restaurant in London, something he'd never contemplated before. He'd reconciled that for whatever reason, his favourite child refused to return to Manchester and he yearned to reduce the gap that had grown between them. The gap had grown into a chasm. *Why can't Sorayah be more like Shazia?* Ajmal had kissed the Holy Man's hand and narrated the story of his wayward daughter.

"She has a jinn in her," the Pir had announced in Urdu laced with Pushto. "It will take much to rip the demon out of her. It's a powerful demon with ten heads and has a heart made of fire."

"What do you need from me? You can have anything you ask. Please, bring my daughter back to me."

The Pir looked into the distance, contemplating the infinite depths of the seven heavens. Then the old man had leaned close and whispered, "She will surely return to you. Her return is as inevitable as death." The Pir explained how Ajmal would drive the demon out and bring her back to be a perfect and dutiful child. Thousands of pounds and several amulets later Ajmal finally heard the good news. A week ago, his eldest and best-behaved child, Shazia, informed him that Sorayah would be coming home.

He should have felt the sharp tang of victory, secure in the knowledge that Sorayah was returning to him, but the moment had been snatched away. A late-night phone call revealed Sorayah's true reason for returning to Manchester. One of his many confidants on the Curry Mile, a source connected to Jafar Ali, disturbed his evening and ensured a sleepless night. "Ajmal Saab,

Jafar's been boasting that your daughter is coming to Manchester to attend his daughter's wedding." The spy's words drove a splinter into Ajmal's soul and sleep fled into the darkness of the night.

She's going to Jafar Ali's daughter's wedding. That kutti, Yasmeen. She finally comes home, and instead of respecting me she's going to do my besti again! He wanted to throw all the Pir's amulets into the River Medlock. *He promised she'd return, but at what cost!* He felt the same anger, horror and desperation he'd felt the day he'd seen for himself what his London confidants had been telling him. "Your girl is seeing a boy – he's not even a Muslim!" *I should have brought her back with me.* He'd momentarily lost his Killer Instinct.

Jafar was amongst Ajmal's greatest enemies. *He's always been itching to take my crown and he's laughing at me now.*

The restaurant trade was a cut-throat world with competitors copying designs, menus and décor and even poaching staff. If one restaurateur hired a magician, a neighbouring restaurant would hire two. Competition was fierce, but where Ajmal and Jafar jostled for position, it was at its fiercest. Their enmity was infamous on the Mile, and Ajmal's informants were eager to supply the information he craved most. Anything on Jafar Ali. Ajmal couldn't believe that they were once friends. *He was as close as my jugular vein. Why didn't Sorayah listen to me and end her friendship with the haramzada's daughter?* Ajmal had never understood his children's friendship with the Alis. *Why can't she grow out of her childish fancies?* With regret he realised he hadn't spoken to Sorayah for two years.

He was forced to rise from his bed in the middle of the night and puff an illicit cigarette in the bathroom.

He'd sat on the toilet seat lid and watched himself, bloodshot eyes showing more than he wished to reveal. The cigarette was ecstasy and his trembling fingers automatically sought a second before the first was consumed. His nicotine addiction had reawakened and sleep would be impossible without a second cigarette. He had worked long and hard to eradicate his addiction. *"Save my life," that bloody kanjar Dr Patel says.* He quit the habit for several months through a fog of suffering, but the dam had broken and each puff of heaven rejuvenated the addiction. Mumtaz would complain if she found out. *But she isn't going to.* A deodorant disguised the smell. The cigarettes dipped him into sleep, his nerves straightened for the remainder of the night. He dreamt nightmares. Later, he would recall a vision of his office collapsing on top of him and then his children, Sorayah, Imran, Basharat, Shokat and Shazia standing around him, looking down as if he were in a well of darkness, and he was looking up into their unnaturally bright faces and begging them to help him. But they were chatting amongst themselves and then the brightest light appeared in the corner of his eye until it grew into a beamer of a comet, falling straight at him, dazzling him awake.

Looking at himself in the mirror, Ajmal cranked up his famous megawatt smile, but it failed to light up. *Come on, Killer Instinct! I have to be ready for Abdullah!* He was certain Abdullah Shah would solve his financial predicament. He had a mental file the size of a country on each of his competitors and friends. He knew how Abdullah breathed, walked and slept, how much he was worth, how much he owed, to whom and most importantly, why. *If anyone can lend me the money to pay that scoundrel David Mirza, it's Abdullah Shah.* None of Ajmal's enemies inspired the fear David Mirza did. *It was a mistake to borrow the money from that haramzada in the first place. But what choice did I have?* The problem with dealing with the shaitaan was that he would soon call to collect. *Killer Instinct yaar, I'm going to need you today. Don't let me down again.* He would twist his friend's arm if needed; after all, that was the code of the jungle, survival of the fittest, Killer Instinct takes all.

He rehearsed the spiel he'd prepared for Abdullah. He calculated the different avenues his friend would take, practised the replies, weighed the endgames he'd require to conquer Abdullah. He licked his lips tasting the sweetness of victory. *I'm going to get him out for a golden duck.*

Satisfied with his plan, he carried out a few minutes of callisthenics as Doctor Patel had advised, gentle stretching exercises that seemed as useful to him as spitting at the North Sea wind. He was nearing his sixtieth year and Doctor Patel had never stopped telling him to take it easy. *How can I take it easy? How? That kutta doctor doesn't understand.* He was the proud owner of a dozen restaurants, six on Manchester's Curry Mile, and with his fingers in other businesses around the north-west and Yorkshire; he had a growing kingdom to govern.

Doctor Patel's remarks had begun innocently enough, "Don't eat so much, Ajmal Bhai. Take it easy on the oil," the Indian would say in Hindi. His words changed their tune to, "You must eat fresh fruit and vegetables every day." *What am I? A Hindu like you? I eat meat!* When he objected to the doctor's demands, he was vilified. "You're overweight Ajmal, your heart can't take it. You're not young any more." *I've got the heart of a lion, I can do anything. I'm an all-rounder.* When the doctor told him, "You'll have to stop smoking, Ajmal", that was the hardest thing. *I have a jungle to rule, laws to lay down. My job continues twenty-four hours a day. I have hundreds of employees, kutta. I make more in one week than you do in a year.*

He relented despite his wounded pride. Doctor Patel cajoled him into seeing specialists who prescribed him 'magic' pills for high blood pressure and cholesterol that he dutifully took around the clock. He felt the medication had dulled his Killer Instinct, a sixth sense honed over decades that kept his creditors, competitors and family in check. He practised one more smile before putting on his black blazer, then he left the bathroom and trudged downstairs. On opening the living room door, he was assailed by the pungent aroma of breakfast. His mouth watered. His restaurants were renowned for the exquisite sensations they aroused, but nothing matched his wife's cooking. Mumtaz was making parata and his favourite morning snack, fried andey with onions, chillies and of course, garam masala, his very own recipe. His expert nose picked out the individual spices; cinnamon, cardamom, cloves, coriander, cumin, ginger, chili pepper, garlic.

He sat down in his armchair. Impatiently, he waited for Mumtaz to bring him breakfast, food fresh as a newborn baby.

Ajmal nodded to himself as he ate, his mouth enjoying the layered textures and tastes. He paused for a moment to touch the amulet around his neck. Inside the black cotton square pouch were selected verses of the Quran, protecting him from the Evil Eye, protecting his business and shielding him from the Angel of Death. *Thank God for Pir Barakullah.*

After breakfast, he checked the Ceefax business pages. He didn't understand the list of figures, but he enjoyed the feeling of belonging to the wider business fraternity. The text blurred as he dropped into a brief doze, the caffeine losing against the tide of tiredness. He resurfaced when his wife brought in another cup of tea.

"Mumtaz, what time is Shazia picking *her* up?"

"I think she said this afternoon."

"Achchha."

Mumtaz returned to the kitchen. Soon Ajmal would give Shokat a ring. His eldest son was the de facto operational manager of the restaurants and he'd be up already, ensuring the delivery of meat to the Manchester fleet of restaurants, the infamous mid-week drop. Shokat surprised him by finding the cheapest prices in the strangest places. *And he doesn't even have the Killer Instinct.*

To Ajmal's regret, none of his sons, Shokat, Imran or Basharat, had the Killer Instinct. *Basharat has a drop of it, but it's all used for the wrong things.* Although Ajmal felt he'd been carrying the bat alone for more than twenty years, he was reluctant to declare knowing none of his sons would come to the crease. Despite disappointing him with his spinelessness, Ajmal had always been glad Shokat had followed him into the trade. Shokat was a good son, loyal and hard-working, a perfect twelfth man. Ajmal trusted his eldest completely, but he was as placid as English sheep.

Imran was a doctor and lived in London. He was his cleverest child, but Ajmal felt he'd never understood

Imran. Ajmal sent his middle son to Manchester Grammar School and it had been (mostly) worth it. Ajmal boasted about Imran to friends and family and called him "puthar doctor". The big English words Imran used made Ajmal feel lost. He wished he'd spoken more Punjabi with his children. *They wouldn't be so westernised now.*

He swore to himself when he thought of Basharat. He was the youngest and a vagabond. Whenever he was in an evil temper he'd say to Mumtaz, "What kind of a son did you give me? He's useless, absolutely useless! You should have strangled him at birth." He wondered if the midwife had made a mistake and given him the offspring of a jatt, either in ignorance or as punishment. His youngest child never did an ounce of work and spent all day racing cars and chasing girls. "Couldn't you have given me a girl instead?" he shouted at Mumtaz each time Basharat got into serious trouble. Last Eid his son was arrested for getting into a fight on the Curry Mile. Ajmal had used his connections with the Greater Manchester Police to get him out. It was severely embarrassing and damaging for Ajmal's reputation, but a few phone calls to the local papers ensured the story never leaked. *But a son is still worth a thousand daughters. Daughters are good as long as they behave, but if they go bad then…* he didn't want to think about that. Such thoughts inevitably led to Sorayah.

Only Shazia had lived up to his expectations. She married the man he ordered her to and she delivered a grandson every couple of years like clockwork.

His children were a growing disappointment. *Who'll take over once I'm gone? There's nobody. All my life's work will sink into quicksand after I'm in my Kabrr.* He'd pretended to himself that his time on planet Earth would go on and on for forever like 'Eastenders'. His fears had become acute over the last few months. Thoughts of mortality brought an acrid taste to his mouth. He quickly drowned his anxiety in a mouthful of hot tea. He snapped up an old copy of the Daily Jang, the Urdu daily, and began to re-read it. The tiny Urdu script jiggled before his eyes, eluding final understanding, tormenting him with implied importance. He kept reading.

As he collected his briefcase in the hallway, he went over the coming day in his head. He felt a surge of anticipation in his loins as he thought of Sameena, his secretary. His reflections turned darker as he exited the house and noticed a dent on the passenger door of his Mercedes. *Bloody Basharat.* He suspected his son had bumped into it when parking his BMW in the dead hours of the night. He walked around the car, carefully inspecting every inch of it. There was a scratch on the back bumper. *I'll pull the donkey's ears off when I see him.*

He got into the car and reversed onto Wilbraham Road. A passing car almost hit him. He swore under his breath and thrust a finger in the air. Smiling, he began the journey to his largest and flashiest restaurant, the Kohinoor. It was the HQ for his restaurant empire. The Kohinoor was the rock around his neck, drowning him in debt. *Killer Instinct, come to me, come to me.*

He went through the day's programme. *Correspondence, followed by Abdullah Shah. Then some more tea, followed by Rusholme Council.* Business would begin picking up at the Kohinoor after lunch and he'd be with the punters, oiling his audience. He'd finish in the early hours of the morning and hopefully, at some point, he'd have secured the finances to repay David Mirza. In the afternoon he might meet Sorayah. *If she has the courage to show her face.*

He switched on the CD player and listened to the Sufi sounds of Nusrat Fateh Ali Khan. 'Meri Ankhon Ko Bakhshe Hain Aansoo' greeted him, exactly where he'd left it. It was set to repeat. Ten minutes later, he arrived at his flagship restaurant. As he stepped out of the car he rummaged for his mobile phone. He hissed. He'd left it at home. Cursing, he hurried to the back door of the Kohinoor and opened it wide. The screaming head chef welcomed him in.

3

National Express coach 540 – London to Manchester – arrived at Chorlton Street Station at precisely 12:41. *Flipping Manchester. I hope it's worth it.*

Yasmeen Ali was Sorayah's friend for keeps. When their fathers fell out, the girls' friendship survived in secret. Then Sorayah was transformed into a bad kuri overnight and nobody wanted to touch her, see her or speak to her. Yasmeen was the only Mancunian friend to visit.

"We've always been best friends," Yasmeen assured her. "We always will be."

"Do you think I'm bad?" she'd asked.

Yasmeen hadn't hesitated. "No. Course not! I'm jealous!"

Now Yasmeen was going to marry a doctor from London, a distant cousin. Clan ranked high amongst the restaurant tribes of Manchester. Yasmeen emailed Sorayah pictures of Raheem, her fiancé. Sorayah thought he was cute. *How could I not return to Manchester for Yasmeen's wedding? I'd be betraying her. I can't let her down.* She imagined Yasmeen arrayed in a red wedding dress, glowing hennaed hands, head bowed, yellow-gold jewellery glittering beneath the studio lights of an Asian wedding hall. Friends surrounding Yasmeen and wedding music filling the hall, drowning out the rumble of voices. Tears welled in Sorayah's eyes. *How could I miss that? I'm going to make sure Yaz has the best possible wedding.*

Familiar sights appeared – the Siemens Building, Southern Cemetery, Hulme Arch, the Mancunian Way. She remembered the day she'd left Manchester. She'd felt the same trepidation, confusion and hope. For a moment, she was lost. DJ Chino brought her back, effervescent Asian beats bringing her blood to the boil. *Has nothing changed? Am I still the same British-born confused Desi?*

Her cheek was pressed against the cold window of the coach and she watched the people hurrying and scurrying.

It felt surreal being in Manchester. She'd avoided thinking about coming home. She'd always been good at avoiding the inevitable. *I did it with Rav. Don't I ever learn?* She feared how her family would react. *Will they throw me out?* She anticipated the ferocious argument her mother would launch into on seeing her.

Shokat, the eldest, had told her not to worry. "I've spoken to Mum and Dad," he'd said in his slow deep voice. "They aren't going to say anything to you, kasam." Shokat rarely made promises and when he said 'kasam' it was usually for keeps.

Her eldest brother had never been talkative and phone calls were often punctuated with long silences. *He's still under Dad's thumb. He'll never be free. The perfect protective big bro and he isn't even his own man.* She felt guilty. Shokat was good to everyone and respected for his down-to-earth approach. *He's the backbone of the Butt restaurant empire, but nobody knows.* As much as she trusted Shokat, she doubted if he'd had any effect on their mother.

Basharat was the black sheep of the family. He'd been so cute as a baby. As a kid he'd entertained everyone with his antics and his infectious laughter, but teenage hormones mutated him from sweet to sour. Bash, as everyone called him, was always getting into trouble. Sorayah loved her desi beats and despised

Basharat's gangster rap drone.

She wondered if her jeans and tight 'CrushedOnU' top fitted into Manchester's more traditional Asian climate. *They can take me as I am or not at all.* She drew her long black leather coat tighter around herself as if trying to hide from watchful Asian eyes. *Anyway, I'll be out like a shot straight after Yasmeen's wedding. Of course, Mum will have a field day, cussing me for wearing tight kapre and Shazia too.* But she didn't care. Sorayah almost snorted in derision. *Mum doesn't live in the real world. She lives in the glory of the Butt clan welcoming the endless queues of arse-lickers. And Baji Shazia lives in her own world.*

If Shokat had pacified any of her parents, it would be her abbu. Even if her father had stopped talking to her, she was his favourite. But the day he had knocked on her flat door remained the saddest in her life, the moment frozen in her heart. She remembered answering the doorbell, expecting one of her university friends. Instead she'd found her abbu at the doorstep. Then Ravinder had appeared behind her, undressed. She'd looked at her father, seen the shock hit him. Her abbu hadn't said a thing. But the expression in his eyes had broken her heart. He'd left the presents he'd brought at the door and walked slowly away. They hadn't spoken since.

She ached to go back to how things once were. She felt guilty for rejecting her father's requests to work for him. The business flowed in her veins, she felt more at home in a restaurant than anywhere else, but she'd turned her back on Manchester. Finally, her family had turned its back on her.

Sorayah pulled out her Antler bag from the luggage rack and followed the stragglers to retrieve her well-worn Samsonite suitcase from the coach's luggage compartment.

Outside, she could hear it and smell it above the noise of the city before she finally saw it. Rain.

I shouldn't have borrowed the money from Uncle Jafar. Her predicament had begun one Friday evening at the Southall Spice Palace. All the London posse were there: Nazia, Rubeena, Priya, Kulbinder, Anita, Aminah and Tanzeela. Friday nights were kicked off at the Southhall Spice Palace. Despite Sorayah's official aversion to anything reminiscent of Indian restaurants, the Palace had become their den. They fed there before hitting the night scene. The best thing about the Palace was that it was a man-free zone. No boyfriends allowed.

As they stumbled into the Palace, Sorayah diligently observed the décor, the seating arrangement, the colours, the dirty napkins, the grey couples and groups of women and men, peeking, ogling and rubbernecking. The Palace wasn't in the league of some of her abbu's restaurants, but it harboured one thing the girls loved: a fat and hairy owner named Varinder Singh who kept up a frightening stream of invective for his workers, but who had only words of welcome for guests.

Varinder singled her out as she entered. "Ah, Sorayah!"

"Hi, Uncle Singh." She turned to the girls. Smiles were pasted on their faces. "What's going on?" Sorayah asked the posse, "Guys, what have you done this time?" She noticed people being turned away at the door by one of Varinder's workers.

"Sorayah, my Sorayah," Varinder rumbled, "today is special, my friends, your friends, han ji, have told me it is a special day for you so I'm doing the works, init, han ji."

"Can't you guess, darling?" Nazia asked. "We thought you deserved a treat to help you get over that idiot, Rav."

"You booked the Palace for me?" Tears came to her eyes and she hugged her friends fiercely. Somebody turned up the music and when she looked up she recognised friends from university coming in from the kitchen. "Well," Sorayah said, bemused, "let's party."

A table had been beautifully laid out. They all waited for Sorayah to sit down. She took her time.

"Hurry up, darling!" Nazia cried, "we're starving!" The girls laughed.

It was past midnight when her friends began to depart. Sorayah stayed until virtually everyone had left. She was light-headed, stuffed and satisfied. She spotted Varinder sitting at one of the tables. He looked drained.

"Thanks for letting us book the place."

"Anything for you, sohniye," he replied, looking distant.

"What's the matter, Uncle?" she asked.

"Nothing, han ji, nothing that I can't deal with, init."

"Money problems?" she enquired.

He looked sharply up at her.

The posse had been regulars at the Palace for over three years and it had always been full. She didn't understand how it could be facing money problems.

"My father passed away last year and I have to go back to sort everything out. I haven't got the means, init, to hire people or trust them to carry it on for me. I got to get money to hire extra staff, init. My family's depending on me."

"Have you thought of selling?"

Varinder jumped to his feet. "I know you don't mean to insult me, han ji, but this place is my life. I'm not selling her to nobody. Anyway, I don't like any of them."

"Who don't you like?"

"The insects who want to take away what I built here, init. It took me twenty years, twenty years to build this thing up, there was nothing here once. And now it's a matter of honour, you know, izzat."

His passion for the business reminded Sorayah of her father. She pecked him on the check, said goodbye, but she'd couldn't ignore his problem. As she was getting into the taxi she stopped.

"Hold on a moment," she told Nazia, "I need to thank Varinder." She ran back inside and found him mopping his brow.

"Did you forget something, sohniye?" he asked.

"No, no, I thought that I could," she hesitated, "I could maybe help you out with your restaurant."

Varinder looked surprised. "No puttar, it's not an easy life and I need people with money, init. You're all students. Not to offend you, but it's a tough life and most of you like partying, which is nice sometime, but it isn't real life."

Crestfallen, Sorayah nodded. She touched him on the shoulder. *What was I thinking? Where would I get that sort of money anyway?* If she'd been under better terms with her abbu she would have had the money the next day. She rushed through the rain and into the taxi.

The following morning she was woken by voices coming from the kitchen.

"Immy!" she hissed. She had a pulsating headache. She crawled out of bed, ready to give him a roasting. As she neared the kitchen she vaguely remembered Imran telling her that there would be visitors in the morning. She returned to her room, made herself respectable, before traipsing into the kitchen. Uncle Jafar and his son, Javed, were chatting with Imran. Javed and Imran were going on holiday that weekend and Uncle Jafar had come to drop Javed off. They stopped talking when Sorayah entered.

"How are you, daughter?" Uncle Jafar asked in Urdu.

"I'm fine," she replied in Urdu. She felt self-conscious. She managed to sit down without falling over. Imran kindly poured her a cup of coffee and passed her a sugar bowl.

"Toast?" he asked. She shook her head.

"What you up to these days?" Javed asked brightly.

A drum was beating in Sorayah's temples. She tried not to squint. "Just between jobs."

"How come you're not working with your father in his business?" Uncle Jafar asked.

"I wasn't that interested in the restaurant business."

Imran pushed back his chair. "Jav, give us a hand with the suitcase. I can't get it to shut." Imran and Javed left Jafar Ali and Sorayah Butt together. She felt betrayed by Imran.

"Really? You're not interested in the restaurant trade? That's not the Sorayah I remember. You have the trade in your blood, daughter. Even more than your father."

"Maybe. But who'd take a chance on me, eh?" She felt reckless, irritated. "You need money for restaurants."

"Oh money is easy to get hold of, but getting hold of the right people isn't that easy. You should know. You could always come and work for me."

Sorayah almost choked on her cornflakes. Silence stretched between them. She sipped the coffee and tried to ignore Uncle Jafar.

"I can tell that you're interested in the business. You're like my own Yasmeen to me. If you want to try out a restaurant idea, I can spare some loose change. More than your father would."

She munched on her cornflakes briefly pondering the possibility of helping out Varinder or perhaps even buying The Palace from him. *The girls would love that!*

"Listen, daughter, I've known you as long as I've known my Yasmeen. The business is in your blood. If you want some money to start up your own business, I can help you."

It was tempting. Jafar's eyes bored into her. "Let me think about it."

His eyes flashed. Jafar fished inside his shirwani suit and brought out a golden business card. *Flippin' cheesy.* She took it and scanned the mobile number.

She rejected the idea as soon as she'd put the card down next to the bowl, but over the next few days she couldn't stop thinking about it.

A week later they met at a café near Covent Garden.

"I'm glad you saw sense, daughter," Jafar Ali said in Urdu.

Sorayah nodded, still not trusting him. She switched to English. "Tell me one thing."

"Yes, of course, daughter."

"You promise never to tell my father."

"I promise."

"And I never have to come to Manchester?"

"Why would I need you to come? And just to be clear, Varinder doesn't owe me, you do."

They solemnly shook hands. He drank tea and she drank black coffee. It rained all that day and the day after. Sorayah had helped Uncle Singh save his life's work, putting herself in debt.

"My own daughter wouldn't have done this for me," Varinder had wept. "Sohniye, you and your friends can have a meal here free every time you come."

Reluctantly, Sorayah stepped down from the coach and into the crowd of milling passengers. She weighed up returning immediately to London. *Come on Sorayah, you can do it.* She elbowed past people and tapped the coach driver on the shoulder. "My suitcase, the black one." On retrieving her suitcase, she stood in the chaos of Chorlton Street Bus Station, the street famous for coaches and infamous for prostitutes. *What do I say to Baji Shazia? I can't just ignore the past.*

When she first moved to London she returned home monthly. Sometimes Shokat would pick her up and sometimes Shazia. Abbu never came; he was too busy with the business. He wouldn't leave the business even if one of the children were dying. It was one of those things that the Butt family accepted, like the rising and setting of the sun. Abbu always denied it when she accused him, "the only thing you care about is that stupid title, Curry King!" She was the only one who dared say it to him. 'Curry King', that's what the north-west papers called him. The *Manchester Evening News* coined the title in the heyday of Indian restaurants, much to Sorayah's regret. In 1999, her father had a clipping of an MEN article framed at the entrance to all his restaurants. 'Curry King Brings In The Millennium.' It showed him receiving a community award from

Prince Charles. Sorayah was so embarrassed. Ajmal sent a dozen original newspaper cut-outs to VIPs and, Paijaan Shokat had told her, abbu had thousands of photocopies ready for clients and customers.

When she was a child there'd been no difference between the family and the business. In fact, she spent more time with abbu and the business than at home with her toys.

One world became two after her abbu broke his friendship with Uncle Jafar. Her father claimed he'd discovered Bilal snooping in his office over ten years ago, "spying for that bastard, Jafar Ali." Sorayah longed to go back to the way things were when Yasmeen lived as much in Sorayah's home as she did in her own. Her father never stopped telling his stories about how the Ali clan was out to bring his restaurant empire down. "Don't you see," he'd cry, "the Alis are trying to make me crumble, but I'm a fighter, I've got the Killer Instinct. That's how I know."

"Paijaan!" Sorayah shouted, seeing Shokat. He was wet from the rain and carefully making his way though the crowd.

"How are you?" Shokat asked. He hugged her, surprising her. Shokat had never been the touchy feely type. "I had to come and see you. It's not every day a long-lost sister comes home. I told you everything would be alright when you got home."

Sorayah nodded. "I'm finding it hard to believe I'm here."

"Let me give you a hand with your luggage – you don't have anything to worry about. You're still my little sister."

Sorayah nodded dumbly. She was relieved to see him expertly handle the suitcase Imran had huffed and puffed to get in and out of his Mini.

"I'm really glad you're back, Sorayah. Things have been, you know, hard."

"What's happened? Is everything OK? How are things with you Paijaan? How's Pabhi? How are the kids?" They made their way through the crowd.

"Everything's alright, I suppose."

"Has some'at happened?"

"You know. Life."

"Life?" Shokat could be pretty deep sometimes. They stepped into the rain and Shokat bundled her luggage into the boot. Sorayah briefly noted the number plate. BUTT2. *That just says it all.* Their dad retained BUTT1. Shokat didn't say anything until they got into the car. *It's such a shame that abbu doesn't take him seriously.* Without Shokat the business would collapse within days. Their father was the face, the living embodiment of the Butt curry empire. Shokat was the behind-the-scenes guy. Shokat complained how Abba constantly interfered with his decisions. Friends and foes alike acknowledged Shokat's ability to price every dish to meet the shifting demands of the market. He instinctively knew how much a prawn karahi should cost, if chicken dopiaza should be on offer or if the popadoms should be free. It was an instinct honed through years of working on the Curry Mile. In fact, the reason their father had won the National Curry Awards more times than anyone else was because of Shokat.

"Dad lets me set the prices now for the Kashmir, Maharajah and Curry Wala and those restaurants have been busy all summer even when the students were out

44

of town. But the Kohinoor's in trouble." The Kohinoor was the biggest, boldest and proudest achievement of her father's to date. "It only picked up since last week when the uni students began drifting back into town. I can't understand abbaji's thinking when it comes to pricing the dishes in the Kohinoor. I should put my foot down."

"But you won't," Sorayah said. Shokat nodded.

"Bushra's really stressed out at the moment. She suspects me of trying to get off with every woman in the universe. She just doesn't believe me when I tell her I have to stay behind late sometimes for work." Shokat laughed. "Would you believe, someone tried to get me to leave abbaji and go and work for him."

"Really?" The competition was fierce on the Mile and Sorayah could imagine others wanting what Ajmal Butt had: Shokat Butt.

Her brother pulled the car out into the rain.

"Yeah, it was a few months ago. You know Bilal? He works for Uncle Jafar. He rang me and said he had an offer I couldn't refuse. He rang me so often I eventually gave in and guess what? He offered me like a quarter of a million straight up to set up a restaurant. But it would be in partnership with Uncle Jafar, you know, Imran's dad."

Sorayah felt a splinter turn in her heart. *What if abbu finds out I've taken money from Uncle Jafar? What if the stories abbu used to tell us about him were actually true?* She couldn't believe Yasmeen's father would stoop so low. Many years ago Bilal, who now worked for Uncle Jafar, worked for Ajmal Butt. *Could the story actually be true?*

"Guess what?" continued Shokat. "Bilal even turned up at my house, he actually came and spoke to Bushra, can you believe it? Now he's got her head filled with money ideas and setting myself up in business. She says abbaji should retire and leave me the restaurants, but he won't cos he's too stubborn. She reckons I should go in with Uncle Jafar. She's doing my head in."

"So what have you decided?" *What would her brother think if he knew I'd borrowed money from Uncle Jafar?*

"I told him to get lost."

"I think you did the right thing," then changing the subject quickly she asked, "By the way, how come Baji didn't come to pick me up? Not that I mind you coming," she said, smiling.

"Nobody wants to talk about it, but Baji Shazia's going through trouble at home. Don't let her know I told you that. She'd kill me."

"Baj?"

"Yeah. I think that her and Ahmed aren't seeing eye to eye."

"Oh my God," she blurted, then, "Where we going?"

"Can't you guess?" replied Shokat grinning.

It took only a few moments before the answer sprung to her lips. "Rusholme."

Sorayah leaned forward, her worries forgotten. She yearned to flit through the intervening streets and walk the Curry Mile again. The journey was accompanied by the sounds of seventies' Indian movie songs playing on the car radio. Shokat nudged the car southwards towards Oxford Road and hit the early afternoon Manchester traffic. The streets were filled with students and commuters. Sorayah had heard Manchester University and UMIST were merging into one university.

Even before they hit Wilmslow Road, she spied her

first Abdul's Takeaway of the day. It was one of several Abduls eateries on the Mile. There were four at the last count. She couldn't help grinning. *Only in Manchester.* Then out of the traffic of Oxford Road rode the princes of Wilmslow Road, neon crowns dimmed by daylight. Sorayah knew them all. They chanted their names to her: Sanam, Sangam, Shere Khan, Tabbak, Hanaant, Royal Naz, Tandoori Kitchen, Shezan, Lal Haweli, Lal Qila, Dildar, Darbar, Kashmir, Maharajah, Curry Wala and the Spice Hut. She used to write their names in her diary when she was a child. These were old friends. And there were new ones. There was Marble Arch, a blast from London, Ali Baba's, Jaffa. *When did the Mile turn Arab! Flipping hell, I can shisha in Manchester!* The Asians of Wilmslow Road built an empire in Manchester, but Sorayah saw the emergence of a new tribe within Manchester's curry district. *It's become more like London.* Once, she knew it so well she could shut her eyes and name each restaurant, each shop, tell you where every bus stop, lamp post, bank and petrol station was. This was where her father would bring her as a child. She hung out with friends showing off her father's empire. She spent and lost her kidhood here. She knew many people who worked on the Curry Mile, from Haji Khan to Katie Doyle in Kwik Save. It brought tears to her eyes.

When Sorayah was born her father owned one restaurant.: the Lazeez on Wilmslow Road. It was the beginning of the rise of curry restaurants. It would take another decade before Mancunians began calling it the Curry Mile. The family now owned six restaurants in Rusholme and from recent news gathered through the family grapevine, the Butt curry empire stood at twelve.

Of course, if abbu had listened to her he'd have had hundreds of restaurants.

Sorayah learnt to cook in her father's restaurants. She absorbed how to balance a ledger, order meat, hire workers, all this before she could even write properly. And she used to spend weeks away from home with her father when he was setting up restaurants outside Manchester. She'd witnessed first-hand one of her father's few failures. On hearing about the success of the Mumtaz in Bradford, her father decided to set his own equivalent in the Yorkshire city. That was his first restaurant outside Manchester and for two years he'd poured energy and money down the drain. She'd spent two weeks living in a rented house with her abbu while he struggled to get the restaurant on its feet. She'd loved those times, but she'd experienced the dark side of the business, the long hours, the frustration and the heartache. Her father sold the Golden Chapatti to a local tradesman. Abbu returned two years after that episode and this time the venture was a success, but he didn't take Sorayah with him the second time. Her mother forced abbu to leave her behind, because she was struggling at school.

As they hit the Curry Mile, Sorayah saw it. The Kohinoor. It was the Eiffel Tower of Wilmslow Road, twice as large as any other restaurant. 'Kohinoor' was emblazoned in unlit neon blue between the first and second floors. The twin marble pillars were as tall as the building.

The Kohinoor was inspired by an idea Sorayah had when she was a teenager and even three years after its opening, it remained unsurpassed. She felt the stirrings of pride; a warm tingling that left her giddy, empty and full at the same time. It was one of those 'wow' moments Nazia was always telling her about. *I wish Naz could see this!* She realised with a start she'd hardly mentioned her family business to her London friends. It seemed seedy and backward, like driving taxis or working in a mill. It wasn't the high status job Asians hankered for; her abbu wasn't a doctor, a lawyer or a teacher. She looked away from the Kohinoor, pride smothered by shame.

It fell into place then, how Pakistani Manchester was. London pulsated to a different Asian rhythm. From Edgware Road to Green Street, Southall and all the other boroughs and districts in and around the capital, there was a greater Indian or Bangladeshi influence. Here life was more earthy, more alive. With the growing number of Arab boutiques, takeaways and restaurants springing up on the Mile she could see the glimmer of London's Marble Arch rising above the skyline.

"It's really changed," Sorayah murmured.

"It looks different every day. New people come. The old change. Even Sanam. It's being refurbished."

"Sanam's having a facelift? That, I can't believe!"

Then Sorayah saw the local grocery shop, Haji Khan's. She felt a pang of nostalgia. Haji Khan used to give her sweets as a child and even as a teenager.

"You okay, Sorayah?"

"Yeah, I'm fine."

"You looked a little lost then."

"I was, but now I'm found," she said. *I've come home.* She'd never thought about it before, but home was always Rusholme. *Home is where the dil is* – something the RDB might say. Most of her closest and dearest friends were connected with the Mile. She grew up with

Yasmeen Ali whose father owned his fair share of restaurants and also with the Khans, particularly Kareema Khan, Haji Khan's granddaughter. She was now living in Abu Dhabi married to a Pakistani civil engineer.

They continued driving down Wilmslow Road. *I left all this for London.* She felt a twinge of regret. When she left Manchester, she wanted it for good. She'd broken up with Haroon, her childhood sweetheart, she'd dreamt of London's sultry lights and they beckoned to her winsome heart. If she'd stayed, it would have meant an arranged marriage, seeing the same old faces, same old places, and now she'd come full circle.

"Have you missed Manchester?" Shokat asked.

She lied. "I've been too busy to miss anything." She gazed back at the restaurants.

"You were away for so long, I missed you, you know," Shokat said. Sorayah wanted to say she missed him too, but couldn't find the words. *I stayed away cos of what Baji Shazia said to me. You guys didn't want to know me and now you're telling me you missed me.*

As they neared home Sorayah's thoughts turned to meeting her mother. She guessed Basharat would be asleep or perhaps he never returned home last night. Abbu would be at work. *Why didn't Immy listen and come back with me? I don't think I can do this by myself.*

She wanted to tell Shokat to take her back to the coach station, but it was too late. *I can imagine what ammi will say when she sees me.* She'd run the dialogues in her head so many times they were as worn as her favourite Levi's jeans. In her mind's eye she saw her mother, hands clenched and gaudy yellow gold bracelets shaking with indignation, "How could you return to this house?

You're a naked white girl, get out, get out of here! Go back to your effeminate boyfriend. Whore!" The acid bubbled in her stomach. They turned at the final traffic lights. The family home was only a few metres ahead, hidden from view by an oak tree.

"Mum's been up since early this morning getting ready for you," Shokat informed her. "She even rang me to make sure I wouldn't be late in picking you up."

She couldn't believe it. She'd never got on with her mother.

"She's cooked your favourite, lamb curry and carrot halwa."

Her mother had never made anything for her. Suspicion reared its ugly head. *She probably thinks I'll agree to marry the first mangatar she puts in front of me. No thanks. No mangoes for Saz.*

"Does Dad know that I'm going to Yasmeen's wedding?" Sorayah asked.

"You know Dad, he always knows everything that's going on."

Sorayah sighed.

"Have you got clothes for the wedding?" Shokat asked.

"No, not yet. I brought some stuff with me from London, but I'm hoping to get some new clothes this week. I'll check out some of those places on Wilmslow Road. There's always Longsight and Cheetham Hill."

They pulled into the four-car driveway of the family home. Basharat's bright red BMW was parked in front of the garage. Sorayah looked in dread at the familiar front door. She heard Shokat get out and make his way to the back of the car. She sat frozen in the passenger seat. A shape formed behind the smoked glass of the front door. Ammi! She threw open the passenger door, breaking a nail in her haste. She winced and sucked her finger. *Who said coming home was painless?* She stood before the front door of the house she grew up in, breath frozen in her throat, bag clutched, mobile phone inside ready to be pulled out in case of emergency. It began to rain again, cold fat droplets bringing her home at the fastest speed in the universe: the speed of memory.

4

Ajmal Butt's hands were trembling. Abdullah Shah would spot any quiver behind his thick black spectacles. *Where will I be then? My friend will eat me alive. Abdullah won't lend me a single paisa if there's any doubt I can't repay him.* Thirty years of friendship would be discarded. A bad taste rose in his throat and he pressed his hands on the desk to steady himself. He itched to loosen his belt and free his gut, his tie was strangling him, but he couldn't. The telephone rang. Ajmal snatched up the phone. "I told you I didn't want to be disturbed," he snapped in Punjabi.

"I'm sorry Ajmal!" moaned Sameena Choudhry, further annoying him with her squeaky voice and by replying in English. He always spoke to her in Punjabi and despite regular rebukes she never replied in the mother tongue. "But I have a message from Mister Shah." Sameena lapsed into silence.

He paused, letting her wallow in discomfort. "OK, tell me what he said."

"He rang to say he'll be a bit late."

"Late! How can he be late! This is a very important meeting." Ajmal's words disintegrated into curses. "Haramzada, kutta…! Finally he hissed, "How late is the scoundrel going to be?"

"He said he'd be about half-an-hour late." Then she asked, "Do you want some tea?"

Sameena made a lovely cup of tea, not the filthy watery English chaa, but the soothing nectar that refreshed his immigrant lips.

"Okay, bring me some tea, but do it quickly." He'd broken out in a sweat. He wiped his forehead with a dirty handkerchief. He took out a small round mirror from the desk drawer. He was pleased with his dyed black hair, no grey showing. He jerked his wide face from side to side and practised looks of sincerity and concern. He smiled, showing all his teeth. "Good," he muttered in English.

He took out his black filofax from his briefcase, placed it on the desk and began drumming his fingers on it, impatiently waiting for the tea. He enjoyed impressing people by showing them how full his filofax was. He loved it when people said: "You're so busy, Ajmal Saab, you're so successful." Lately, the only entries were his appointments with Doctor Patel.

He squeezed his eyes shut. When he opened them, he had a vision of Manchester through the window: the grey streets, grey sky, grey people. *Where did all the colour go?* Only the marble pillars on either side of the office window showed any vitality.

England was a total shock to him when he first arrived in 1967. The early years were hard, but he worked day and night, using his considerable guile to amass enough money to hire a stall in Longsight Market. He scrimped and saved and then with money begged and borrowed from relatives he took a huge risk. He bought his first restaurant on Wilmslow Road. He'd been amongst the vanguard foreseeing the potential of the restaurant trade. He'd earned the title of 'Curry King' by working tirelessly, a name he intended to keep no matter the cost.

At the height of his fame, he owned twenty restaurants in northern England. *Everyone knew my name.* He'd appeared on countless documentaries and loved to talk about how curry was "allowing everyone to come closer." *That's total bakwaas, but the goray love to hear it.* His apna food fed the masses and cost mere pennies to make. Regretfully, the profits he'd made on bottled water in the eighties was a money-making opportunity never to be repeated. *It was all good before bloody apne stopped taxiing and started up restaurants instead. The kutte always know a good thing when they sniff it.* Over the years, his favourite sobriquet, Curry King, had became a potent phrase allowing him entry into places and pockets he normally would not have reached. *Until now.*

He cursed Abdullah Shah, simultaneously hoping the ageing factory owner would lever him out of his dire predicament.

He once owned eight restaurants on the Mile, but he had been forced to sell two due to the haemorrhaging of cash. Losing Rangeela, one of his first curry houses, had prompted him to take the gamble of his life. He wanted to create the Titanic of all restaurants. All his friends, even Dilawar, had advised him against it. He ignored them. *I'm a businessman and by God I have to take risks!* It took three years to raise enough capital for his flagship and he'd lost three more restaurants in those terrible years, one swallowed up by the Kohinoor itself. One disaster followed another and with his back against the wall he was introduced to David Mirza.

Sameena had been in London to arrange visas for new restaurant workers with the aid of a brilliant immigration lawyer named Waseem Azad. Sameena met David Mirza in Waseem Azad's Ealing waiting room. On her return, She advised Ajmal, "David's a very rich businessman and he's looking to invest his money. I don't think he'll turn you down – your name is known everywhere. Do you want me to give him a call and find out if he's interested in meeting you?" It made sense that a London entrepreneur with no links to Manchester would be more amenable to filling the hole in his finances. *But it was too easy.* Since the Kohinoor's doors had opened, money had been sucked out of his fifteen bank accounts as if a giant vacuum cleaner were sucking money into financial oblivion. A timely benefactor was a sign of providence.

"Yes! Tell him to call me," he commanded Sameena. "But make sure you keep him sweet so he doesn't ask too many questions about the business."

The Asian entrepreneur's telephone call six months ago had changed his life for the better. Or so he'd thought at the time. *What a stupid mistake I made.* Ajmal travelled to London to the Indian's large detached home in Hounslow and was impressed with the smartly dressed middle-aged man. He thought he was dealing with a consummate gentleman – like himself. He would have taken Sameena with him, but she couldn't find a babysitter for her six-year-old.

"I'll pay you back within six months," he promised David.

"Of course you will. You're a decent businessman. I can trust you to keep your word," the Indian replied handing him a glass of whisky.

Within a day Ajmal had received a black briefcase at his London hotel. In hindsight, his desperation, the unending supply of whisky and the brazen Asian woman that David Mirza provided that evening had been his doom. He couldn't remember the name of the young Pakistani woman who accompanied him to his hotel, nor what she looked like. *The fiendish Indian was so clever!* He had been confident he'd repay the Indian before the six-month deadline expired. *How could I be such an idiot!* Within two months, he discovered he was trapped in a cage wrought by his own hands. He'd made a monumental Mancunian mistake: he'd forgotten most students left in the summer. The six months in which he'd promised to return the money had become a life sentence. And it was impossible to procure additional loans: every window was barred, every door was locked and someone had thrown away the cha-bee.

"You haramzadi, you got me into this mess," he accused Sameena. Sameena's weeping and endless apologies finally convinced him that meeting David had simply been bad kismet.

In his calmer moments he realised there was only one solution. To sell the Kohinoor. But he'd never sell it. *Izzat di gal hai.* He continued seeking prospective lenders through his contacts. Only one person was willing to loan him the money he needed, the one man he'd never deal with: Mohammed Jafar Ali. *Let earth and heaven become one, but I will never do business with that stinking khanzir.*

Sameena carried in the tea on a metal tray. Ajmal heard the sound of music behind her. Asian Sound Radio. He tolerated her listening to the Asian radio station as he occasionally got to hear a song by Mohammed Rafi. He liked Rafi, because he was an Indian Muslim and had the voice of an angel. He told his friends that all the best Indian actors and singers were Muslims. Imran once asked him, "Is that a good thing, Dad?" Imran was very intelligent, but sometimes he couldn't see the jungle for the trees. Imran even asked him if he'd consider allowing Sameena to run one of his restaurants. *Stupid boy! How can a woman run a restaurant? It's a man's game. Only men have the Killer Instinct.*

Sameena back-heeled the door shut. She walked over to the desk and placed the tray on his desk without stumbling. She poured a fresh cup of tea from the dented metal teapot and placed it in front of Ajmal. She dutifully added three sweetener pills and stirred for precisely ten seconds whilst humming a tune. She placed the spoon noisily on the tray.

"Ajmal," she said, "are you okay?" She walked round behind him and Ajmal closed his eyes as her familiar hands worked magic on his shoulders and neck. He pushed her hands away.

"Are you feeling nervous about the meeting?"

"I'm fine," he replied in Punjabi, "just tell me when Abdullah arrives and then I want you to bring in some more tea. I don't want you taking minutes today. There won't be any need."

Sameena took the tray and walked across the room, mesmerising Ajmal with her swaying hips. It amazed him how he never tired of her.

She closed the door behind her and moments later he saw her sit down at her desk reading a magazine. Ajmal watched her closely through the window set in the wall at the end of the office. He let out an involuntary *mashallah*. Sameena's heaving bosom was a welcome respite from the travails of running the business. He boasted about her charms to his closest friends, after all "every successful businessman needs ways to relax, han ji?" As most of his friends were of a like mind they slapped him on the back and begged him to bring her with him next time he visited them. He promised to, but never did. *A lion doesn't share.*

He remembered the first thrilling year when he used

her domestic difficulties to procure delightful favours from the twenty-eight-year-old. He barely gave her time to heal from her marriage to a Pakistani import, the type of mangatar who hankers for the mother country and loathes England. Her husband had returned to Pakistan dumping her with a young girl, no money and the dishonour of divorce. *Thank God for the baradri system.* They reached a comfortable status quo where his occasional physical demands on her were not too much to cause her undue anxiety. She never complained. *How many men would have been kind enough to give a job to an apni divorce? No, I have been more than generous; she owes me her body and soul.* His friends agreed whole-heartedly and their lives were filled with the clicking sounds from the high-heels of divorced Asian women marching in and out of their offices, taxis and shops. *Mashallah.*

Sameena was the kind of woman most Asian parents had nightmares about. She was nothing like Ajmal's eldest daughter, Shazia. Shazia was the perfect dutiful daughter every Asian home should have, but who would soon join the dodo. Nowadays, apnes had daughters like Sameena, caught in the lifeless land between one culture and another. Of course, that never halted him from sampling the wares of the new culture while simultaneously cursing it and expounding the beauty of the old.

Sameena had worked well for him for three years and he couldn't imagine a day without her. He trusted Sameena with his deepest secrets and she was a wily negotiator. And her bosom – he dreamt of it. He licked his lips, but they remained as dry as the Sindhi desert.

Ajmal blew across the top of the steaming tea and took his first sip. He savoured the pungent mix of tea brewed to perfection. The little gas stove he'd bought for the office was priceless. With the cup warming his hands, he walked over to the window overlooking Wilmslow Road. He looked down and watched the traffic, people walking, talking, standing, white, black, Asian.

The Kohinoor was located at the extreme end of the core restaurant area of the Mile. Directly opposite the Kohinoor was Jafar's restaurant, the Shaandaar. His dushman's restaurant looked shabby in comparison to his. Ajmal smiled grimly. His accountant of twenty-seven years, Ghani Bhai, urged him to stop donating huge sums to the mosque. "It's a question of honour," he told Ghani in Urdu. Ajmal believed he was destined to have ten houses in paradise with luscious gardens, where virgins would make him nectar-like tea. He believed he was promised such an elevated rank in heaven because he'd regularly donated money to the mosque for three decades: he'd funded extension after extension, new carpets, painting, lighting, heating bills and teachers. *And the Pir promised me I'm destined for Paradise.* Sadly, influence had grown more expensive to buy. *My Lord, why are you punishing me?* Worse, Jafar Ali was now the treasurer of the mosque committee and had made record contributions for the last four years, lashes of humiliation to Ajmal. *Where does the khanzir get the money from?* Ajmal felt God was trying him for his sins. At such moments he considered firing Sameena, selling his business and donating all the money to charity. Such moments were thankfully rare.

He ambled back to his chair. He wanted to drift into a perfect place where he'd be free from worries, but peace was as likely as a Bollywood movie without a playback song. *All I need is enough to pay David Mirza back and then I'll be done with him forever.* Failure filled Ajmal with dread and part of the fear was that he was tiring, that he was an old zakhmi lion, that he was the last man standing and nobody would keep his memory alive. When he was angry he swore at Shokat and just to prove Ajmal's point the boneless child said, "ach-cha abbaji." Ajmal sighed. He always wanted tigers, instead he had pussy cats.

The tall and cadaverous Abdullah Shah arrived two and half hours late, and without a drop of apology on his lips. Ajmal was angry and flayed Abdullah Shah with a thousand gaalz, but all were lodged silent and seething in Ajmal's heart. Abdullah sat in the leather chair on the other side of Ajmal's desk, occasionally tugging his thick grey beard, his long legs crossed, cupped hands placed in his lap. Two cups of tea sat in front of the men, steam floating between them. Thankfully, Abdullah hadn't paid any attention to Sameena's scandalous clothes. That would have been a bad start to the meeting. Sameena had left them alone to talk business and taken the tray with her.

Both men spoke in Punjabi.

"I understand the problems you're facing," began the tall man and Ajmal winced. He felt as though he had been punched in the stomach. *The kutta's not going to give me the money.*

Ajmal tried not to frown. He opened his arms in a universal gesture. "It's been a difficult few years with competition and everything," he said.

"Yes, we've all tasted the competition," interrupted Abdullah, laughing gently, peering closely at Ajmal from behind thick rimmed spectacles. His eyes were pinpricks of darkness. "By God, I would like to help you, but I simply can't. I have too many burdens."

Nobody does anything in the name of God! Ajmal mistrusted anybody claiming to work for a Higher Purpose. Despite Ajmal's membership of the mosque committee and praying the five prescribed prayers on schedule, it was all done to bolster his claim to his position in the community. People were always watching. Clean shaven and impeccably dressed in high-quality Western suits, Ajmal was considered an upright and successful apna businessman. The local Asian press printed his photo in every edition as a mark of his standing. Bile rose in his throat at the thought of Abdullah Shah playing with him and rage threatened to engulf him.

"Abdullah Bhai," Ajmal hated himself for begging. "I only need the money for a very short period of time." His voice trailed off as he realised he'd been close to shouting. In his peripheral vision he could see Sameena looking in his direction.

"I understand," Abdullah said, pursing his lips and looking sympathetic.

Damn you to hell! I'll kill you! You'll burn in the lowest level of dozakh for eternity!

"If I had the money I would give it to you, but I don't. I have my daughter's wedding in two months and you know how it is, the dowry, the hall, the cards."

Ajmal lost interest and patience as Abdullah explained how his wonderful graduate daughter would be wedded to his brother's son, equally successful, a doctor of impeccable moral character and who was Canadian by nationality. *Why are you telling me all this? Just tell me yes or no, you donkey.* Ajmal took a slow deep breath. *Killer Instinct, where are you?.*

He looked at his friend straight in the eye. "Abdullah Bhai," he said interrupting the flow of his friend's little speech, "We are close friends, aren't we?"

"Yes."

"We go back a long way. Don't we?"

"Yes?"

"We are businessmen, two of the best – you are certainly a better businessman than I could ever be," *that's it, flattery!* "I've often admired you from afar and I've learned much of what I know from you." Ajmal caught a fleeting smile on Abdullah's face. "We live tough lives, you probably have a hundred different burdens. I've often wondered how you achieve so much!"

"I do what God allows me to do, everything is thanks to Him."

"Do you remember seven years ago when you came to me for money for your factory that burnt down?"

"Yes, but I was desperate, my situation was terrible, the insurers wouldn't pay. But I paid you back after a year, didn't I?" Ajmal smiled inwardly. *He's losing his cool. Good.* When Abdullah Shah's factory burnt Ajmal had saved him from disaster. The debt of gratitude remained.

Ajmal smiled magnanimously. "Yes, you did pay me. And I trusted you at a time when all my other friends said, 'Don't give him the money, his business is in ruins. How can he pay you back?' Abdullah, I'm not asking for a gift, I'm asking for a loan and I will repay and unlike your situation of seven years ago I have a thriving business, but I need a little fuel injection to grow a little faster."

Abdullah appeared to be mulling this over, forcefully tugging his beard. *I'm almost there. One little more push is all it'll take.* Of course, his friends had made no comment at the time, because none of them had known he was loaning money to Abdullah Shah.

"However, I understand your pressures and if you're unable to help me at this delicate stage I have other friends who can help, so it isn't too bad. You know, I can go and see Tariq Imtiaz. Yes, he's quite helpful."

Abdullah's hand stopped pulling his beard, his eyes huge behind his glasses. *Yes, you old donkey, I know all about Tariq Imtiaz and his drug money and I know all about your connection with him.* Ajmal's informants had provided a killer piece of information about one of the most respected Asian businessmen in Manchester. Abdullah Shah was involved with drug money, perhaps not directly, but he was certainly dealing with Tariq Imtiaz, one of the biggest and craftiest businessmen in the UK and by introducing him into the conversation, Ajmal had subtly informed Abdullah that he knew his secret. Abdullah worked for Tariq.

Abdullah blinked rapidly.

"But we're friends, and it's better to deal with one's friends than find new ones who you can never be sure about." Ajmal controlled his laughter. *Almost there, come on, take the bait, take it!* He forced himself to keep his face impassive. *Abdullah will probably go to Tariq to get the money for me in order for me not to spill the beans!*

"OK, my brother, my friend," Abdullah said sighing, and then flashed a quick smile. "My hands are tied, but I think I can speak to one or two people and give you what you need."

Ajmal rejoiced inwardly. The deal was done. Only the details remained. Immediately he calculated how quickly he could pay off the scoundrel David Mirza and begin work on the next restaurant project. The Floating Palace. Ajmal exuded an uncaring exterior to wind down the meeting. He couldn't wait for his Faislabadi friend to drink his tea and depart.

After concluding the meeting, the two old friends shook hands, rose and Ajmal accompanied his friend to the ground floor.

"Thank you once again my friend," Ajmal told Abdullah as they shook hands once more at the VIP entrance, "I won't forget this."

Abdullah nodded and shot him a quick smile before tugging his beard and slipping into the rain.

"Boss, Boss," a voice shouted in Urdu behind him. He turned to see the restaurant manager.

"What is it, Saleem? Did some of those crazy students break one of the tables again last night? I've told you to stop them dancing on them when they're drunk. Yesterday, I told you to move the bigger tables to the side." One of the biggest hazards of the trade were the overly zealous students, high on loans and spice. They caused as much damage sometimes as they spent – corporate customers were sometimes even worse, but they usually spent more money.

"No, Boss – there are some people here to see you."

Ajmal frowned and walked to the front of the restaurant where three people were sat, all Asian; an old man and two middle-aged women. People came to the restaurant each day to beg for his help. Somehow, he'd never tired of meeting them, listening to them.

They stood up as he approached. "Ajmal Saab," the

old man began in Punjabi.

Ajmal motioned for the people to sit.

"How can I be of assistance?"

The old man's hands were trembling. Ajmal took the man's hand in his own. "My son, he's in trouble with the law. I've done everything to keep him straight, but it's drugs. He can't stop himself. I've done everything. I'm helpless. They took him away yesterday."

"Which police station is he in?" The old man told him. "Okay, I'll speak to someone. He should be home by tomorrow. Send him to me. I'll speak to him."

"Thank you, Ajmal Saab, may God bless you."

Ajmal waved him away, guilt and happiness churning in his belly. He'd never understood these emotions.

The two ladies remained.

"Ajmal ji," the older of the two began. "My son has been looking for work for several months, but he can't find a job. I want him to get a good job. Can you give him one? Can you help us? I hear you always help people."

Ajmal nodded. "Send him to me. What's his name?" The old woman sighed and told him. "Tell Rehan to come and see me this evening. I'll speak to my manager. I might not be able to get him a job here, but definitely in one of my restaurants."

The old woman grabbed his hand and kissed it. Ajmal froze. The women thanked him profusely before shuffling out of the restaurant. A heady mixture of remorse and regret filled his heart. He watched them leave. Whenever he looked into the eyes of those who came to him and heard their cries for help he remembered Pakistan. He remembered everything he wanted to forget: the bite of poverty, the dust and the heat and then the Killer Instinct would raise its ugly head.

"Saleem," he shouted in Punjabi, "why haven't you moved the bloody tables yet?"

5

Sorayah shut the car door. Raindrops were falling gently and she found solace in their cold wetness. She glanced in the direction she'd come. *How could I be so pagal? Why did I listen to Immy?* She clutched her Gucci bag for comfort, but it didn't shield her from the sight of her mother behind the smoked glass of the front door. The handle turned slowly, time trickled. The door opened. Her ammi was wearing a red salwar and kameez: she'd always worn red. Something clicked in Sorayah's head and she switched to Punjabi. It was a neglected place inside her. In the London circles she rotated in, Urdu and Hindi were more common than Punjabi, because they opened doors between the Hindus and the Muslims, bridged one generation with another, between the Pakistanis, the Indians and the Bengalis. The world in Punjabi was rancid red.

"Assalamualaikum ammi," Sorayah said. Her mother took small steps out of the house into the cool Manchester air touching Shokat briefly on the head with her right hand and then opened her arms and hugged her. Sorayah was shocked. *Am I the prodigal daughter?* She struck off the thought. *We daughters don't inherit much. Sweet F. A.* An old bitterness ballooned inside her. *For us kuris there's nothing, just an arranged marriage and our brothers inherit the earth.* She loved her brothers deeply, but she suspected she'd been denied something vital at birth, the last clue in a cryptic crossword. She hugged her mother half-heartedly. *Don't you understand? I'll be gone straight after Yasmeen's wedding. I wasn't meant to come back. Tusanoo samach ni andi?*

"Sorayah daughter, come in, you must be tired," her

mother said in Punjabi. "Getting up in the mornings is very tiring." The voice was soft and delicate, afraid of itself, the sentences banal as Manchester rain, but her ammi's words stirred up memories. Sorayah tried not to pout. She was quickly bundled into the house and she tried to hold onto some control, keeping an eye out for her bags – Shokat put them down in the hallway.

The doorbell rang and she heard Shokat say, "Shazia's here."

Shazia was wearing a dazzling smile, the kind Manchester is rarely exposed to, her head covered in a green hijab matched by a forest green salwar and kameez beneath a long brown leather coat. *God, she hasn't changed.* Sorayah was sure Shazia would start whingeing soon: "Your clothes are too tight, why don't you wear something decent, I mean really! You're not a gori!"

The sisters were close as children, being the two daughters of the Butt empire. When the inevitable suitors came knocking on the door Shazia was engaged and married within a year of leaving Loreto College, chained to a family import who possessed what mattered most: a psychological subservience to his Uncle Butt.

Sorayah had discovered love by then. She didn't switch paths even after her teenage love ended. She'd maintained a lasting and loving relationship with Shazia until their father's visit to London. The more religious Shazia considered the cycle of dating, clubbing and drinking scandalous and unacceptable of a Butt daughter, but Shazia had looked the other way. The crack became a chasm when abbu disclosed to Shazia what had happened in London.

"How could you do this to us? I always thought better of you," Shazia shouted at her two years ago, following abbu's visit to London. Sorayah had bitten back a tart reply. "Do you know how upset abbu is? When ammi finds out it'll really hurt her." *That's all she cared about. Them. Not me. And Bash can do anything he wants cos he's a boy, and cos I'm the girl I'm a filthy throw-away thing.* Inadvertently, Shazia confirmed what Sorayah had feared most – their father had shared the news with the rest of the family. The gates of her family home had irrevocably shut. *Manchester is dead. Long live London.* The words which cleaved them apart burst in Sorayah's head. "After all the freedom Mum and Dad gave you, you do this? What kind of person are you? Have you got no decency? Was anything ever denied you? You always got away with everything when we were kids, but not this time, you're not welcome here any longer. Abbu might not be able to say it to you, but I can. As far as we're concerned, you're out of our lives. *In our eyes you're dead.*"

Sorayah had spent sleepless nights staring up at the ceiling of her bedroom in London reliving what Baji had said to her and it hurt so much she'd have to get up and go into the bathroom so she could cry without waking Ravinder.

Last night's phone call had been a surprise. Shazia promised she'd come to the coach station to collect her. "It'll be just like the good old days – I'm just so happy you're coming home!" Sorayah was speechless and bemused and Shazia had continued chatting away on the phone at a hundred miles per hour as if two years of silence hadn't built a wall between them, that everything was forgiven and forgotten. *But nothing's forgotten, is it, dear sister? When the crap hits the fan, you'll bring it up just like everyone else. Flipping hypocrites, all of them.* But despite hesitating, she wanted to return home to see her family. She didn't blame Shazia for her stance. *We might only have six years difference between us, but it's more like a generation. What do I say to Baji Shazia? Do I pretend that nothing happened? I'm not like her; I can't ignore the past.*

Then the two sisters were face to face. Before Sorayah could react, Shazia hugged her with arms hardened by house labour. Sorayah smelt lavender and her body tried not to respond to all the memories the smell evoked. Sorayah felt awkward hugging her sister.

"I'm so sorry I couldn't come, something came up and I just – anyway, it's good to see you," Shazia said.

How am I meant to ignore all the things that you said to me? But at least she's here for me now.

It was only then she noticed the little girl looking shyly up at her. "Is that Rubeena?" Sorayah picked up the girl who appeared so deliciously cute and docile, wearing a red sequined salwar, kameez and a denim jacket. "Hi Rubeena, how are you?" She pecked her niece on the cheek. "She's grown." The little girl regarded her with wide-open eyes. The she squirmed and Sorayah reluctantly put her down. Sorayah felt warmth spread through her belly.

Then Shazia was talking at a hundred miles per hour. "Oh yes, I didn't tell you, got a new car, well Ahmed got it, you know, he likes his cars," Shazia giggled as they made their way into the living room. Their mother had disappeared into the kitchen and Shokat was nowhere to be seen. She heard a distinctive voice shouting in Urdu. "Shokat! Where are you? Stupid idiot." It was coming from upstairs. *Pabhi.* Sorayah heard footfall on the stairs. The door opened and Shokat's wife entered. Bushra gave her a cursory hug. Shokat had gone. Sorayah felt sorry for him. He'd probably escaped to avoid more scolding from Bushra. Her sister-in-law went into the kitchen and returned just as promptly. *Probably looking for Paijaan.* She left before Sorayah could say another word to her.

Shazia rattled away in Punjabi as effortlessly and as unstoppably as she did in English.

Their mother interrupted Shazia's monologue. "Come Sorayah, sit down. I've made you lunch." It felt odd. Her mother had never cooked for her. Her ammi used to rise early to cook breakfast for Shokat and Imran, but never for her. Her mother placed the food tray on the table. Sorayah smelt the rich aroma of the lamb curry. *She really did make it for me, just like Paijaan said.* A flood of smells washed over her: sweet, aromatic, fiery, bitter-sweet, earthy, hot and intoxicating. Her mouth watered.

"Sorayah daughter," her mother urged, "don't be shy. Eat." Sorayah didn't need to be told twice. She'd missed good food. She savoured the first gush of texture and taste. It took an inhuman effort not to gulp it down. She took a swig of Coke. As she continued eating, she noted how the living-room had evolved. The photo of Mecca remained, but the studio lights were new, a cool blast of fluorescent white. The old Sony television had transformed into a Phillips Plasma TV.

Despite her protests, her mother brought more food. Carrot halwa, an assortment of Asian sweetmeats and a pile of rotis appeared as if by magic. Sorayah pushed away the feelings of strangeness, of oddness, but they clung. *This can't be happening.* She'd expected recriminations, heated words, not kindness, happiness.

She itched to phone Imran. She wanted a voice, a familiar awaaz to bring her back to planet Earth. *This is weird. Why are they being so nice to me?* A cynical voice in her head told her: *they've got a mango waiting in the wings.*

Rubeena was sitting on the sofa, banging a Nintendo Gameboy as if her life depended on it. Shazia and ammi talked. Sorayah was half listening to the conversation. Family stuff bored her. She had never grasped the infinite permutations of relationships that were second nature to the rest of the family. As a young girl, she'd learned to sidestep household chores and submerge herself in her own coterie of friends with whom she could simply be Saz and not have to be careful with her words. She felt discomforted in the presence of her mother and sister, but as the minutes passed she felt herself slowing down to the Manchester clock. It was an older rhythm, not enslaved by the arrival and departure of Tube trains.

Rubeena had pulled out a doll, an Asian Barbie. Sorayah ate as her niece played by herself, discussing crucial child matters with the doll. After she'd finished eating, she took the tray of food into the kitchen, but was shooed away by her mother.

"You don't have to wash up. Go and play with Rubeena." Nodding, she dutifully returned to the living room and sat down with the little girl. She watched emotions race across her niece's face. Rubeena was adrift in the doll's world whom she'd named 'Bunny'. Sorayah joined in, spinning a tale of how Bunny once got lost in a dark forest and was trapped in a monster's castle. When Rubeena became bored, she put a finger to her lips and said, "Shush Khaalah. Bunny needs to rest or her arms and legs might drop off."

Sorayah laughed. "That's true Rubeena, you should put her to sleep straight away."

"I am! Hush! You'll wake her up and then she'll start crying. Don't you know anything?"

Later, Shazia showed Sorayah upstairs. She was itching to walk around the house and rediscover each nook and cranny. There were five bedrooms in total, hers was in the back overlooking the garden. She'd adored her room as a child, spending hours looking out onto the verdant horizon.

Her room was unrecognisable. It had been redecorated in pastel green and looked barren. She stood in the doorway. The bed looked strange. It all felt wrong. *Unlived in, unloved.* An unfamiliar chest of drawers was on one side of the bed. A wardrobe dominated the space next to the window. She wondered what had happened to her treasured furniture. Her mother loved to donate to charity, her way of balancing the size of the family fortune with the family's debt to God.

Shazia threw on a bed cover and disappeared to get pillows.

Sorayah sat down on the bed. She'd lived in this room dreaming deeply, craving to go a million places at a zillion miles per hour. She'd thought she'd made a clean getaway, but it had become a drowning albatross. *Where did it get me? Rav?*

"I need to unpack my things, Baj," she told Shazia when her sister returned, hiding her face. She pretended to be inspecting the wardrobe.

"I'll see you downstairs then. Just shout, I mean really, just give us a shout if you need a hand."

"OK Baj. Thanks."

"You don't have to thank me. Really. What are sisters for?"

Sorayah forced a smile and was glad when the door closed. She put her suitcases on the bed. She unpacked her belongings and put them neatly into the wardrobe and the drawer. She pulled down the net curtains. *So flippin' TP.* She found her mobile phone and discovered a queue of text messages from Ravinder and a dozen friends querying how things were going in Manchester. She deleted Ravinder's messages without viewing them. Too tired to text her friends, she sighed and connected the phone to recharge. She then locked the door, took off her jacket, kicked off her shoes, lay down on the stranger's bed and wept.

She met Basharat as she came out of the bathroom. For an instant she didn't recognise her skinhead goatee-bearded brother. His shiny earrings brought her back to her senses.

"Oh, Baj," he said, sounding surprised. "When did you get back?"

"Hi Bash – I got in earlier this afternoon, about two hours ago."

"Right. Need the toilet. Like the haircut?" He winked and entered the bathroom before she could think of a reply.

She banged the bathroom door. "What time do you call this? It's the afternoon. Haven't you got a job or something?"

"I missed you too, Baj. Did you bring me a present?"

She heard him chuckling as she made her way downstairs. She shook her head. Basharat had looked much older. *He's been doing a lot of living without me to keep an eye on him.* When they were children, she'd mothered her youngest brother to distraction. *Did I spoil him?* She was dismayed at herself, they were close as children and now they were strangers.

She spent the rest of the day refamiliarising herself with home and ringing her Manchester friends. Most were at work and Sorayah sat in the living room thumbing text messages as Rubeena watched her.

She hadn't rung Yasmeen. She felt too tense to call. *What would I say to her?* Sorayah would have to visit her soon, but today wasn't the day to do it. She'd just arrived and needed to set down some roots.

She attempted to help her mother with the cooking, but was shooed away again. "You're tired. The journey was long and you should rest. Watch television." *This is so bizarre.* In the past, her mother moaned when she watched the TV. A couple of hours later, Aunt Gulshan arrived with a string of friends. Her Auntie, fat, friendly and girly had lent an understanding ear when she was younger.

"Come, my daughter," declared Auntie Gulshan in Punjabi, hugging her, "we are all so happy to see you."

And then Shazia returned with all her children. "Auntie!" Sara exclaimed on seeing Sorayah. Sara, almost ten, fiercely hugged Sorayah. Haris, eight and a half, tolerated a peck on the cheek and wiped off the saliva with his shoulder, dug out the PlayStation 2 from underneath one of the sofas and professionally began to connect the games console to the television.

"You never let me play!" Rubeena cried.

"Get lost," Haris replied. "Go and play with that stupid doll of yours."

"Ammi!" Rubeena shouted.

The living room was a frenzy of playing and shouting children. More children entered with Bushra. Sorayah's spectacled sister-in-law didn't make small talk with any of the women. Sorayah made a mental note to ask her brothers and sisters what was wrong with Bushra. Shokat's children were twin boys, both equally mischievous and both rushed off after greeting Sorayah to play with Uncle Basharat in the front room and took Haris with them. "Wait," Haris shouted, "let me unplug the Playstation. We don't want the girls playing on it."

"Faisal and Kasar look just the same," she told her sister-in-law in Urdu.

"Don't you think they look like their grandfather?" Bushra asked her. Sorayah couldn't place the strange tone in her sister-in-law's voice.

Sorayah didn't think the boys looked like her father, but diplomatically said, "I hadn't noticed, but you could be right."

Shokat arrived. Sorayah noticed Bushra was ignoring him. *How come she isn't helping out in the kitchen?* The tension had risen in the room and unexpectedly Sorayah felt it was nothing to do with her.

"Good to see you settling in," he said in his calm and slow voice. He awkwardly touched her on the head in welcome. "I told you everything would be alright when you got home."

Sorayah nodded. "I'm finding it hard to believe. I expected it to be much harder, you know. I was up this morning at six o'clock. It's been a really long day."

"Tired?"

"Yeah."

Shokat shot off on receiving a call on his mobile

from one of the Manchester restaurants.

When the guests had gone, Sorayah went upstairs to phone Imran.

"Immy, it's going okay," she said, cradling her mobile phone in the nook of her shoulder. She was sitting on her bed, back against the wall.

"You're not just saying that, are you?" he asked.

"No. Honest. Ammi's been very nice, everyone's nice, everything's okay."

He poked and prodded her in his relentless way until she said, "There's one thing though."

"What?"

"You should have come back with me."

"Oh, don't start that again!"

She was grinning when she heard her father's voice waft upstairs. The grin disappeared.

"Abbu's here," she told Imran, "gotta go."

She slowly descended the stairs and stood in the living room doorway. Her father turned on hearing her footfall and they looked at each other for a long moment. He nodded briefly and turned back to her mother. "Have you seen my mobile phone?"

Sorayah felt rebuked and lowered her head, caught between coming into the room and racing back to the safety of her bedroom.

"I put it on the dressing table upstairs."

"Well go and get it," he ordered.

Sorayah seized the chance to get out of the room. "I'll get it," she said and rushed off before her father could tell her not to. When she returned downstairs, her father was sitting in his favourite armchair eating dinner. Basharat had appeared and was munching away like a hungry beast. Sorayah put her father's mobile phone on the table and sat down on the sofa across from him. In her head she replayed the last time she'd seen her father.

"So you're back," her father said after a few minutes.

"Yes," Sorayah replied, startled.

"You've come back for that whoreson's daughter, eh?"

Offended, Sorayah bristled. "She's my best friend," she replied in English knowing her father disliked it when she did.

"Best friend," Ajmal said, switching to English, "The Alis aren't anyone's friend. They're dogs. All of them. You should know what that bastard did to me. Don't you have any respect?"

"She's my friend."

"You can all go to hell then and take your friend with you." Her father wasn't even looking at her.

She wanted to stop herself from replying, but she couldn't: "I'm going to Yasmeen's wedding even if you don't like it. She's my friend – I'm not her father's friend. She's never done anything wrong to me, so I'm going." She was surprised by the vehemence in her voice.

She saw Basharat looking stupidly from her to her father as if watching a tennis rally. It was rare for anyone to say anything to their father. *Well, I'm not stepping down just cos he thinks I should.* Her dad looked angrily at her. She felt guilty that she was already arguing with her father and she hadn't even been home for one day.

Her abbu opened his mouth to say something then closed it. He then shouted in Punjabi, "Mumtaz, don't make any more rotis, I have to get back to the restaurant."

Her father looked at her. Sorayah held his gaze for a

moment. She stood up to go into the kitchen and then caught her sister-in-law standing in the doorway, gloating.

"Bushra daughter," she heard her father say, "tell Mumtaz that I'm leaving now."

Sorayah walked past the leering Bushra into the kitchen. Moments later she returned to the living room to pick up the empty plates. Her abbu had gone. Basharat was still eating and flicking through the satellite channels. He found MTV Base and turned up the volume.

6

Late, bloody late. Late, because of the lafanga! I should chop his ears off! Stupid boy! Ajmal glared at Basharat in the rear-view mirror of the Mercedes. Basharat was sitting in the back. *Khanzir.* Shokat was in the passenger seat, quiet as a chuha. They were late for the most important weekly religious observance. The Friday prayer. The car was clogged in traffic. Ajmal's grip tightened on the steering wheel, words seethed in his heart.

On Fridays, Ajmal returned home like clockwork to pick Basharat up. Normally, he only needed to park in the driveway and his son would jump in. Basharat didn't appear today. After several minutes, Ajmal got out of the car, hissing under his breath and went into the house.

"Where's that djinn of ours?" he asked Mumtaz.

Mumtaz put her hand over her mouth and hobbled upstairs. She knocked on the bathroom door: "Son, you know your father is waiting."

"I'll be down in a moment, Mum," came back the muffled voice in English. Ajmal stood fuming at the bottom of the stairs. The bathroom door opened and the gunda appeared.

"Hurry up, we're late!" Ajmal shouted. Basharat looked sullen, a look Ajmal thought his son was born with. Basharat sloped off to his room, "What's he doing now?" Ajmal asked his wife in exasperation.

"I don't know," she said tremulously from the top of the stairs. She gently knocked on Basharat's bedroom door.

"Tell the idiot I'll be waiting in the car. If he isn't down in one minute, I'm off." But of course he had to wait for Basharat, because Mumtaz looked as though she might weep.

Ajmal regretted having to come back for the charlatan, but Friday was the one time in the week when he and his two sons were together. If Imran were in Manchester he would accompany them too.

Basharat was infamous for sleeping all day as if practising how to hibernate, but the habit had never extended to Fridays. Ajmal was certain Basharat was a good-for-nothing, but at least he went to Friday prayers. Nowadays, many jawans didn't bother to pray even if they went to the mosque: they stood outside smoking spliffs. The ones who prayed were usually members of openly anti-Western organisations. Ajmal loathed the zealots. They often sought him out and told him he was hell-bound for selling alcohol, voting and pandering to kafirs. Ajmal told his friends that, "It isn't possible to do everything halal in this country. Who'd come to my restaurants if I didn't sell sharaab? It's no sin to take back the money you've rightfully earned, is it?" Ajmal cursed the zealots and was glad his sons hadn't become one of them.

Ajmal waited in the car with Shokat. "I don't want you telling Sorayah anything about the business, okay?" Shokat nodded and Ajmal grunted.

Basharat arrived and got into the back without saying a word. A bandage was wrapped around his left hand.

"What happened to your hand?" Ajmal snapped in Punjabi.

"Nuffing, init. I fell, init," retorted Basharat in English.

The boy's useless. It would be so good if he helped out in the restaurant instead of mooning around town and getting up to trouble all the time. I give them everything and how do they repay me? These children have no respect. Ajmal wouldn't be surprised if his son had been in another fight.

He drove in angry silence and made a point of staring at the rear-view mirror every few minutes to glare at Basharat, but his son wasn't paying the slightest attention. Ajmal knew he had lost his favourite parking space and to add insult to zakham he was forced to park in a side street, five minutes walk away from Victoria Park Mosque. *Late, bloody late and the car might get bloody scratched.* He normally arrived early so he could park his car near the Imam's BMW. *It would have been better to stay at home.* It was too late, people had seen him. He swore in frustration. Basharat and Shokat quickly disappeared ahead of him, perhaps fearing his wrath. *Kutte.* Ajmal rushed to catch up with them and was soon huffing. He slowed into a shuffling walk. He was sweating profusely by the time he arrived at the mosque gates. He paused for a moment to regain his breath.

Victoria Park Mosque was the closest to the Curry Mile. It was where business met religion – and won. The faith centre was also known as the Central Mosque even though it wasn't situated in Manchester's centre. It had been the Butt family's masjid since it first opened and as far as Ajmal was concerned, all other Mancunian mosques paled into insignificance.

Ajmal was proud of the mosque. His hard-earned pennies were set in its bricks and mortar. He often told his friends, "I built it." But the truth was Ajmal had no choice. For a man of Ajmal's standing to distance himself from the mosque would be slow social suicide, like joining the Conservative Party in Cheetham Hill.

The mosque had been constructed over several

decades and had a dome and minarets. It could accommodate over a thousand souls and was crammed on Fridays. Eid festival prayers resembled a United football match, intense, raucous and energetic.

The mosque was packed. The congregation was mostly of Pakistani origin, some in western suits, others in traditional dress. There were young and old, men and women. Many in the congregation recognised him. A feral-looking old man with a wizened beard implored, "Ajmal Saab, please pass, there's a place for you." *Qurban Elahi*. Ajmal smiled, and politely asked him about his sons. The man whispered a thanks and let him pass. Ajmal continued his slow progress towards the front. Finally, he sat down cross-legged in the second row of the congregation. He'd lost his place in the front row.

Imam Mazhar caught his eye. Ajmal winced inwardly. He stared down at the intricate weave of the prayer carpet, trying to disappear from view. *There's nothing that can be done. If anyone asks I'll tell them that I was in an accident.* He practised the lie in his head until it became fact.

A headache droned like a fly droning in Ajmal's skull. Then he noticed Jafar Ali sitting in the first row. *He's taken my place.* Jafar's son was there too. The young man turned his head and nodded. Ajmal blinked. *Doesn't the boy realise that we're enemies?* Jafar turned, perhaps noting the movement of his son's head, but only to give him an insolent look. Ajmal glared back and was greeted by a spiteful smile from Jafar.

Imam Mazhar, speaking in Urdu, was standing on the mimbar, ceremonial staff in his hand. His voice rose and fell like the ebb and flow of a deep ocean tide. The Imam's large golden hat shimmered beneath the fluorescent lights. His mellifluous voice mesmerised the flock. Ajmal's mind was elsewhere. He was thinking about business: he pondered repaying David Mirza, punishing Basharat, straightening Sorayah out and Sameena floated in and out of his thoughts like a wraith, tantalisingly distant, but within earthly reach.

The Imam gesticulated wildly, nearing the finale of the sermon. "God does not need your charity! Any good you do is for your own souls, God does not gain any profit from it." The Imam's voice shook the chandeliers. Ajmal saw men's heads nodding and wished the Imam would stop talking about charity. It was a dangerous topic, one that would doubtlessly lead to requests for more money. "My brothers, we are as one nation and each of us must do one's best to help one another…" Why did the Imam's words sound so hollow today? Ajmal could not put his finger on it.

Once upon a waqt, Ajmal and Jafar were best friends. The two men became enemies eleven years ago. Their well-known animosity was the reversal of the firm dosti they'd once shared. *We were almost like brothers.* Once, Ajmal imagined his children would marry Jafar's, but that dream had fled. He'd locked his regrets away.

So strong had their friendship been that they'd joined forces to create a restaurant franchise. It was the heyday of the curry trade when restaurants were sprouting up everywhere to feed the insatiable indigenous goray's appetite for ex-colonial cuisine. Their partnership beyond the bounds of blood kin was unknown. They could have dominated the market by creating the first Asian chain of restaurants to rival McDonalds, Wimpy and Burger King. *Together we could have gone further. But I'm still the Curry King and he's the King of bakwas.*

On the eve of the final agreement to pledge their assets to the new enterprise, Ajmal had returned to his offices in the Lazeez restaurant and caught his manager, Bilal, rifling through his most confidential documents, papers he wouldn't even have shown his accountant. Trembling with indignation, he seized Bilal and threw him to the ground.

"Who are you working for, you khanzir?" he shouted and began strangling the short man. Bilal kicked and thrashed, finally freeing himself from Ajmal's grip. As Bilal lurched away, Ajmal tripped him, jumped on top of his back and brutally pulled his ears. "Tell me now or I'll kill you!"

"Ali... " was all Bilal managed to say. Ajmal, horrified, let go. Capitalising on his shock, Bilal writhed free, clutching his bleeding ears and shot out of the office never to set foot in Lazeez again. Ajmal soon learned that Bilal had joined the swelling ranks of Jafar Ali's staff, confirming his treachery. *How long had Bilal been working for Jafar? What information did he glean? What did he use it for?* Ajmal suspected he was walking into a trap. He considered all the times he'd been with Jafar. They'd lived out of each other's pockets. Without explanation, Ajmal backed out of the deal and worked ceaselessly thereafter to ensure that Jafar Ali found it impossible to establish himself further on Wilmslow Road. By removing financial support for his ex-friend he guaranteed Jafar would struggle for many years. It heralded the beginning of the end of his family's relationship with the Ali clan. Ajmal had wanted it to end totally, he wanted a clean break, but his children wouldn't accept the new status quo. *It was my fault for having let my children grow up with his. I should have always maintained my distance.*

Sorayah had been most outspoken. "Why can't we go to their house? So what if he was spying on you! You probably spied on him. I know what you're like abbu!"

"That's not the point. I'm your father and I'm telling you that I won't have you going to that haramzada's house again. Do you hear me?"

"I hear you alright, I'm not deaf you know. I want to go to their house. Yasmeen's having a party and I want to go."

"No, you're staying here!"

"Why are you so mean to me? Why don't you love me any more?"

His will held firm and reluctantly his family accepted the separation. Sorayah and Imran flouted his absolute will by continuing to meet Jafar Ali's children. He'd been glad when Imran distanced himself from Javed, but again it was Sorayah and her firm dosti with Yasmeen that had been a constant chilli in his eye.

All had gone according to Ajmal's master plan. For most of the last decade he had the edge, but from nowhere Ali had opened a restaurant in the Trafford Centre and won a contract to provide Asian pensioners in Stockport with meals on wheels, something Ajmal had never considered. And he had failed miserably to make the Kohinoor the jewel in his crown. There were vague rumours that Jafar was using less than legal means to finance his new-found financial freedom, but Ajmal's sources couldn't substantiate the stories.

The prayer began behind the Imam and his electronically boosted voice rippled as the congregation bowed and prostrated.

After the delightfully short congregational prayer, Ajmal made his personal dua in Punjabi. He prayed, "Oh God, please help me to repay this debt that I owe so that I can make my business stronger. Make my position in the community stronger. God, please help save me from the eyes of spies and flush out any of those who wish to betray me." He wiped his face with his palms and felt refreshed, safe and ready, the world a harvest waiting to be reaped.

He then completed the individual set of prayers, praying quickly and efficiently, his arms and legs sweeping through the air, pistons of a well-oiled machine. After he'd finished, he stood up, tightened his bright red tie, pushed the mosque hat tighter onto his head and surveyed the prayer hall. Some were still praying, but from the volume most had finished. He caught sight of Basharat. His son melted into the horde leaving the mosque. He suspected Basharat would seek out his good-for-nothing friends and resurface tomorrow afternoon to feed.

He saw Jafar Ali with Javed. *The khanzir looks so happy and relaxed.* Their eyes met. Jafar glanced in the Imam's direction and Ajmal realised Ali wanted to speak to the Imam. In a split second, Ajmal determined he had to get to the Imam before Jafar did, no matter what. *Killer Instinct.*

Imam Mazhar was still praying. Many used the post prayer period to speak to the faith leader and a small group was gathering behind him. Time crawled as Ajmal approached the Imam. Ajmal pushed past people and they made way for him. He was well known to everyone in the mosque, even to newcomers, his name going forward like a tsunami. The Imam finished making his dua and turned.

"Assalamualaikum Imam Saab, that was an excellent khutba!" Ajmal said loudly in Urdu, his right arm outstretched, his hand wide open to grasp the Imam's.

"One has to try for the congregation, but the words of God speak for themselves. We're as nothing before Him. I haven't seen you at the weekly study circle recently. My friend, you should come more often to the House of God and learn about the Divine Book."

Ajmal cringed. Being rebuked publicly was galling. Clasping the Imam's hand firmly with both of his, he replied, "I've been very busy, but inshallah, this week I'll be coming along. It's after Maghrib as usual?"

"Yes, of course." To Ajmal's horror, the Imam turned away. "Ah, Jafar Saab," the Imam said. Jafar had approached from the opposite direction, "you wanted to speak to me about something? Your support for the mosque has been most generous. Allah will surely repay you even more generously in the after-life for your important contribution to the community. "

"One must do everything one is able to do in the way of God," Ajmal heard his enemy say. The Imam hugged Jafar. *He's hijacked the Imam from me!* Jafar Ali didn't even glance at Ajmal and his blood ran cold. He took a deep breath like Doctor Patel had instructed.

"Hello Uncle," he heard someone say behind him in Urdu. It was Jafar's son. Javed looked nothing like his father which only good as far as Ajmal was concerned. Jafar's eldest boy was of medium height, but built like a palwaan. *Strange, he was so thin as a child.* The earliest memories Ajmal had of him were playing with Sorayah. "How are you, Uncle-ji?"

At least the boy is respectful. "I'm fine, and how are you, son?"

"I'm okay," Javed said. Ajmal was trying to listen to Jafar's conversation with the Imam. "We have a Quran study circle at our home on Sundays. You can come if you like. Please, bring your family." There was a wistful tone to the boy's voice. *How can the boy be asking me to bring my family to his house? Doesn't he know that his father and I are enemies? The young nowadays, absolutely no idea of family loyalty. Izzat noo bilkul ni samach de.*

"No son, I'm very busy on Sundays and I don't think I'd be able to come along," said Ajmal, unexpectedly finding patience. *He's very respectful. How can he be the bastard's son?*

Perhaps understanding Ajmal's reproachful tone, Jafar's son fell silent. Javed then said goodbye and disappeared into the departing crowd.

Ajmal had to get the Imam back from Jafar, it was a battle he simply had to win, but his enemy had his arm around the Imam and was guiding him to the back of the prayer hall. Ajmal guessed they were going to the Imam's office. He clenched his fists. *That Jafar gets everywhere, he has his finger in every curry. The man is a damned nuisance.*

"Ajmal Saab!" he heard someone say in Urdu. Ajmal turned to see an old man with a large mosque hat on his head. It was Haji Khan. Ajmal smiled, feeling genuine warmth for his old friend. They hugged and firmly shook hands. "You're looking well," Ajmal told the old man in Urdu. The old man was looking tired, but Ajmal thought it wiser if he lied.

"It's good to see the masjid full. It wasn't like this once," the Haji said.

"Yes, the community is very big now. Even the young

come to the congregation." Ajmal looked up to the first floor balcony, "And ladies too."

"Yes, God has brought good into the world."

The Haji asked about the business and Ajmal gave non-committal answers that revealed nothing, hid everything. "How is your family?" Ajmal asked. He knew all the Haji's children and grandchildren having met them all at some time or other.

"As well as they can be," the old man said, "God takes and gives as He wills."

"Is everything alright? You know you can come to me if you have any problems."

"I know, my son,." Haji Khan was the only man who called Ajmal 'son'. "You have a reputation for helping people and many come to you for your protection, but forgive me son if I suggest something to you. Forgive an old man for making suggestions."

"Of course, you can say what you like to me, Haji Saab. I respect your words."

"Then listen to me when I tell you to end this enmity with Jafar."

Ajmal looked away. He did not feel the anger he normally did at the mention of his enemy's name.

"I know I've mentioned this many times in the past… "

"I can't end this – he insulted me and I'll never forgive him. You know what he did, you know what he's like. Don't ask this of me. God can forgive, but I can't."

"Son, it's better to forgive. I'm not saying that you have to forgive him now, but if you need someone to broker an understanding between you then let me know."

Ajmal nodded curtly. *There's no way in dozakh that I'm*

going to do that.

"Do you need a lift?" Ajmal asked, changing the subject.

"No, you're very kind son, I came with my grandson and it's better if I walk. I'm going back to the shop for a while."

Ajmal nodded and the two men shook hands once more. He watched the stooped old man amble into the crowd. Then Ajmal was surrounded by acquaintances and, suddenly feeling indulgent and more like his old self, he gave them a willing ear.

It was chaos in the entrance hall as people searched for their shoes. After locating his brogues, he elbowed his way to the door. A huge crowd was milling outside the doors of the mosque. He heard names being shouted, swear words being exchanged. "Move out of the way," Ajmal shouted, but his voice was lost in the din. When he broke through the crowd surrounding the main doors, he was astonished and dismayed to see Basharat talking loudly to a group of young men in the centre of the throng. *Stupid idiot, what's he doing now?* Ajmal didn't recognise any of the boys. They all looked the same to him with their shaved heads.

A scuffle broke out and Basharat punched a youth with his unbandaged hand. There were shouts and cries as men tried to stop the fight. A large man held Basharat back. Ajmal saw a jawaan, perhaps aged sixteen, being held by two burly men. The youngster had a black eye and was mouthing obscenities, "I'll get you, you fucking bastard! You think you're hard, but I'll get you!" Ajmal lost sight of both boys as the crowd surged forward.

He tried to make his way through the horde to have

strong words with his youngest son. It was impossible. Everyone was excited by the scuffle. He gave up exasperated. "Bloody stupids," he muttered in English. He wanted to head back to the car, but he was hemmed in. Slowly, the crowd dispersed, cars pulled out, men took off their mosque hats and began walking back to their lives. The groups of young men broke up, the excitement gone. The mosque emptied. Ajmal searched for Basharat and found him with his friends near the mosque gates.

"Yeah, I got him good. It was sweet, man. Sweet!" he heard his youngest brag.

"What was all that about?" Ajmal demanded in Punjabi. Basharat turned, startled. "Why were you fighting outside the mosque? You're showing me up deliberately to the Imam! Everybody knows who I am and because they know who I am they know who you are. Anything you do reflects on me."

Basharat didn't meet his eye.

Shokat arrived then. "Bash, you been fighting?" he asked.

"Your brother's always fighting," Ajmal told him.

"You know you shouldn't be fighting, Bash," Shokat said. Basharat looked away. His friends were crossing the street and he looked longingly in their direction. "You might get hurt, or hurt someone."

"Who was the boy you were fighting with?" demanded Ajmal in English.

"How should I know?" Basharat answered petulantly.

"You don't know? How can you not know?"

"I don't know who it was; he just took a swing at me, init. What do you expect me to do, kiss him?"

"I don't want to see you fighting again!"

"Okay, okay, I get the bloody message!"

"No, you don't get the message and as punishment you're not getting any more cash this month!"

"Oh, Dad, that's not fair! It wasn't my fault, he just came at me, init. I had to defend myself. You would have done the same. I got into a scuffle last night, init. I was only playing snooker, kasam, Dad, and that twat's brother got jealous of me game, init. Then his young brother has a crack at me today – see it wasn't my fault, yeah."

"Well, I don't care. You're disrespectful. And I don't want you talking to that bloody Jafar or any of his children! And why do you have to play snooker till five in the morning?"

"I don't play till five, bloody place closes at one! It's not fair. And I didn't speak to Uncle Jafar or Jav, Paijaan Shokat did," grumbled Basharat.

"That man is not your Uncle, he's a scoundrel. And what's this, Shokat? Why were you talking to that kutta, Ali? Have I not told you to keep away from that bastard?"

"Sorry, Dad. He just happened to be there, when I was putting my shoes on."

Ajmal stared at both of his sons.

"I don't believe it. Both of my sons totally useless. What good are you to me? Stupids."

Basharat turned away, making his way to where his friends were waiting on the street corner. Ajmal shook his head. *He'll probably be out again till five in the morning and come back after having another bloody fight. Idiot.* "They're all insolent. And mad," he muttered to himself and walked back to the car with Shokat. His eldest didn't say a word.

His son's insolence grated on his nerves all day. Even Sameena had the sense to leave him alone in the office, only coming forward to ask him if he wanted tea. And the humiliation his enemy had served him had left a terrible taste in his mouth that even Sameena's perfect tea couldn't remove. He knew he shouldn't go over events, "it isn't good for your heart," as Doctor Patel would say, but he couldn't help it. *That's the way God made me.*

He returned home that evening to change suits and freshen up for the evening trade. He wasn't prepared for what he witnessed when he entered the house. The front-room door was slightly ajar and he heard the sounds of dreadful Bhangra music.

He threw the door open. Sorayah, wearing tight black leggings and top was inspecting some clothes with a frown on her face. The sofas were covered with her junk. *She's been home now for only a few days and she's wasting all her time and money on getting ready for the haramzadi.*

"What are you doing?" he snapped in Punjabi.

Sorayah turned, "I'm just deciding which dress I'm going to wear."

Ajmal said, "You're not going." Sorayah stared at him. Ajmal hated the imperious look on her face. "I'm your father, and while you're in this house you won't be attending that haramzadi's wedding, do you hear me? I'm not having any of your spoiled antics this time. You're not going."

He recognised the tilt of her head and could feel his own fury rising as she shook her head. "I'm going whether you like it or not," she said crossing her arms. "You can't stop me. Just try."

Ajmal's blood turned to fire. "How dare you, you

randi!" he told her, and then stopped, shocked by his own words. His mouth dropped open in a rictus of horror. He felt an ocean of regrets in the brief terrible silence that built a wall between them. Then Sorayah was rushing off out of the room, away from him. *Oh, mere khuda, what have I said? Why did I call her a whore?* His thoughts were thick with remorse and he stumbled towards the door, but Sorayah slammed it shut behind her. "Puttar stop, I didn't mean to say that!" he cried, but he knew she wouldn't hear him. He heard Sorayah sobbing as she ran up the stairs.

Moments later Mumtaz appeared in the room. "What's wrong? What's happened?" she asked. Ajmal looked down, ashamed.

Mumtaz left, chasing after Sorayah. Ajmal followed helplessly. *Why did I say all those things?* He heard his wife knocking on his daughter's bedroom door and then heard the door open and the creak of the floorboards as Mumtaz entered.

Agitated, Ajmal hurried upstairs to change and decided he'd return to the Kohinoor and skip the evening meal.

He heard the sounds of sobbed conversation coming from his daughter's room. He undid his red tie. He pulled off his black jacket and trousers. He removed his shirt. He pulled open a drawer and selected a carefully folded crisp white shirt. He took out one of his many spare black suits from the wardrobe. He noticed he couldn't hear the muffled conversation any longer. *At least she's stopped crying.*

A few seconds later Mumtaz knocked on the door. She pushed it open without waiting for his reply. He knew she was waiting for him to turn. He didn't bother.

He could see her reflection in the mirror. He couldn't face her. Guilt rolled in his stomach. He wanted to say he was sorry, but couldn't.

"Ajmal," she began.

"What?" he said, straightening his tie.

"Don't call my daughter that again." And then she was gone and the door was closed before he could reprimand her. Ajmal swung round and glared at the door. *They're all plotting against me! I'll show her how to respect me!* For the first time in his life he considered beating his wife. He took rapid steps towards the door and stopped dead in his tracks. A shocking thought occurred to him. He realised that if anything would make his children tigers it would be if he set himself up against Mumtaz. *I want tigers, but not like this, not against me — for the business, for the bloody business.* He sat down on his bed and assessed this new discovery. He didn't like it.

He fled the house, rushing through the hallway into the rain and into his car, speeding towards the nearest newsagents to buy a packet of Benson & Hedges.

In the car, the puff of cigarette sweetness calmed him a little. He glared at the busy Mancunian road, rain streaking down the car windscreen. The traffic and rain soon disappeared in a haze of cigarette smoke. The engine was running and the windscreen wipers streaked dizzily.

He sighed and engaged the gears. A tear ran down his face. He wiped it away, mistaking it for a raindrop.

7

Sorayah was standing in the heart of the Curry Mile, on windswept Wilmslow Road. *Why did I have to wear a Lengha tonight?* She'd bought the dress from Eleganza in Longsight and hadn't regretted a penny, but felt like a twerp in the freezing cold. Thankfully, her sister's black brolly had shielded her so far from the rain. She was waiting for the old college gang: Dina, Farzana, Ghazala, Tayiba and Shabnam. She'd coaxed them out on the reunion.

She'd phoned Dina first. Her old Punjabi friend had just become a mum. Dina had been a stalwart e-mail buddy who'd migrated to MSN Messenger, but the chats had gradually disappeared as married life rose in the ladder of priorities. Sorayah was surprised she didn't have to twist Dina's arm. "What about your baby?" Sorayah asked. She was dying to see the baby.

"Don't worry, my husband will look after her," Dina said and giggled.

Tayiba, or Tabby, as the friends called her, was the shyest of the bunch, but always had the craziest ideas. That call lasted several hours. "Of course I'll come," Tayiba agreed almost as an after-thought when the conversation drifted to a close.

Shabnam was eager for the reunion because it presented two irresistible commodities: food and gossip. "Tell me who's coming again! I can't believe it! I love you, Sorayah. Can I bring my sister?"

"No Shabs, just bring yourself."

"OK, don't shout at me, I get a headache when you shout."

Farzana was more cautious; "I'll have to ask my

husband."

"If Dina can come, why can't you?" Dina and Farzana were best friends. Farzana caved in instantly.

Ghazala was the hardest to locate. She'd married her boyfriend and with their respective clans on opposite sides of the tribal landscape – he was a jatt she was a syed – they were promptly disowned.

"I don't know," Ghazala said, "I want to come, but it's short notice."

"What? You got another meeting arranged on a Thursday evening? Give Azeem the phone."

Sorayah didn't waste any time: "Listen Azeem, we're old friends of Ghazala's. You know her family won't talk to her so how come you're stopping her from meeting up with us? I thought you cared about her? What kind of husband are you? We're the closest thing to family she's got. I never knew you were so heartless, Azeem!"

"I'm not! I never said she couldn't go. Ghazza, what you been telling Saz?"

After that it was easy.

Sorayah had left her best friend till last. "I'm so sorry," Yasmeen told her earlier in the afternoon. "I want to come, but my future in-laws are coming. It'd look really bad if I was out, but I really want to be with you guys."

That's what you get for counting your andeys. "You sound like a married woman already."

"Oh, don't be like that."

"Don't worry, we'll have a great time out."

"That's great, rub it in."

"OK, we're going to have a wonderful time out," Sorayah said, and Yasmeen laughed despite herself.

They had agreed to meet outside Rusholme Chippy. It was a neutral meeting point. Sorayah had told everyone to arrive by seven, but like good Asians they were already late. Shabnam arrived first. They hugged and pecked each other on the cheek. "Oh Sorayah, it's so cold! Let's go inside one of the restaurants!"

"No, we're going to wait for the others."

"Don't do this to me, you know I hate the cold. I'll die if we're out for two more seconds."

"What if someone arrives and we miss them?" Sorayah guessed that like herself, Shabnam had dressed to impress, and like her own selection, Shabnam hadn't considered the cold. She was wearing a bright red salwar and kameez.

"It's a lovely dress," Sorayah said, knowing Shabnam was eagerly waiting for compliments.

"Is it?" Shabnam said, "I wasn't going to wear it, but I ran out of other things. You know how it is." Shabnam grinned. "Well, are we going to wait and die in the cold or are you going to give me some gossip?"

Sorayah laughed. What Shabnam meant by gossip only meant one thing. Men.

"Go on, I know you Sorayah, you can't sit still for two minutes without a guy!" Shabnam giggled.

"I'm not like that! That's a nasty thing to say." Sorayah's cheeks burned in the frigid air.

"But it's true, well, if you don't have any gossip, I've got some of my own. I was saving it for the others, but cos they aren't here I'll tell you instead – I'm going to get married!"

"You're getting married?" Sorayah asked slowly.

"Oh, I knew you'd be surprised! Now don't be jealous. He's wonderful, he proposed to me and everything. It was romantic, like one of those Bollywood movies. I swear I could hear music when he proposed. And he looks just like my favourite Bolly star, Hrithik! Well, when it's dark anyway."

"Is he one of your Internet pen pals from Desi Delight?"

"No! Those guys were too weird. He's from here. We met, well, we were introduced by my sister, Ambreen. He's really cute."

Sorayah didn't want to hear more. She couldn't believe that Shabnam had found true love. Sorayah felt ashamed. *Why can't I feel happy for my friend? Is there something wrong with me?*

"He works in a factory, but he's not a factory worker, he's an engineer, fixes the valvulas."

"Valves, you mean?"

"Yes, valvulas, and he's really cute. You'd want him too, but he's mine and you're not getting your hands on him. I know what you're like when you want a bloke!"

Shabnam giggled and Sorayah forced a smile. *She deserves to be happy.* She hugged her friend. Then took a deep breath. "So, when's the big day?"

It took another half hour before the other girls arrived. Sorayah's teeth were chattering from the cold. As Dina, Farzana, Ghazala and Tayiba were dropped off there were hugs and kisses. She savoured the glow of happiness on her friends' faces. But she felt out of place. *After Shabs gets married I'll be the only one left.* Her dark thoughts were turned by comments like, "God, you look so thin!"

"Thanks," she replied, warming slightly. "Listen, we need to chose a restaurant. I haven't been in Manchester for a while so I think you guys should choose. I don't know what's decent here any more," Sorayah said.

The friends conferred for a few minutes. "The Kohinoor," Tayiba finally said. "Let's go there!"

Sorayah was surprised. The last place she wanted to go tonight was the Kohinoor. There was a high chance of meeting her father and she wanted to avoid any awkwardness. She hadn't spoken to abbu since the incident. She was still angry with him. "Are you sure?"

"Do you *not* want us to go there?" Dina asked.

"No, it isn't that, it's just that…okay, why not?" She allowed herself to be carried on a wave of nostalgia, arms linked with the other girls, towards the shining neon crown of the Kohinoor.

Saleem, the Kohinoor's manager, looked astonished to see her, but responded quickly. "We're not that busy tonight. We can give you a table on the first floor. Do you want me to tell the Boss you're here?" Saleem said in Urdu. Sorayah, resigned to her fate, nodded and Saleem led them upstairs.

"It's really beautiful," Ghazala said as they went upstairs. The others murmured agreement. The plush interior matched the extravagant exterior. Piles of satin fabrics, Mogul brocade and luscious burgundy drapes exuded luxury. The girls ordered popadoms and soft drinks, took turns to look through the menu and made suggestions to each another. Saleem disappeared. *Probably gone to tell abbu I'm here.*

"What's the difference between a jalfrezi and a dopasanda again?" Shabnam asked. It was an old conversation. She found herself explaining how curries were made. She explained why curries "don't taste like ammi's cooking," and why, "the gorays love it so much." Then she said, "Look how much Manchester has changed just because of apna food? Food has a lot of power, it brings people together and– " She stopped mid sentence. *I sound just like abbu.* She was glad when a waiter brought the starters and the girls settled into an evening meal laced with tangy gossip. A flower seller popped up and made a slow circuit of the first floor, waving a rose in his right hand whilst clutching a bunch with the other. The girls ignored him and he didn't approach them. Sorayah noticed that he didn't make a single sale and fluttered downstairs. She frowned wondering why her abbu still let the flower sellers in.

The girls had just received their main course when Sorayah spied her father in the distance. He was looking directly at her. His furrowed forehead left no doubt how he felt. She looked away, anger rising in her belly.

"You okay, Sorayah?" Shabnam asked, chomping on a buttered nan.

"I'm fine."

Her father approached a nearby table and made conversation with the guests. Sorayah recognised two of the men. They were Manchester United players. She thought it was Gary Neville and Ryan Giggs, two of Ravinder's heroes. She didn't know the two women with them. *Probably wives – or girlfriends.* Her father chatted amiably with them.

"Hey, Saz," Ghazala said, nudging her under the table with her foot, "it's your dad."

"Oh, yeah." She hoped he wouldn't come to their table.

Then her father was there, a hulking presence over her shoulder. *Please, don't show me up, abbu.* "Salam beti, I see you've come with your friends - hello girls," Ajmal Butt said in English. Sorayah mumbled something unintelligible and nodded meekly. His hurtful words rang in her head and she had to look away.

"Hello, Uncle," the girls chorused in English.

"Your restaurant is wonderful," Dina said.

"Thank you, beti, it's Dina isn't it, Azhar Rasool's daughter, no? Give him my salam. Tell him to call me, we haven't spoken in a while."

"Yes, I will," Dina promised.

Her father spoke to each of her friends, surprising her each time that he knew who they were. Sorayah watched her friends fall for her father's charm. "You know, I am in restaurant trade for more than twenty years now and I tell you that food is bringing people together," Ajmal said. Sorayah winced. His words were a replica of her own, but her friends didn't shoot her any glances. The next ten minutes were spent with "Uncle…Uncle…"

A waiter approached her father to call him away. Ajmal Butt turned back to the girls; "It was nice to see you all after so much time. I hope to see you again soon." He smiled dazzlingly and left with the waiter.

"Your dad is great," Ghazala said, "at least he treats you like a real person." The girls murmured agreement. "My dad spits when he hears my name. God, I wish I had a dad like yours."

Sorayah couldn't believe it. *Can't you see how manipulative he is? How he gets people to do what he wants and doesn't give an inch?* She yearned to tell them what he'd called her only a few days ago, but she couldn't. She nodded, not wanting her friends to know how bad things were between father and daughter.

The girls continued talking after the meal was finished. An hour stretched into two. Sorayah went to the ladies and returned to find her father at the table again. She paused. Her father noticed her, nodded in her direction and then walked away. She sat down. Her friends were sitting quietly. She looked at each of them suspiciously. *What did he say?* Tayiba asked, "What's the time?" And the girls started talking again.

Soon it was time to leave and ring home to call their rides. They slowly made their way downstairs. They waited in a huddle outside the restaurant and promised they'd meet again at Yasmeen's Henna Party. One by one they left, cars pulling up outside the restaurant; there were hugs and promises to go shopping in London.

Finally, two remained. Shabnam and Sorayah.

"What's the matter, Sorayah?" Shabnam asked.

"Did my father say anything when he came to the table?"

"Eh?"

"When I went to the toilet he came over to the table again."

"Oh that. He just said that we should respect our families no matter what the differences and that they always want the best for us. Your daddy's so cute, don't you think?"

Maybe this was his way of saying sorry to me. Over the last few days, she'd learned from Shokat that their father was half the man he used to be. He'd started to forget important meetings and make small errors. That worried her. Despite what he'd said to her, she still loved him.

If he ever finds out that I took money from Uncle Jafar he'll kill me. But now she was stuck, there was no way out except to pay Uncle Jafar off as quickly as possible.

After Shabnam had been picked up by her brother, Sorayah's mobile phone rang.

"Hello, daughter," Uncle Jafar said in Urdu. She'd been expecting his call. She murmured a cursory hello. "I've been waiting for you to call me. Where have you been? Don't we have some business to discuss?"

"I heard you approached my brother to work for you? What are you playing at?"

Jafar Ali laughed gently. "Daughter, it's business, just business. Anyway, he won't leave your father. I knew that."

"Then why did you try?"

"This is wasting time. I want to discuss payment and I want to do it soon. Come to my house tomorrow."

"I was coming tomorrow anyway to meet Yasmeen."

Jafar was silent for a moment. "I'll see you in the morning then. Don't make it too late. I've got other things to do. Don't waste my time and I won't waste yours." He ended the call.

Sorayah sighed. *I should never have borrowed the money from him. I was such a stupid idiot!* She'd had a couple of days of bliss. She'd almost forgotten why she'd returned to Manchester. She needed a drink.

The drive to the Ali's was a well-worn route. After the Butt clan broke ties with the Alis, her father refused to take her to his enemy's home. Shokat had obliged in secret. Now, standing in the hallway of Jafar Ali's house, Sorayah recalled long and passionate conversations with Yasmeen. Smiling, she looked around the hallway: it was unrecognisable. Clean, muted marble had replaced the Asian floral motifs. Uncle Jafar always had taste.

She was waiting to be called in to meet with Jafar when she heard footsteps on the stairs and looked up to see Yasmeen running downstairs, hair flying behind her. Her best friend flung her arms around her and she almost fell. Yasmeen yanked Sorayah towards the living room.

"It's so good to see you again, beti," Yasmeen's mother said in Urdu when they entered. She looked worn and tired, but genuinely happy to see her. "I'm so happy you've stayed friends...through everything." Yasmeen grinned like a maniac.

"When are you getting married, beti?" Yasmeen's mother asked.

"My family's looking," Sorayah lied.

"Inshallah you'll find a good boy," Yasmeen's mother said. *Whatever.* Sorayah would have loved to marry and have a life filled with children, exotic travel and romantic meals, but it was all gone. Love had left an aftertaste of heartache. She didn't want that anymore. *Maybe I should could get an arranged marriage.* She stubbed out the thought, refusing to accept her sister's fate.

They climbed the stairs to Yasmeen's bedroom. It hadn't changed. She recognised the plain beige painted walls, the quilted pastel coloured patchwork bed cover, the full length mirror, the tiny bookshelf, the photos of friends and family. Sorayah started to cry.

"Are you okay?" Yasmeen asked.

"It's just...I can imagine myself here, sitting right there on your bed, talking about stuff. Your room has hardly changed – you should see my room."

"I liked things the way they were. Are, I should say."

Sorayah hugged her friend fiercely, "I missed you, Yaz."

"Hmm? Thank you for the phone calls."

"I'm sorry I didn't call you more often."

"Hey, I was only joking, I know you missed me. Everyone does."

They laughed.

Then they sat down on the bed and talked. Sorayah talked about how she felt being home, she mentioned the friends' get-together, how her abbu had treated her, how things had changed with her mother, how Baji Shazia was being so supportive and how Paijaan Shokat was as wonderful as ever. She mentioned Basharat.

"He was always a bad one, that one," Yasmeen said, "but he was so cute as a kid!" Sorayah nodded mutely.

Yasmeen showed Sorayah the wedding dress, still in its plastic covering. Sorayah was speechless with envy.

"It cost over a thousand pounds," Yasmeen told her. "I bought it from an Asian wedding fair in the NEC. It's gorgeous. Isn't it?"

"Oh yes." It was absolutely divine. Red silk with golden brocade. "Some women would kill to have that."

"Hmm? What you hinting at?"

Sorayah laughed. She took a brush from the trellis table. Without being asked, Yasmeen turned around. The two friends used to brush each other's hair when they were girls. She began brushing her friend's lustrous long hair.

Sorayah noticed her friend daydreaming, her eyes all cloudy. "What you thinking about?"

"Hmm, nothing."

"Don't give me that, Miss Yasmeen Ali."

Yasmeen turned round. "I'm just nervous."

"About the wedding?"

"The whole thing. I don't think I can go through

with it."

"Come on, you're bound to feel a little bit scared. It's the big M after all. Most people feel nervous. Your husband-to-be is feeling nervous too. Flippin' hell, I'm feeling nervous and I'm not even getting married."

"Yeah, I know, but I don't think I'm ready yet. It's too much."

"You're just afraid, it's natural, you won't be afraid after your shadi. You'll look back thinking 'what was I so worried about?'"

Yasmeen looked away. "I don't know him."

"Yaz, I can't believe you. You do know him, don't you?" Yasmeen was marrying her uncle's son. "And he's not un-cute."

"No, he's a hottie, but...oh, I don't know Sorayah, it's such a big change – and I don't love him." Yasmeen started crying, tiny silent tears. Sorayah hugged her friend.

"Why didn't you tell your mum that you feel like this?"

"Come on Sorayah, I can't tell my mum. She'll kill me."

"You know, I don't get it. Three months ago you were raving about Raheem, that he was the best thing since mango lassi and now you're telling me you don't want to go through with it. If nothing else, let me see you wearing the dress you bought for the wedding!" They both laughed. "Come on," Sorayah continued, "let me help you with the dress you're wearing to the party tonight."

The dress was maroon, interlaced with a complex golden weave. It had been brought over by a family friend a few weeks ago from New Delhi. Normally girls wore less ostentatious affairs for the painting of henna on their hands.

"I loved this dress so much I just knew I had to wear it at the mehndi," Yasmeen said. Sorayah caught Yasmeen looking at her with an odd expression in her eyes. "What's the matter?"

"I was wondering what things would have been like if I'd gone with you to London." When Sorayah had left Manchester, her plans had included Yasmeen, but her friend had stayed behind.

"I can't leave my family," Yasmeen had pleaded. She'd stayed and enrolled at the University of Manchester.

Meanwhile, in London, Sorayah discovered new friends. It was a mark of their firm friendship that they could continue a conversation exactly where they'd left it no matter how much time passed in between.

"I really hated you for a while," Yasmeen said. Sorayah opened her mouth to speak, but couldn't find the words. "I really did. That's why you couldn't get hold of me sometimes. I'm sorry."

"I don't get it. I begged you to come with me."

"Yeah, I know. But as much as I love you, I hate you sometimes too."

"Why would you hate me?"

"Not all the time, just sometimes. I'm sorry, I shouldn't have said anything."

"But why, Yaz?"

"Cos you got away. You escaped! You were free. I always wanted that – to get away, just like you."

"I didn't get away from anything."

"Yes you did," said Yasmeen her voice rising slightly, "you got to live your life in London. You had the parties, boys, you had it all. What did I have? I had to stay here and be a good kuri."

"Yaz, look at me. Don't hate me. Please, don't hate me. I'm no different to many girls who leave home."

"I know Sorayah, I know that. I just can't help feeling the way I do. I wanted to be like you – no, that's not true. I wanted to be you. I wanted to be as beautiful as you, but I couldn't be, I wanted to be as free as you and I couldn't be, cos I wasn't strong enough."

Sorayah's mouth hung open. She put her arms around her friend, but her friend didn't respond. She wondered if she should return home. "You think I had everything? Parties. Boys. The high life? That's what you think? I went to parties, most of them were shit. Boys? They all broke my heart. You want to swap a life of things-you-never-did with one where-you-did-em-and-paid-for-em? Do you know what it's like to have your boyfriend cheat on you for years behind your back? While he's so sweet in front of you he's having a twenty-four hour party with every kuri that comes his way…" Sorayah was weeping. It was Yasmeen's turn to put her arms around Sorayah. All the pain she'd felt when she broke up with Ravinder came back, a dark and searing pain. "You know," she said through her sobs, "I'd swap my life for yours and I wouldn't have any regrets."

"I'm sorry, Sorayah. I didn't know, I didn't know…" and then Sorayah filled in all the gaps about Ravinder as Yasmeen supplied her with tissues.

Sorayah then knew she had to tell her friend about the business deal with her friend's father. "I needed to help a friend out. Your father agreed to give me a hand, but he'd only lend the money to me, not to my friend. I trust Varinder so I agreed." She realised with a start that the real reason she'd delayed coming to Yasmeen's was because of Uncle Jafar.

"No way! You're kidding me. I don't believe it. Your dad wouldn't have let you… oh, he doesn't know, does he?"

Sorayah shook her head.

"Was it a lot of money?"

Sorayah nodded.

There was a knock at the door. Sorayah, thinking it was Yasmeen's mother, went to the door. It was Jafar Ali looking immaculate in his shirwani suit.

"How are you girls doing?" he asked in Urdu.

It was an awkward moment. *I'm lucky I told Yasmeen about borrowing the money.* Sorayah looked back at her friend. "Is it okay if I go and speak to your father? We need to have a chat."

Yasmeen nodded, concern in her eyes.

Sorayah followed Uncle Jafar downstairs into the front room.

"What have you told my daughter?" he snapped as soon as the door closed behind them.

"Why, what would you like me to tell her? Should I tell her everything about our deal? I'm sure you'd like that," Sorayah taunted.

Jafar Ali cleared his throat and sat down on the large leather sofa. He motioned for Sorayah to follow suit. "Okay, so you're in Manchester." A smile rippled on his face. Sorayah tensed.

"Yes. I'm here for Yasmeen's wedding. *Your* daughter's wedding."

He snorted. "You came because I told you to come. Because I want the repayments now. You were late last month and you're probably going to be late this month."

Was this to prove how powerful he is? "Summer's a slow time for the trade. You know how it is."

"Listen, don't be clever with me. I want my money all paid back by the end of the year."

"We agreed a three-year repayment deal."

"Well, things change. Don't they, daughter?"

"I can't do it. I won't do it."

"Then I'll tell you father that I lent you the money. He'll love that, won't he? His own daughter borrowing money from his worst enemy?"

Bastard. She loathed his gloating. She wanted to slap him. "Well, if you break your promise to me – "

"You were already late in paying me once."

"Once! And only by two days! You're shortening our agreement by almost two years."

"That's life, daughter."

There was a knock at the door and Auntie Rashida entered. "Jafar, is everything okay? Yasmeen said you wanted to speak to Sorayah."

"I was just asking about her father – I heard he wasn't too well," Jafar Ali said.

He looks tense. Good.

"Is everything okay, daughter?" Yasmeen's mother asked Sorayah.

"Oh, he's been a little ill, but he's okay." Sorayah said.

"I'll bring some tea," her auntie said brightly.

They were left in peace once more. "So, you want the money back by the end of the year?"

"Yes. You're a bright girl."

"I won't do it."

"What?"

"I'm not doing it. How are you going to make me?"

"I only need to make one phone call to your father."

"Oh yes, and I only need to have one conversation with Yasmeen. Perhaps I should have a word with Auntie Rashida as well."

"What are you talking about?"

"I'm sure they'd love to know about your women."

"What bakwas is this?"

"I know where you stayed last time you were in London. Oh yes, you didn't think I knew." They'd had a business meeting three months ago and following him had been easy. "I'm sure your wife and daughter would love to know all the things about you."

"You're cunning just like your father."

"Don't bring my father into this."

He swore under his breath. "You're quite a foe aren't you? I see." He smiled. "I underestimated you. You have ways of getting what you want."

She watched him carefully. "What do you want?" she asked bluntly.

He laughed. The door opened and her auntie came in carrying a tray, with two cups of tea, a little metal teapot and a plate with Asian sweetmeats.

"Yes, he's improved a lot," Sorayah said, continuing the pretend conversation. "But you know how it is running so many restaurants, having to travel so much. And it's so hard to get the right people. Plus, everyone needs to relax sometimes?" She peered carefully at her uncle. He was looking at Aunt Rashida. *Afraid I'll tell his wife about his women, eh?*

"Auntie," Sorayah said, "Uncle has come to London quite a few times to visit." Sorayah looked Jafar Ali straight in the eye. His eyes looked fearful. "After all, my brother lives in London and is a good friend of Javed's."

Jafar visibly relaxed when his wife left. They sat in

silence, sipping home-brewed tea. Sorayah let the silence build.

"No," she finally said.

"What do you mean, no? I haven't told you what I want yet."

"The answer is no, anyway."

He laughed then. "Let me finish, daughter. I've watched the way you've handled business between us, you're a formidable opponent, I grant you that. The loan was mere pennies to me. I wanted to see if you were worthy of investing in. You're better than I expected. Better than your father would have expected."

"You don't need to mention my abbu in every sentence."

"Of course not," he said placatingly, "but perhaps because I'm not your father I can see the good in you." *Lying bastard.* "I've watched you and I think you... let's say I would like you to come and join forces with me. Why don't we open a restaurant here in Manchester. Just you and me?"

How dare he? What makes him think that just because I borrowed some money off him that I'll become partners with him? "No. And I told you the answer would be no."

"Listen, daughter. You know Manchester as well as anyone. Why not join forces with me? You don't want to, because it would hurt your father's feelings? Does he care about yours? Would he have lent you the money that I did?"

"So, a few minutes ago you were twisting my arm and trying to get me to cough up the money years in advance and now you want me to be your partner?"

"It was a little test, that's all. I wanted to see if you were worthy."

"I don't need to pass any test of yours. I'm more than worthy." Despite her strong words, she knew he'd spoken the truth. *Abbu would never have lent the money to me. He'd never make me a partner.* But she'd never enter into a partnership with Jafar. "I'm here for your daughter's wedding. It's her mehndi tonight."

"Yes, yes, I know. But a little business can be mixed with personal items sometimes."

"Oh yeah, I know you like to do that. I know about that woman of yours on Hartley street."

His smile became brittle.

"Let me think about it," she lied.

"Yes," he said after a moment. "Think about it. But I'm only giving you twenty-four hours."

"I'm here for your own daughter's wedding and I'll take my time about it, thank you." He was about to reply when there was another knock on the door. Yasmeen came in.

"Shabs and Tabs are upstairs and asking for you!"

Sorayah looked at Uncle Jafar. "Okay, I understand," she said, "I'll give your salam to my father." She left the room, feeling relieved, angry and upset.

"What were you talking about?" Yasmeen asked.

"Business." She saw a cloud pass over Yasmeen's eyes.

"Is everything okay?" Yasmeen pressed.

"Yes, everything's fine."

She followed Yasmeen upstairs, remembering she hadn't finished her tea. At the top of the stairs she saw Javed. As she approached the landing he opened his mouth to say hello, but she looked away. She'd seen that look too many times on men's faces. She felt Javed watching her as she entered Yasmeen's room.

The henna artist arrived at precisely seven o'clock. She was a Kashmiri woman from Birmingham and had a long ponytail, a hairy chin and thick glasses. Her name was Kulsoom and she could do magic with henna. Sorayah made Yasmeen comfortable on a pile of cushions and pillows. Yasmeen was smiling, yet distant.

Music played loudly. Someone, probably Shabnam, had brought a mehndi compilation CD. She heard one of her favourites 'Aai Dekho Mehndi Ki Rat', followed by another: 'Banne Ke Ghar Se Mehndi'. There was others: 'Mehndi Se Likh Do', 'Menhdi To Mehndi He', 'Mehndi Wale Sab Ke' and 'Mere Angna Mehndi'. Sorayah effortlessly mimed the words to the songs, but her gaze was fixed on Yasmeen. She heard Shabnam shout: "Yaz looks so beautiful, I'm going to die!" A cameraman swooped in and out of the room. His long grey beard didn't dupe her. *God, he's horrible. I swear he's dribbling.*

The mostly female guests were chewing on tandoori chicken and lamb kebabs smothered in ketchup and everyone praised the intricate henna work growing on Yasmeen's flesh. Yasmeen was fidgeting beneath the ministrations of the henna hand painter.

"Don't worry," Sorayah assured her, but Yasmeen looked uncomfortable.

Javed appeared in the distance a couple of times, pulled in by aunties eager to show their daughters to him. Sorayah felt irritated that he was getting so much attention from aunties seeking a rich son-in-law.

All the girls were there. Dina, Farzana, Ghazala, Tayiba, Shabnam and other friends from Loreto College: Abida, Sharon and Tazmin.

Sorayah looked around the living room and counted the number of heads. She lost count at fifty-seven and then saw Parveen enter, the cameraman at her heels. Yasmeen's sister was wearing a pink dress that would look terrible on anyone else, but Parveen could pull it off.

"Parv wanted to speak to you," Yasmeen told Sorayah.

"What does she want to talk about? Come on Yaz, you know I don't get on with her."

"Yeah, I know that, I think she must have decided you were worth getting to know cos you're my best friend."

Sorayah was sceptical. *We were always best friends – what's so different now?* She met the gaze of Parveen who made her way across the room to sit down with them.

"Hi Sorayah. How are you?"

"I'm fine, that's a nice dress."

"Thanks," Parveen replied. *She knows how gorgeous she is and can't even be flattered.*

They made small talk. Parveen then asked, "How's your family?"

"They're fine…Imran's fine too." She saw the flush spread across Parveen's cheeks. *So it's true.*

"Oh, I'm glad they're okay," Parveen said.

Sorayah was irritated with Imran, not because he'd refused to come to Manchester with her to Yasmeen's wedding, but because it was to avoid Parveen.

Later, the friends gathered around Yasmeen as the henna painter completed her evening's work. Yasmeen looked magnificent. The designs were so intricate they hurt if you stared at them too long.

"You're so beautiful I'm going to die!" cried

Shabnam.

"Yes, you're beautiful," added Sorayah.

"Me, or the henna design?" Yasmeen said and they all laughed.

8

Ajmal drove like a madman along the Curry Mile. It was past midnight and the Kohinoor like the rest of his restaurants was still open, but he'd called it a night and left Shokat in charge. He was in a celebratory mood. Abdullah had thrown him the lifeline and he was on cloud nine. Neon sliced through the air. Wilmslow Road rippled into Oxford Road. He passed Manchester's universities in quick succession.

He pulled up outside Sameena's council flat. The light was still on in the front room. *She's waiting for me.* He licked his lips. He sat in the car as it cooled in the cold night air, and looked out for any spies. He tightened his red tie and cleared his throat. He left the car and waded through the street light into the darkened entrance of the rundown Chorlton-on-Medlock flats and up the smelly concrete steps.

He knocked once on the front door, a dull thud barely heard above the sighing wind and the distant groans of traffic. Thirteen heartbeats later, Sameena opened the door. His heart raced with jawan passion as he saw her, soft and yielding in the light of her living room. She was wearing a see-through salwar and kameez. He controlled his passion with an effort. In the past, he'd been followed. He didn't want an incriminating photo of him in a passionate embrace with Sameena.

"You're earlier than usual," Sameena said. He stepped into the house. She promptly closed the door behind him.

"Come here," ordered Ajmal and she was in his arms, filling all his emptiness.

Breaking from his embrace, Sameena urged, "Amina's asleep, don't make any noise."

He wanted to tell her Amina would be fine, either asleep or reading Harry Potter, but he only nodded and let her lead him into her flat. He recognised the rug, the television, the video player, the stack of Indian movies, all bought by him for her. *Without me she'd be nothing.* They stumbled onto the sofa and the night stretched around Ajmal and he felt he was home, no more restaurants to think about, nobody to pay, he didn't have to worry about rivals, the uselessness of his children, these nightmares were gone and only feverish jawan heartbeats remained.

"Please don't smoke. You know it isn't good for you," Sameena pleaded.

Ajmal puffed on regardless. She always complained about his smoking. He opened the kitchen window and puffed smoke into the rain. He savoured the sight of her beneath the dim electric light of her flat. Sameena was one of the most beautiful women he had ever met. Many of his friends would give their right arm to be with her and he still remembered the first day she came to him. A friend sent her in his direction three years ago. Luckily, Dilawar had different tastes, preferring demure, traditional girls.

"She'll be perfect for you," his friend had promised. They were speaking in Punjabi. "She makes excellent tea as well. And from what I know of your tastes, I think you'll find she doesn't look like a donkey." Dilawar had gone on to tell him that Sameena had recently been divorced, providing him with the leverage needed to extract his heart's desire. She had been disowned by her family in Bradford and was struggling to make ends meet. Ajmal was sceptical, but that was before he met her. The stunning and provocatively dressed Sameena had opened doors in his dirty heart. He'd lusted after many women before, a common dalliance amongst some restaurant owners, but to have a dish as delicious as Sameena was something he couldn't turn away.

Many of his assistants in the past had been women so it did not arouse suspicion and she made a useful contribution to the running of his little empire. But it had taken more than a month to swing the relationship in the direction he wanted. It began with the odd box of chocolates, red roses delivered by courier to her flat. Sameena had finally invited him to her home, of course at his urgent insistence. He'd checked out where she lived beforehand. Her flat was suitably distant from his home and it was wonderful she didn't live in an Asian area. She knew the score, that he was married and would never leave his wife of thirty years for her, a twenty-something divorcee.

Ajmal watched Sameena dress and walk barefoot into her tiny kitchen. She filled a kettle with water and turned on the gas cooker. He glanced at his watch. It was almost two o'clock. He felt the tiredness in his bones, but was still content. He sighed, pushed himself up into a sitting position on the sofa and pulled on his trousers. He usually stayed longer, but was itching to leave. Unfortunately, he couldn't sleep at her place.

"What's the matter, Ajmal?" she asked from the kitchen. He grunted.

She walked to the doorway of the kitchen, her long black hair a waterfall of delight. Ajmal felt a familiar stirring in his loins and smiled.

"You've got something on your mind, haven't you?"

"That David Mirza hasn't shown his ugly head yet," Ajmal said at last.

"You're tense," Sameena said coming back into the room. "Don't worry, I'll relax you." Sameena kneaded his shoulders. Ajmal sighed contentedly, closing his eyes for a long moment.

"He's bound to contact us sooner or later."

"Why worry about him, you're with me. You must forget about all your worries."

"Yes, but he's a dangerous man to deal with."

"I know, I know. You've told me a million times."

Friends and informants had told him the loan shark was as close to a disease as a human being could be. *Why didn't I learn this sooner? If only I'd known I wouldn't have made the stupid mistake of borrowing money from the gunda.* David Mirza had deep connections in the Asian underground. Over the last few months Ajmal had gleaned the startling extent of Mirza's reach. He was involved with prostitution, drugs, money laundering. What worried Ajmal most was that Mirza was rumoured to be connected to the killing of the Birmingham businessman, Wazeer Azam, the multi-millionaire burnt to death in his Mercedes. The official report was that it was an accident. Rumours said Mirza personally torched his car.

Dilawar, Ajmal's best friend, had asked: "Why didn't you come to me if you had troubles?" Ajmal had no reply.

Sameena continued massaging his shoulders. He felt himself melting. "Don't worry. He can't do anything to us, we've got the money to pay him," Sameena told him. "Do you want some tea?"

Ajmal shook his head. He'd decided to leave and catch up with the sleep that had eluded him for weeks.

"How much did we make today?" Sameena asked him quietly. Ajmal was lying on his front on the sofa as she massaged him. At one time he would never have allowed her to ask him that question – let alone consider answering it.

"Just under ten thousand when I left." He always liked to know how much was in the till. It was quite a feat combining all the totals of the Curry Mile restaurants in one go, but it was a challenge he enjoyed and Shokat was competent enough to handle the loose change.

"That's an improvement on last week," Sameena commented.

Ajmal grunted beneath her ministrations. He knew it was a tremendous upturn. *But what does one day count?* There was a time when ten thousand was a small fortune, but with his competitors opening million pound restaurants, ten thousand pounds was nothing.

Sameena's tone changed as she said, "Ajmal, I've been meaning to ask you something."

"What?" Ajmal guessed what she wanted.

"I could really do with a pay rise. Amina's growing up fast now and I want to send her to a good school."

"I pay you well enough." Ajmal was used to these conversations with staff. "I give you gifts and I let you come in late sometimes, don't I? I've given you your own office space. I've even lent you my car when you needed it. I helped you open a bank account; I paid for your holiday in France last year. Am I or am I not a generous boss? I don't do all these favours for all my workers, you know. I don't think you appreciate what

I've been giving to you."

"Yes, Ajmal, I do, but you're such a successful businessman. I was so lucky to find you. I thought my life was over in Bradford, but you made everything right for me, just like you promised. But you're so successful; you make even your problems seem small." Ajmal finds himself glowing. *That's more like the praise I deserve.* He was consciously slipping into her net. *Why not? What do I have to lose?* "Let me think about it."

"Thank you, Ajmal," Sameena said, "I'll make it worthwhile."

Ajmal smiled.

Later, Sameena helped him with his tie. It was something Sameena had always done from the start of their affair. He felt guilty being with Sameena, but he hadn't shared any intimacy with his wife for several years.

Ajmal relaxed on the sofa. He was contemplating leaving when there was a noise from the stairs. Ajmal turned. Sameena's daughter, Amina, was clutching a teddy bear. She ran to her mother who hugged her.

"Mummy, I woke up and you weren't there."

"It's okay…I was just talking to my friend."

"You always talk to your friend at night, mummy. I want you to come back to sleep." With a look, Sameena implored Ajmal to not say anything. She took her daughter upstairs and Ajmal helped himself to a cup of tea. Sameena had brewed a pot. It was as good as ever. He had a lot to thank his friend Dilawar for. *I'll have to return the favour one day…let me sort David Mirza out and then I'll see what I can do.*

Sameena soon returned. He stayed for another ten minutes before pulling himself up from the sofa.

Sameena helped him put on his jacket.

"Don't be late," he told her at the door. She nodded. She looked tiny without her high heels. She touched him on the chin. He felt a surge of affection for her.

As he got into his Mercedes, he saw her in the living room window. She waved and he waved back. As he pulled away, he saw a shadow in the rear-view mirror. He blinked. It was gone. Cursing himself, he put the car into gear and hurriedly drove away.

On the way home he began to feel intensely tired. He pulled over and closed his eyes. His heart was racing. He felt a tightening across his chest and fear leapt into his mouth. *No, not now, I don't want to go now!* He felt the pressure building up in his chest and imagined his heart exploding. *No! I have the heart of a lion!* He clenched his jaw in an inhuman effort to contain the explosion he was expecting.

He saw his future rolled out before him, his family at his funeral prayer and loyal and spineless Shokat looking down at him, dark tears streaming from his normally docile face and whimpering, "*Abbaji! Abbaji!*" *Oh no! Jafar will eat him alive! What chance does he have?* His fear of a rudderless business eclipsed everything. The pain capsized, the moment was gone, but it left Ajmal with ashes in his mouth. *What chance do I have if my children can't take over after I'm gone? When I go my business will all crumble – Ajmal & Sons will be finished.*

He felt dejected as he put the car into gear and made his way home. The warm feelings from Sameena had fled, leaving the same emptiness that was there before she opened the front door.

He kicked the accelerator, switched on the CD player and the mesmeric voice of Nusrat Fateh Ali Khan filled the darkness of the car.

9

The house was silent when Sorayah awoke.

She tumbled out of bed, blurred figures dancing before eyes. In the bathroom, cold water revived her. She squinted at herself in the mirror. *There goes my market value*. She grinned at the thought. She'd returned late from last night's mehndi, and although she had been tired, she could not sleep. She'd pulled out her journal and written for an hour. She wrote everything she could remember about the henna party, noting down what the girls had said they would wear to the wedding. Now, in the harsh light of day she rummaged through her wardrobe looking for the right dress. She selected a beautiful blue kurta pyjama, an unexpected bargain from a tiny Indian clothes shop in Rochdale. Most of the girls would be wearing gaudy colours. *You never get a second chance at a first impression.*

After she'd changed, Sorayah went downstairs and stood waiting in the porch.

"Damn! Where's that flippin' Shabnam?" Her friend had promised she'd pick her up on the way to Yasmeen's nikah, the marriage ceremony. Sorayah was ready, preened to perfection, poised on the porch and Shabnam was nowhere to be seen. "Where is she?" Sorayah regretted listening to Shabnam's request to go together.

Her mobile phone rang. It was Imran.

"Are you off shift?" she answered, surprised.

"Oh, yeah, how was the mehndi?"

"How come you're so curious? You know what happened to the cat?"

He laughed, but sounded nervous.

"Everything was okay, but your friend was acting a little weird," Sorayah said.

"Which friend?" Imran asked.

"Javed."

"Weird? How?"

"Well, I think he's sweet on me."

"There's nothing wrong with that, is there? You know he likes you. So what if he likes you a teeny weeny bit?"

"Come on. It's Javed we're talking about."

"He's a nice guy. But then you don't seem to like nice guys."

"What do you mean I don't like nice guys?"

"You prefer the ones who're nasty, you know, the tear your heart out types."

"Is there something you want to say, Immy? Cos I've got a wedding to go to."

"I just reckon you guys would be kind of cute together."

"What? You're crazy."

"Okay, okay, I shouldn't have said anything."

"He's Uncle Jafar's son for crying out loud!"

"Since when did you care about things like that?"

"That's not fair, Immy," Sorayah said, then added, "are you saying all this cos you want to have a better chance with Parveen?"

"Parveen," Imran coughed, "Parveen, you mean, like, Javed's sister?"

"You're so crap at lying."

"This hasn't got anything to do with that."

"You seeing her?"

"Sorayah!"

"Are you?"

"No. Yes. No, I mean."

"Well, Mr Confusing. Is this all about Javed or is this all about you and knowing abbu won't like it so you're trying to make it easier for yourself?"

"Whatever's going on between, well, you know, between Parveen and me, has nothing to do with this."

"Oh, pull the other one," Sorayah said.

"Honest. I wouldn't lie to you."

"You're a right one. Hiding it for all this time."

"Look, honest Sorayah. This isn't about me. I don't care what Dad or Uncle Jafar think anyway."

"Really?" Sorayah was surprised.

"Well, I guess I didn't realise it till I said it. Now come to think of it. I don't. They live their lives. We live ours. Kind of good that way, eh?"

"So what's this all about?"

"It's about Javed. He's always liked you, Sorayah."

Sorayah blinked quickly. "Come on, he hasn't. It's only since I moved in with you and went out with you guys a few times. I know guys. This one in particular. He was always the one to be led by the nose."

"He isn't like that. He'd make a good choice for you."

"What? I can't believe this. You're my brother. You're meant to protect me, I'm your little sister, remember. And you're trying to hitch me with your mate."

"I am protecting you! You're the one who doesn't protect herself."

"Look Imran, much as I love to talk to you, I've running late for a wedding. How come you're calling me now? Did he phone you or something?"

"No."

"He was being really creepy last night – and just to inform you, I'm over guys. I'm not interested."

"Look, Sorayah. My diagnosis is you need to settle down."

"Don't go telling me what I need to do."

"You just don't get it, do you, Sorayah? One of these days you'll realise, but it might be too late by then, you always go for the bad ones, Sorayah, You can't control yourself."

"How dare you!"

"Why can't you go for someone who actually loves you?"

"Loves me?"

"Yes, why don't you go for someone who loves you for you instead of these wannabe Salman Khan types? Eh?"

"What do you mean 'someone who loves me'?"

"You're really thick today, aren't you?"

"Thick? You mean Javed?"

"Yes."

"No way! I've already been through this with you. It's no, in capital letters!"

"Why not?"

"I think I want to forget this horrible conversation."

"He'd follow you to the ends of the earth."

It sounded nice, but she couldn't believe it. "Men are all the same. They're all phoney."

"Me included?"

"No, you're my brother. But maybe I should speak to Parveen."

"Why would you want to do that? That's crazy!"

"Someone definitely called you yesterday about this. Was it Parveen? I bet you speak everyday."

Imran didn't reply straight away. "No, it was Yasmeen."

"What? She phoned you about this? Are you all talking behind my back trying to set me up? I can't believe you guys. You want me to stay in Manchester, trapped here forever. I can't trust any of you. I'm going to kill her!" She ended the call. Imran tried calling her back, but she ignored the ringing mobile phone. She was fuming.

"I knew I should have gone by myself!" Sorayah told Shabnam.

"Don't be angry Sorayah – I came as quickly as I could. I swear. I'll die if you don't forgive me!"

"Just hurry up!" Shabnam pulled out of the driveway and hit the accelerator.

Sorayah felt more stressed than before. She took a deep breath, the music pushed up her blood pressure. The girls hurtled towards the Alis' house. The journey to Cheadle Hulme passed in a blur. Sorayah didn't know how she'd apologise to Yasmeen if she didn't make it.

They arrived in a screech of tyres. Sorayah jumped out of the car, almost tripping over her dress. There was a line of cars filling the driveway and people milling outside the house. Sorayah was impressed at the numbers.

"Oh no, I think she's already married. Flippin' hell."

She didn't wait for Shabnam, she picked up the bottom folds of the dress and raced to her friend's house, zipping between cars.

Then she saw the ambulance. She stopped.

Shabnam knocked into her, but she didn't notice. Fear erupted in her belly. She noticed people looking glum, troubled. There was subdued talking. She asked an auntie what had happened, but the woman only shook her head.

"What's going on?" Shabnam said, her voice sounding small and scared.

Sorayah shushed her. The front door was open and people were on the stairs. *Has something happened to Yasmeen?* She desperately looked for someone she recognised. Then she heard movement behind her and saw Javed running up the drive. She stopped him and asked him what had happened.

"She tried to kill herself," he said quietly, almost whispering.

Horror filled her. "What?" Then, "Why?"

"She didn't want to get married. She's your best friend, didn't she tell you?"

Sorayah looked away. She felt ashamed.

Sorayah's mother appeared in the doorway and Yasmeen was brought out on a stretcher. "Please move back," the paramedic said. People moved grudgingly. It was a funeral procession. Yasmeen lay sickly, pale and unconscious on the stretcher. A pall fell over the crowd. Sorayah felt the tears trickle down her face and angrily wiped them away. A shiver went down her back when she saw the look of terror on Auntie Rashida's face. And then the incongruousness of Yasmeen phoning Imran hit her. *Why did you do it? Why this way? She said I was free and she wasn't. Maybe I just didn't get it.* All the anger she'd felt towards her friend was gone.

She wanted to ask if Yasmeen would be okay, but couldn't and she couldn't look away as her friend was bundled into the ambulance. Sorayah could imagine the things already being said. She was certain that many within the Ali clan were fervently praying for Yasmeen to die to stamp out the shame she'd brought on her family. Sorayah noticed her friends milling around. They looked scared and lost. The ambulance left like an afterthought. Sorayah hugged a muted Shabnam and they both wept for Yasmeen.

The next few hours were frantic. Imran phoned again and she answered this time.

"I'm really sorry for anything I might have said," he began.

"Shut up and listen."

"Uh?"

She quickly explained what had happened. "Shit. I'm really sorry, Sorayah, I really am. Is she okay?" Imran asked.

"I don't know." Sorayah felt responsible. *I should have listened more to her.* She got Javed's number from Imran. She phoned Javed and asked him which hospital Yasmeen had been taken to and she made her way there alone. Shabnam was in no state to accompany her and had stayed behind at the Alis. Sorayah phoned home, but nobody answered. She phoned Shazia and Shokat. They were all afraid: afraid for Yasmeen, but also afraid for what it would all mean.

Yasmeen's family were already there when she got to Wythenshawe Hospital. Sorayah felt like a vulture, but nobody said anything to her, nobody shooed her away.

Javed walked over to her. "Thanks for coming," he said. She frowned.

"Why are you thanking me? She's my friend. I came for her. Don't you think I care for her?"

"No, it's just, I wanted to thank you for being here."

"Is she okay?"

"The doctors haven't told us yet. She's lost a lot of

blood." Javed paused. "Sorayah," Javed said looking directly at her for the first time. "will you marry me?"

She was shocked. *His sister's lying dying and he's asking me to marry him. He isn't just weird, he's stupid.* She heard the sound before she realised what she'd done. She slapped him across the face. She saw people turning at the sound.

"How dare you!" she hissed. She turned on her heels and walked down the corridor.

"Sorayah, I'm sorry, I don't know what came over me," she heard him say, but she ignored him. *What an idiot.* She stopped around the corner and rested against a wall, breathing deeply. She felt her insides were going to explode. *He's crazy. Why would he do such a thing? What if others had heard?* Slowly, she walked back. The chagrined Javed avoided her and she stood silently amongst the other family members.

Several hours later, Yasmeen was allowed visitors. There was subdued chatter in the corridor. The news placed smiles on people's faces. Relatives began to drift away. Sorayah entered the hospital room. Her eyes sought her friend out. Yasmeen's eyes were closed, but she looked peaceful.

"Daughter, come and sit down and talk to your friend," Yasmeen's mother said in Urdu. Sorayah was touched. She sat down and Yasmeen's eyes fluttered open.

"It was quite a party last night," Sorayah began.

"Yes, got a bit freaky at the end, hmmm?"

"Definitely." They watched each for long moments. Then Sorayah said, "You're a cow, you know. Who would I have done shopping with if you weren't around, eh?"

Yasmeen laughed, but ended up coughing. Anxiously, Sorayah handed her a cup of water.

"Why, Yasmeen?"

There was silence.

"Why else? I told you, Sorayah."

Sorayah nodded. There wasn't anything she could add to that. "I was angry with you this morning," Sorayah confessed. "I was upset you spoke to Imran last night."

"You can't blame a sister for trying to help her brother." Yasmeen paused. "He's always loved you, Sorayah. He just couldn't tell you, that's all, and I wanted to help. I saw the way he was acting last night. You didn't think I'd noticed. You can't kid a kidder, you know."

Sorayah smiled grimly.

"He just proposed marriage outside. He's an idiot."

"A big idiot. He should have at least waited for me to wake up first!"

"I don't love him, Yasmeen."

"I know, Sorayah. Don't you think I know that?"

"Then why tell Imran?"

"Sorayah, that's the saddest story of the world. You know you loved Ravinder but he never loved you?"

"But he did. He told me."

Yasmeen paused as if weighing something momentous. Finally, she said, "No, Sorayah. I never told you this, but he made a pass at me two years ago when I came to your birthday party."

Sorayah didn't want to hear it, didn't want to believe it. She held the delicate hand of her friend and knew it was true. She wept then, knowing the love she'd felt for

Ravinder was finally broken in a hospital room in Manchester. It was gone. There was nothing.

"I slapped him."

"Who?"

"Your brother."

"He probably deserved it."

"Probably?"

"Definitely." There was a long silence between them for several minutes and Sorayah thought Yasmeen had fallen asleep. "Forgive him. He's awkward around you. He just doesn't know what to say when you're there."

"I can't promise you anything, Yaz," Sorayah said. Yasmeen smiled, closed her eyes and slept.

10

Son of a bitch. Ajmal forced a smile, but inwardly he was enraged. Ahmed Iqbal, the proprietor of *Greater Manchester Asian* was sitting on the other side of the desk. The journalist had arrived a scant ten minutes ago, openly leered at Sameena and demanded a cup of hot tea be brought up immediately.

The need to donate funds to the local mosque was one problem, but the perennial obligation to advertise his restaurants was far worse. He felt he was at the whim of the local ethnic press. As the restaurant clientele had shifted from white to Asian, the press had become judge, jury and executioner and they were accountable to no one. A carefully crafted rumour that a restaurant was serving haram meat could be deadly.

The number of Asian newspapers had grown feverishly. Corner shops, restaurants and taxis were the staple diet of apnes who rarely undertook an untested, untried activity. Ethno-journalism was a brave new duniya that granted something the usual apna trades simply did not – it gave the thickly moustached Ahmed Iqbal the power to grant life or death, honour or dishonour. *How did this kanjar become so powerful? He wouldn't even be good enough for a dog's scraps in Pakistan.*

"Twenty thousand is reasonable for a year. Do you know how many people read *GM Asian*?" Ahmed said in Punjabi, smoothing his moustache with thumb and index finger.

"I paid five and a half thousand last year. Why this massive increase?"

Ahmed slurped his tea loudly. "There is great demand and I can't meet it. The circulation has increased. There's no better Asian weekly in the whole of Greater Manchester."

It was true, but Ajmal still hated him. *The bastard wants to be paid in cash as well.*

"Jafar Ali had no problem paying the amount," said Ahmed bluntly.

Ajmal's temperature rose several notches. "Well, maybe he did, but I'm not Jafar. I'm a businessman and I don't throw money away. I'll pay you seven thousand, that's reasonable."

"I can't afford that. I need twenty."

"No, seven thousand it is, or I'll lower it to five and a half thousand like last year. I don't get any customers from your paper and I had to make lots of concessions for your parties." *GM Asian* held many functions on the Curry Mile each year. Invariably, Ahmed Iqbal turned to the Kohinoor for the most important events and had the gall to demand a discount.

Ahmed bridled. "Well, if you're not interested I can take those functions elsewhere. I'm sure Jafar Ali will be more than interested in new business from me. After all, he's the real Curry King, isn't he?" He got up to leave. Ajmal felt the moment slipping away. He refused to buckle under the pressure. *Killer Instinct, where are you?* Ahmed was striding towards the door.

"Okay, twenty thousand," he blurted reluctantly. He felt depressed. Deflated. Ahmed turned back. He was smiling toothlessly.

"Perhaps another cup of tea?" Ahmed said smoothly.

After Ahmed Iqbal departed, Ajmal riffled through the different Asian papers to check his photos were in every one. It was imperative his face appeared more often than Jafar Ali's. Jafar's restaurants took up the central pages in half of them. "I need to have more function here at the Kohinoor. I need free publicity." *But how? How can I do it? Killer Instinct, where are you?*

Shokat rang him. His eldest son called him several times a day to keep him updated on events. Sameena was filing away press cuttings of Ajmal in the portfolio he'd created specially for visitors.

"Abbaji, you know Uncle Jafar's daughter, Yasmeen?" Shokat said in Punjabi.

"He's not your uncle and yes, of course I know who she is. Your stupid sister was at her wedding. How could I forget, idiot!"

"She didn't get married, abbaji. She was taken into hospital yesterday."

His ears pricked up. "Oh yes, what happened?"

"She tried to commit suicide."

After he put the phone down, Ajmal sat back in his swivel chair. He was knocked for a six. He'd been so angry with Sorayah for attending Yasmeen's wedding and now the shadi was off.

Ajmal would have expected to feel the stirrings of victory on hearing such a calamity had befallen Jafar Ali, but instead he felt sadness. He'd known Yasmeen all her life. She'd played with Sorayah as a child and he'd once felt jealous that Yasmeen was closer to Sorayah than him. *How could this have happened? What did Jafar do wrong?* Ajmal shook his head. It was a sad reality in Ajmal's life that he had total control over hundreds of workers' lives, often paying them a pittance and treating them like serfs, but he had little control over his own children. *Yasmeen is like my own daughter.*

"Ajmal?" Sameena said from the doorway that

separated their respective offices. "Is everything okay?"

"No," he muttered back in Punjabi. "No, it isn't okay." He stood up. "I'm going for a walk." Sameena looked surprised, but didn't say anything. Ajmal knew what he had to do.

On the way downstairs he met the restaurant manager. He informed Saleem Rasool he'd be back shortly. The manager nodded. Ajmal made his way to the Shandaar.

As usual, traffic was heavy and the Mile was filled with students, shoppers, apnes and gorays. He paused at the entrance of the Shandaar. He'd stared at its doorway for the last few years. He knew every inch of it, knew the doormen by sight, even their names, but he'd never crossed the threshold before. There was no doorman present. It was still early and few people would be entering for the Sunday buffet.

Ajmal pushed open the heavy door and stepped inside. It was warm and humid. Large plastic plants stood on either side of the entrance. He looked down towards the till and saw his old employee, Bilal Yusuf. The short man leapt up as if electrocuted and dashed upstairs. *Traitor.* The other workers realised something was afoot and stepped forward to intercept him. Ajmal grinned fearlessly, ignored them and followed the route Bilal had taken. *Yes, traitor, lead me to him.* He walked up the flight of steps. He looked up and saw Jafar Ali waiting for him. There were dark circles under his eyes. He normally looked resplendent in his shirwani suit, but today he looked like a husk of himself. Bilal fidgeted at his side.

"Ajmal Saab," the unctuous Jafar began in Urdu, "what brings you here?"

"Let's speak in private," replied Ajmal in Punjabi. He refused to change languages for his enemy.

Jafar looked at him for a moment. He whispered something in Bilal's ear and motioned for Ajmal to follow. He was quickly led into Jafar's office. Ajmal stopped himself from openly admiring the décor. It was tastefully done, green plants and dark wooden panelling that reminded him of Pakistan.

"So what do you want?"

"I came here, because I heard about your daughter."

There was fury in Jafar's eyes. "Oh, so you've come to gloat, no?"

"No, my brother. I haven't come to gloat. Yasmeen is like a daughter to me."

"Don't you dare say her name. How is she a daughter to you?"

"She's like my own Sorayah."

"Well, perhaps your daughter is more like a daughter to me than mine is to you."

Ajmal was confused. "What nonsense is this?"

"Oh yes, got you now, no? Your daughter came to me last year and asked me for money and I lent her every penny she asked for. She could have gone to you, but she trusted me more than she trusts you! So yes, maybe your Sorayah is more of a daughter to me than she is to you!"

Ajmal was breathless. What was he hearing? *She's a traitor like that bastard, Bilal!*

He shot out of the Shandaar, Jafar's clipped laughter ringing after him. If Jafar's accusation was true he would crush Sorayah's throat in a vice and feed her to dogs. *How could she do this to me, her own father?* It was besti on besti. He was in a daze all the way back to the restaurant.

He pulled out his car keys. *I'm going to find that kutti now and end her betrayal once and for all.* He rushed through the Kohinoor's entrance, surprising Saleem who was rearranging tables with three other workers for a wedding. Ajmal ran through the kitchen and into the car park. He got into his car and sped out of the driveway, fire in his head. He turned the corner without looking or caring and smashed into the rear of a passing car. For a moment he sat dazed, not knowing what had happened.

In slow motion, he watched Saleem Rasool and other employees approaching. An Asian woman stepped out of the car he'd crashed into. She was shouting abuse, but he couldn't understand what she was saying. He heard the roar of blood in his ears. Then Shokat was there, talking to the woman. Someone put their arm around him. Later, he would remember it was his son. Later, he would learn Shokat placated the woman.

Ajmal sat down on the pavement like a limp sack of Basmati rice.

He finally noticed his Mercedes and the huge dent at the front of it. "What's Basharat done this time?" he muttered.

"What happened, abbaji? Are you okay?"

"Go and find Sorayah. Now."

"What, abbaji? Why? What's the matter?"

"Idiot. Find her and… and kill her. She betrayed me. She trusted that bastard Jafar more than me. More than her own father." The words were out and simply speaking them broke some terrible spell. His mind reasoned his enemy was cunning and may have spun a deliberate half-truth to engineer panic. He raised his head. "Okay, okay, just find Sorayah and bring her to me. I want to talk to her and find out what happened. I want to know if she did go to him and if so, why? Do it now, son, do it quickly."

Shokat hesitated.

Ajmal pushed him roughly away. "Quickly. Bring her to me. Or I swear I'll kill her myself!"

Shokat left.

Ajmal looked up at the sky and almost wept. *My khuda, why are you testing me like this? I don't deserve this! Have I not served you and the masjid well?* He was helped up by a couple of his workers back into the restaurant. The police and an ambulance arrived ten minutes later.

11

Sorayah's eyes snapped open. She stared at the bedroom ceiling, the bed sheet wrapped in her limbs. Groggily, she reached for her phone to check for text messages. The battery had gone down. She cursed and tumbled out of bed. She should have been leaving for London today, but that plan had been discarded. She'd forgotten to cancel the ticket. *I have to stay until she's okay. I should have been there for her and I wasn't.* She put the phone to charge, changed, opened the curtains and the window and went to have a shower.

"I'm a doctor, and even I don't know what to do," Parveen told her in the hospital. They were talking quietly in English in the corridor. Only Yasmeen's closest family were there. Uncle Jafar was absent and Sorayah felt irritated by that. *Hurt his stupid izzat, I bet.*

"I know, it's hard," Sorayah said, putting her arm around Parveen. They'd never been close, but Yasmeen's attempted suicide had brought them closer together over the last few days.

"I can't concentrate on anything. How can I? My sister's lying here in the hospital that I work in. It's just so weird."

"We're here for her, that's what counts."

"I'm not used to having things out of my control."

"That's life, Parv."

"But if I accepted that, then I wouldn't do what I do." Parveen was a general surgeon. "What can you do to heal someone's heart?" Parveen looked away. "We should go inside."

They heard footsteps approaching. It was Raheem,

Yasmeen's fiancé, with Javed. Sorayah felt herself stiffen at the sight of Javed, but she was more concerned that Raheem was there.

"What's *he* doing here?" Parveen said in Urdu, her voice breaking.

"I don't know," replied Sorayah.

"Raheem can't meet her! He caused this." Parveen sounded close to tears.

Sorayah realised Parveen was in no state to speak to either of the men. "Raheem, I don't think it's a good idea that you're here," she said in English.

Raheem looked away. Javed spoke. "Look, Raheem isn't the bad guy here."

"How do you know that, Jav?" hissed Parveen. "It's because of him that this happened to our sister."

"I told you this was a bad idea," Raheem said and turned away.

"No, wait, Raheem," Javed said.

Raheem stopped.

"It wasn't his fault. He didn't know Yasmeen was against the marriage. Our father wanted it to happen," Javed continued.

Sorayah knew Raheem's mother was Uncle Jafar's sister and they'd planned the unification of the two families decades ago. "Raheem thought Yasmeen had given her free consent."

Raheem spoke up. "I would never have said yes if I knew she wasn't interested. She could have told me millions of times over last year. I don't want to marry someone who isn't interested in me." He was looking at Sorayah, but he was speaking in Urdu. Sorayah guessed he was really speaking to Parveen. "But I still want to marry her. There's nobody else for me. I don't care about what my mum says about her being worthless."

"Don't you dare say that about my sister," Parveen snapped.

"I'm only telling you what my mum thinks. But I don't care what she thinks. I just want to make sure Yasmeen's okay."

"Raheem," Sorayah said in English, "Yasmeen's not well. It isn't the right time to go up to her and tell her all this. She's traumatised. Your family hasn't been to the hospital to visit and we can guess why. We're not blaming anyone for that. Wait until Yasmeen's recovered a little and then speak to her, but not today. If you say you still want to marry her, then please be patient."

Raheem nodded.

"Sorayah, how can you say that?" Parveen said. "She's in this hospital because of him. *Him*. Don't you get it?"

"No, Parv," Javed said, "she's in here cos she was unhappy and tried to find a way out of her unhappiness. We're glad that she didn't succeed, but what if she has the chance to be happy in the future? Would you deny her that?"

Parveen was silent.

"Okay, I'll go," Raheem said, interrupting. "But she can't get rid of me that easily."

Raheem left, leaving Javed looking uncomfortable. "He came to me, Parv. He said he felt, you know, that he couldn't live with himself if he didn't get to tell her that he hadn't known."

Parveen stomped away down the corridor.

"She's going to take some convincing," Sorayah said. "I'll talk to her."

The day Yasmeen had attempted to commit suicide, Sorayah had returned home late. She hadn't rung home to tell her mother what had happened. When she arrived, the lights were on. Her mother was sitting in the living room listening to a recording of the Holy Quran. Sorayah tensed. She expected her mother to reprimand her for returning so late. When she looked closely she could see her ammi had been crying.

"You should have phoned to tell me," her mother said.

"Ammi, are you okay?" Sorayah asked in Punjabi.

"Imran phoned to tell me what happened. Poor Yasmeen. What a poor child."

Sorayah sat down and put an arm around her mother. "It's okay. She didn't die. She'll be okay."

"Some people will say that she's a bad Muslim, a bad girl. You know that, Sorayah?"

"Yes, ammi."

"They'll say she was a bad girl all along, that she'd wanted to marry someone else."

Sorayah could only nod.

"But she's like my own daughter. Who wants this, this thing, forcing a beautiful woman to marry against her own will? Tell me, who wants this?"

"I don't know, ammi. People just do."

"You know why I didn't go to the hospital, why I haven't rung her mother to ask how her daughter is? Because of your father. Is it more honourable not to speak to someone than to speak to them? But I can't go against him. His wishes have always been greater than mine, just like my father's wishes were always greater than mine before I got married. I wanted to get married so much when I was a girl, young and beautiful like you, but maybe my heart didn't want it either."

Sorayah nodded, not fully understanding. "Abbu hasn't been that bad, has he?"

Her mother looked away. "How can you know what men make women do? You're young, unmarried. Women belong to their men, the men make the decisions and we suffer. That's our lot in life and for most of my life I've never complained. But I want to complain today, because I almost lost a daughter."

Her mother started crying again. Sorayah handed her a tissue.

"Don't cry, ammi. She's going to be okay. You can come and see her with me if you like."

Her mother shook her head. "I can't. Your father would object."

"You don't have to always do what abbu says."

Her mother smiled weakly. "I'm not as strong as you, Sorayah. I have to. I must. My honour begins and ends with him. If I die by his hands that's enough for me. What else is my life worth?"

"Ammi, your life's worth a lot to me. We all love you." *We all love you.* Sorayah had never used those words for her mother before and they felt odd, yet right somehow. "We'd all die for you. Yes, we love abbu too, but you're our mother."

"You were always closest to your father when you were a child, but maybe you're more my daughter now that you're older."

Sorayah could only nod.

Her mother stood up. "It's late and I have to get up early for the morning prayer. Don't stay up too late or your hair will fall out like Basharat's."

It was only after her mother had gone and closed the

door behind her that Sorayah realised her mother had made a joke. Sorayah laughed gently and shook her head. She slowly made her way upstairs to her room and changed. As she lay in bed, she wept for her mother, for her friend and for all the other women she could think of, stories spinning in her head, tales of passion and pressure, violence and dreams unlived.

Sorayah held Yasmeen's hand. "Do you remember when we were kids and we used to play that game?" Yasmeen asked.

"Witch's Cauldron?" Sorayah replied.

"Yeah, that's it. Do you remember the words?"

"I'd never forget them."

Yasmeen lapsed into silence. Then, "We used to argue a lot didn't we – when we were kids, I mean?" Yasmeen said, a far-away look in her eyes.

"How come you're so nostalgic today?" Sorayah teased.

"I suddenly realised that I almost threw it all away. God, I was so stupid. I don't know what I was thinking. I've ruined everything. Daddy will never speak to me again."

"That's not true. He loves you."

"No. He doesn't."

"There's someone who does though," Sorayah said brightly.

"Who?"

"Shabs."

They laughed.

"No seriously, there is someone who does," Sorayah said.

"Who? Are you gonna keep me in suspense,

hmmm?"

"Well, let's just say he still wants to marry you."

Yasmeen closed her eyes and then opened them again.

Should have kept my mouth shut.

"How can he after all I put him through? His family probably never wants to lay eyes on me ever again."

"His family maybe, but not him. I think he'd crawl on his hands and knees for a million miles just for you."

"Really?"

"Really."

"Wow. He really is crazy."

"Definitely."

"Maybe he isn't so bad after all."

Later, when Sorayah stood up to leave, Yasmeen made her promise she'd return.

"You're my best friend. I'll never leave you. You know that."

Yasmeen smiled, but Sorayah was still afraid for her friend.

Life had to go on and somehow Sorayah continued. Later that day she was sent on a shopping trip by her ammi to Longsight Market. She drove down in the spare Mercedes and spent half an hour looking for a parking space. Exasperated, she parked on double yellow lines, close to World Wide Supermarket. She noted the shopping trolleys in the car park. Once, you had to carry everything in thin unmarked plastic bags and double park to do your weekly shopping.

As she was making her way across the car park she saw Haroon. She hadn't seen him since she'd left Manchester for London, all those years ago. He looked older, as if life had eaten away at him from the inside, but she instantly recognised the slouch, the long black leather jacket and the defiant short hairstyle. He was the one whose lopsided smile once made her tingle.

He was with a young woman, who Sorayah guessed was his wife. She looked like an import from her clothes. The style of salwar kameez belonged to a different continent, her facial expression didn't quite fit the climate. The baby Sorayah saw being pushed in the pram sent a tremor through her. Seeing his wife with a baby hurt her in a way she didn't expect. She'd thought the old wound had healed.

She saw Haroon turning in her direction. She attempted to duck her head. It was too late.

Quickly, she walked to the supermarket entrance, keeping the cars between them. Once she'd entered, she looked back. Haroon Yacub was being pulled away by his wife. She was glad he wasn't alone – she was certain he would otherwise have come over to talk to her. She waited for the couple to turn the corner and enter Longsight Market. They were arguing. Haroon tilted his head in a way Sorayah knew meant he was irritated. Old conversations and sensations coursed through her, none of them pleasant. The couple seemed to take an eternity in moving off. Haroon didn't look in her direction again and the two of them finally turned the corner. She wished she hadn't seen him.

By the time she exited World Wide Superstore's car park she was in the middle of Manchester's school run. Her knowledge of the Curry Mile's back streets allowed her to take tight turns and emerge alongside Platt Fields Park. It should have been plain sailing after that, but the phone rang.

Shokat made it clear abbu wanted to see her immediately.

"What's wrong, Paijaan?"

"Just come to the restaurant. Abbaji wants to see you."

"Tell me, or I'm not coming." She was still angry with her father.

"Abbaji's going on about you betraying him or something. I don't know what he means. He just had an accident."

She paused. "Is he okay?"

"It's not serious. Just a little bit shaken up. He wasn't paying attention and hit a passing car. Nobody's hurt."

"Okay, I'll be there in a few minutes."

When she arrived, the restaurant was busy with customers. She ignored the restaurant manager and made her wait upstairs to the second floor. She knocked on her father's office. She heard a grunt and opened it. She noticed her father stiffen as she entered. Her father was alone. He didn't say a word. Instead, he picked up the phone and blasted, "She's here." A few moments later Shokat arrived, breathing hard.

"How could you betray me?" her father began in Punjabi.

"I haven't betrayed you," she replied in English.

"You've gone into partnership with that khanzir, Jafar Ali. I went to his rubbish restaurant to give my condolences about his daughter and instead of thanking me he tells me that you've been working with him all this time. I try and be nice to him and he throws that in my face," he said in Punjabi.

Sorayah refused to speak in the mother tongue. She realised that Jafar Ali had broken his promise to her.

"Abbu, I'm not in partnership with him. I don't know where you get that from. I can't stop you two from being enemies with each other, but I needed some money when I was in London."

Her father switched to English. "Why didn't you come to me for help?"

"You wouldn't have given me the money. You didn't want to speak to me."

Her father paused. "Have I denied you anything?"

"We hadn't spoken for two years, you stopped depositing money in my bank account. You would never have helped me. Tell me if I'm wrong?"

Her father, glared at her. "I want you to come and work for me."

"I can't work with you, abbu."

"Oh, too good to work for your father, isn't it?"

"Have you forgotten what you called me a few days ago?"

"That's right, go and break your father's heart."

He was at his charming worst. She hated it and hated herself for not buying any of it.

"I have to do what I have to. I can't just be your daughter and do whatever you say, I have to live for me. I can't be what you want me to be and do what you ask all the time."

"When have you done what I have asked of you? You always do what *you* want."

"That's not true. I don't. I came here tonight at your request, didn't I? I was busy shopping for ammi, when Paijaan Shokat phoned me. I came straight away."

"Mumtaz, she's spoiled you, she's ruined you. I knew it the moment you stepped home."

Sorayah couldn't believe what she was hearing.

"What are you talking about? Ammi has nothing to do with this, you're just saying all these things, not because you want me to work with you, but because you don't want me to work with Uncle Jafar. You don't care about any of us, just about yourself. You think you're the Curry King, you aren't even the king of your little finger."

"How dare you, you insolent child. After all I've done for you, you still run to the bastard."

"I don't run to any man," *not anymore*, "not to you, not to him. You've never cared for the family. You live your own life and you ignore everyone. That's why you've pushed everyone away from you." She wanted to stop herself, but she couldn't. "You pushed Basharat away, you've stifled Paijaan Shokat, you've destroyed Baji Shazia by forcing her into a marriage she didn't want. You're a dictator, that's what you are!"

Her father shot up onto his feet. "Who do you think you're talking to? I'm your father. Don't you dare talk to me with that tone!"

"You're both the same, you and Uncle Jafar. You're made from the same cloth. Turn you around and I bet you've got Jafar's face!"

He swore. "Don't compare me to that lying deceitful bastard. We're not alike. And stay away from that Yasmeen. It was good she tried to take her own life, it was what she deserved."

Sorayah opened her mouth to say something, hesitated and then decided she'd say it anyway. "You're a cruel person. You're not the father I loved. I don't know who you are, I don't know what you are!" She turned and strode to the door.

"Hey, where are you going?" her father called after

her. "Don't you dare go without my leave!"

"Oh, you can't stop me. You never could. I'm leaving, don't worry about that. I'm going away from you, father. I finally saw you for what you are. A bitter old man who can't see the goodness in others."

"Oh yes, I understand now why you're doing all these theatrics. Run to that bastard and join forces with him against me, go on. You're no daughter of mine."

"What?" She stopped. She couldn't believe what he'd said. She turned to face her father. "Okay," she said quietly. "I was actually going to turn Uncle Jafar down, but I'll go and speak to him now. He's treated me more like a daughter than you ever have."

She turned on her heels and slowly walked out of the Kohinoor.

12

Sorayah awoke, clutching her stomach. She was in her bedroom in Manchester. Moonlight was shining. The residue of a nightmare clung to her duvet, coiled and warped. She recalled the words her boyfriend had used that day. She'd turned the CD player up high in her bedroom. Ammi always listened to conversations.

"It's not my baby," Haroon said. "Get rid of it, I'm not havin' it."

"How can you say that? I didn't make this baby by myself."

"Fucking hell!"

"Don't swear at me."

"Keep your voice down."

"Or what? Scared someone might find out?"

"I'm not saying it's not mine, I'm saying I don't want it."

"Why are you saying this now? What about what you said to me before? You said you wanted a child – you said you wanted to marry me."

Silence.

"That was before," he muttered.

She ended the call angrily, knowing he couldn't ring her back. Boys weren't allowed to ring girls in the Butt household. Haroon always got his cousin Fauzia to ring and pass the phone to him once Sorayah was on the line. As anticipated, the house phone rang a few minutes later. There was a knock on the bedroom door. She turned down the volume and opened the door. It was her sister-in-law Bushra holding the phone. "It's your friend, Fauzia. Again." Bushra said frowning. Sorayah shook her head and closed the door. Sorayah heard

Bushra telling Fauzia that Sorayah was busy. Fauzia didn't phone again.

She sat up in bed, rocking gently, arms wrapped around her knees and wondered if the foetus growing inside could sense her thoughts. *I want this baby, but I can't do it alone. I'm only flipping seventeen.* She'd planned her future with Haroon. She hadn't planned for a baby so soon, and Haroon had backed off as if the baby wasn't his.

She wanted him to go to her abbu and tell him that they wanted to marry, but Haroon was afraid. So was she. *Ammi and abbu will kill me, but what else can we do?* She hated herself for getting pregnant, but she'd never dreamt that the one she most loved would behave so dishonourably. It was more difficult for her than for him – he was a boy and no matter what his parents said, they would accept him. Both families would consider her a pariah, the one who'd seduced and corrupted Haroon.

He's surprised by the news. Maybe he just needs time to get used to the idea.

She heard a tap at the window. She cursed. Experience told her it could only be Haroon. *The idiot.* She rushed to the window overlooking the garden and her heart lurched as she saw that it was her boyfriend, his earrings shining in the dark. She opened the window.

"What you doing here? You'll get me in trouble," she whispered hoarsely. She heard cars passing along Wilbraham Road. That would cover some of the noise. Her father was away in Sheffield, and ammi was a deep sleeper, but it wasn't good to take chances.

"I just wanted to see you," Haroon whispered back.

"After what you said?"

"Yeah. I had to see you."

"Why can't you face up to your responsibility?" she wanted to say to him, but felt awkward. "I'll be down in a moment."

Reluctantly, she slipped on her jeans and pulled on a jumper. She navigated the stairs avoiding the creaking third step and collected the house keys from her jacket. Silently she pushed the front door open, shut it quietly behind her and slipped into the night. She searched for Haroon, heard a hiss ahead. She crept through the gate and followed the shadowy figure. She saw him get into his car. She got into the passenger side of the Toyota Corolla and they drove off without exchanging another word. Haroon stopped the car at Chorlton Water Park and they looked at each another.

"Well?" Sorayah finally said. He raised his hand to touch her cheek and she pushed it away. "Well?" she repeated.

"I can't be a father now, I've got so many plans."

"But it's our baby. You said you wanted a family one day."

"But not now! I can't!"

"We'll manage."

"No, we won't. I don't want it."

"You don't want me any more, do you?" She looked away, blinking back the tears.

"No, it isn't that," he said quickly. "It's not the right moment, that's all."

"Oh yeah, and when's it going to be the right moment? Tell me, cos I'm just dying to know."

"This baby," he said, exasperated, "what would we do, eh? Your dad isn't going to accept me. Mister Curry won't let me marry you."

"How do you know? Have you asked him? He

doesn't even know your name."

"I just know."

"You're a coward."

"Don't fucking call me a coward."

"Don't swear at me."

"Don't you fucking tell me what to do!"

He was snarling at her, shouting at the top of his lungs. Sorayah didn't feel an ounce of fear. She knew he'd never hit her. She'd seen every emotion play across his face. She loved watching the dimples appear in his cheeks when he laughed, she coveted his eyes, which captured every part of her. Then, sitting in his car as he shouted at her and slammed his hands on the steering wheel in anger, her love just died. As if it had never been.

"Take me home," she told him.

He nodded and drove her back at breakneck speed and dropped her off. He rolled down the window. "I'll get Fauzia to phone you tomorrow."

Sorayah didn't say a thing. She wanted to weep, not for the future, nor the child, but because he'd broken her heart. He tried to kiss her goodbye, but she didn't respond and he pulled back. He rolled the window up and Sorayah gazed at him, trying to remember him before she let go.

Just as he was about to pull away, she knocked on his window. He pulled it down.

"I'm going to get rid of it. The baby, I mean," she told him.

"OK. Good. I'll call you tomorrow."

She nodded numbly. *Our baby doesn't mean a thing to him.* She turned and walked calmly back to the house and let herself in. Nobody had awoken. She made her way up the darkened stairs into her bedroom and locked the door. She'd forgotten to close the window and the room was frozen. She shut it and left the curtains open.

She sat on the bed thinking, but tiredness overwhelmed her and she lay down and watched the ceiling. Then she wept. Tears crawled down her face and she didn't wipe them away. She held her belly and wondered if the world would be different in the morning, promised herself she'd never let a guy treat her so badly again. She slept deeply and if there were any dreams, they left no mark.

In the morning, she rang the clinic and booked an appointment. She was lucky to get an early slot. She took the 85 bus and passed her college on the way to town. She couldn't bear to look at it. She'd shared so many precious moments there with Haroon.

After the procedure, she bought a one-way coach ticket to London. Manchester slipped away. She never said goodbye to Haroon. She thought she could hold back the tears, but seeing Imran waiting for her at the London coach station broke the dam inside her. She wrapped her arms around her brother and wept. They took a taxi to the flat he was sharing with medic friends. In the icy light of a despairing kitchen bulb, she told him everything. He put his arms around. "That fella was always a twerp, if you ask me. I'd love to say you're better off without him – so you're better off without him."

Seeing Haroon again in Longsight had reawakened the nightmare. She had dropped by the Alis' place to visit Yasmeen when Fauzia had rung.

"Haroon spoke to me," Fauzia began breathlessly, "he wants to speak to you. Urgently. You've got to call him."

Sorayah didn't know what to say. She'd met Fauzia a few days ago at a maatam. One of her mother's old friends had died and Sorayah went with her ammi, who'd needed comforting.

Haroon, flipping Haroon. Why don't these guys just leave me alone? "What's it about?"

"He wouldn't say. Go on, Sorayah. It might be important." Sorayah had a bad feeling.

Reluctantly, she took the number down. Not really knowing why she was doing it, she dialled the number. "Haroon?"

"Sorayah? Is that you?"

"Yes."

"I'm glad you called."

"Fauzia said you wanted to speak to me urgently. What is it?"

"Erm, well, listen. I think we should meet up."

"Why?"

"I think that we need to sort out the differences we had in the past, you know start again."

"Sorry? Start what again?"

"Us."

"What are you talking about? There is no 'us'! We finished a long time ago."

"Come on Sorayah. You know you still want me."

"What? You're crazy. Not even in your dreams! What makes you think I want to get back with the guy who didn't want his own baby? How dare you call me when you've just become a father yourself! Does your wife know you're trying to reach me?"

"Sorayah, why are you saying all this when you know you still love me?"

She ended the call. *That's the last time I listen to what Fauzia has to say.*

That single phone call precipitated a deluge of calls and text messages from Haroon. He matched Ravinder. Her ex-beaus were hovering around her like vultures. She sat on her bed and contemplated leaving for London. But she couldn't. Yasmeen needed her too much. *Why don't I ever learn? Why do I always go for the same type?* She sensed the men in her life were closing in, the vice tightening around her neck. She felt betrayed by them all. Even Imran had deceived her. She wondered if Paijaan Shokat was hiding something from her. *Why do we women do this to ourselves, let ourselves be used by men?* But she knew the answer. *Because we let them.* The image of her father swam before her, gloating, cutting her out of his life, disowning her. The icon of her father was eclipsed by Jafar Ali, her new business partner. She already regretted signing the contract, but perhaps it had been worth it – she'd made a deal with Jafar Ali to quash the money she'd borrowed for Varinder.

She took a deep breath and phoned Shabnam.

"Sorayah! Do you want to go shopping? I'll really love you if you do! I'm dying to go to the Trafford Centre with you."

"Not today. Do you know any good mobile phone deals?"

13

"I can't pay you!" Ajmal told the gunda and instantly realised he had made a mistake.

David Mirza's laughter, a sharp staccato burst of arrogance, jarred Ajmal's nerves. Ajmal always assumed a position of strength when dealing with rivals, waiting for them to reveal a chink in their armour. *But what if the enemy has no weakness?*

He wanted to slap the kutta, but was helpless. Mirza had brought two mountains of muscle to quell any uprising. *I should have got bodyguards like Dilawar told me.* He had phoned Mirza countless times since obtaining the funds from Abdullah Shah, but the numbers were dead. He had feared a set-up and tonight confirmed it. Mirza had come to collect. He wished a waiter or Shokat or anyone would come running upstairs to his office to save him.

Mirza quickly walked over and bent down so his nose was only centimetres from Ajmal's. Ajmal smelt expensive perfume and a hint of whisky. He thrust himself further back into his leather chair. Fear flip-flopped in his belly. Sweat broke out across his brow.

"That's not the answer I was looking for Ajmal Saab," Mirza whispered.

He hated the way the gunda said 'Saab', so insincere, like he owned the world.

"You know that I can't accept that answer," Mirza said. He walked over to one of the chairs facing the office desk and kicked it aside.

"But I tried to contact you – I did!" Ajmal pleaded. He no longer felt like a king. He was ashamed at his fear.

Mirza shook his head and wagged his finger in

admonition. "What are we to do with you, eh?" Then he ordered his men, "Hold him down and cut his heart out."

Ajmal looked from one burly bodyguard to the next. One moment they were standing on either side of the desk and the next they were moving towards him, their intent clear and deadly. He panicked, rose out of the chair and made a break for the door, but he was trapped. Strong arms gripped him. He wailed. Cold metal pressed against his neck, sharp and ungiving. He took a sudden breath as the blade broke skin. *They're going to kill me.*

"Please, reconsider, Ajmal, I want my money back – immediately – or I cut your heart out and feed it to you. Now what do you want me to do? A good businessman like you should be able to work out what the best solution is, right?"

Killer Instinct, where are you? Where are you, damn it? "Perhaps I can find the money for you," Ajmal said trying to buy time.

"Don't give me 'perhaps', Ajmal. I want the money now."

"Okay, let go of me and I'll get it for you. I'll have to make some phone calls."

The arms held him like metal vices. The knife probed deeper, drawing an involuntary cry from him.

"If you're play-acting Ajmal, I'll tell you what, I'll cut your heart out and feed it to your family – do you get my meaning?" Mirza smiled, his eyes feral. "Did you think I didn't know where you lived? Tut tut, you should know not to mess with me. A guy like you should know who he's dealing with. So what do you say?"

Ajmal's mouth had gone dry. His hesitation brought

fists and slaps. He raised his hands helplessly and whimpered like a bachcha. They stopped. Then the two goons picked him and threw him into his chair.

"You're not leaving this bloody office," Mirza instructed, "You're gonna stay in here and do whatever you need to do!"

Mirza was watching him, grinning. Ajmal looked down. In that moment, time died. Between the space of two rapid blinks, a drop of blood rolled down his throat and fevered thoughts raced through his mind *Shokat must be ready to take over from me…he'll be wolfed down in a day without me!* He decided to sell his factories as quickly as time would allow. He would focus solely on the restaurants. The franchise he had planned with Jafar Ali ten years ago might still become a reality. And he promised himself he would exact revenge on Mirza for humiliating him.

This was the darkest tunnel Ajmal had ever travelled through, but there was a pulsating white light at the end of it. The drop of blood stopped at the white collar of his shirt, and was then absorbed by the cotton.

He took a hoarse breath and looked into Mirza's dead eyes. The money was in his office safe, but he did not wish to reveal its location. He made pretend phone calls to several people.

"I'm losing patience, Ajmal. Don't fucking waste my time or I'll waste you."

He knew his back was against the deewar. He blinked rapidly. "I'll have to give you my life savings," he told David. *Don't worry kutte, your days are numbered.*

Mirza snorted. "I guess you will! See it as your savings actually saving your life."

Mirza's men laughed with him. Each note of laughter

was a kick in Ajmal's ribs.

In despair, he pushed aside his swivel chair and pulled up the carpet concealing the floor safe. He brought out his trusted bunch of keys and instantly found the right chaabi. He slotted it in and grunted as it clicked open the safe. He pulled up the door and revealed the tidy stack of used banknotes. He piled them on the floor. Mirza's men counted them.

"And the rest?" Mirza said when Ajmal stood up awkwardly, pain flaring in every joint.

"What? That's your quarter of a million. That's what I owe you!"

"No, Ajmal Saab, that's what you owed me last week when you should have coughed up. Now you owe me everything that's in the safe."

"But I tried to pay you – I rang the telephone numbers you gave me."

"You didn't try hard enough. Now do I have to repeat myself or shall we take business to a different level?"

Ajmal grimly pulled out the rest of the cash. Abdullah's money had saved him, but at a horrendous cost. Mirza's men commandeered his beloved black briefcase and stashed it with cash after ripping out its rich leather pockets.

"You're a good man," Mirza told Ajmal, walking round to his side of the desk. He held out his hand, but Ajmal refused to shake it. "Ah well, be like that, it was good to do business with you. I'm glad we managed to sort out our differences. In a way, I wished you'd resisted more. I would have enjoyed that."

Then they were gone.

Ajmal looked down at the empty hole in the floor.

Bastard.

He stood there for many minutes, the rage building up inside him. Then he kicked his swivel chair aside and threw the desk over. He smashed the picture frames and threw another chair across the room. He flung papers, magazines in all directions, ripping them to shreds, wailing like a demented beast. When he came to his senses he was standing in a war zone, breathing hard, soaked with sweat, fury urging him to run down the stairs and seek out the gunda.

Then he smiled.

Theft, that's it. I'll call the police in the morning and say the money was stolen. That'll get back some of the money. His scheming mind was in overdrive. *Killer Instinct, finally you're back! Maybe something can be salvaged from this disaster.* He knew insurance wouldn't cover the four hundred and fifty thousand pounds he'd lost, but he'd get something.

He made his way to the first floor. On the stairs, his legs almost buckled. He grabbed the rail and steadied himself. It took him several minutes to reach the bottom.

The Killer Instinct had deserted him tonight. It had fled when he had discovered Sorayah's boyfriend and again, tonight, when Mirza had appeared out of the blue. Mirza had shown great audacity. He had walked into Ajmal's restaurant, Ajmal's territory, and held him to ransom.

He wondered what would have happened if Sorayah had been there. His heart almost stopped. He took his head in his hands. He wished he had not driven her away, but thanked God she was safe.

He walked out of the restaurant like a zombie,

muttering to Saleem that he was unwell. He didn't wait for a reply. He got into his car and slowly drove to Sameena's. When he got there he noticed the light was off in her flat. He turned on the CD player and listened to the voice of Nusrat Fateh Ali Khan ride his way to heaven.

Ajmal Butt, formerly the Curry King, puffed hard on a bent cigarette and contemplated vengeance.

14

Sorayah bundled the last box into the back of the Mercedes then turned to look back at the family home. Her mother was standing in the driveway, forlorn, her arms crossed. She'd forced her to take spices and food for her flat. Baji Shazia had helped her pack and now held Rubeena's hand.

Sorayah's mother asked, "Puttar, why don't you stay?"

"Abbu doesn't want me here." She'd constantly repeated those words over the last week, her decision to move out was final. She knew now she couldn't live in the same house as her father.

"Don't leave an old woman like me. Who do I have?"

Guilt twisted in her belly. Bushra had become the house dragon. Her mother had confided, "She's really kamini," and Baji Shazia didn't come as regularly to the family house as she used to. Since announcing the news of her divorce, Shazia had grown increasingly distant.

"She's not leaving you," Yasmeen said in Urdu, interrupting them. She was sitting in the passenger seat of the Mercedes. "She'll visit you every day."

Sorayah hugged her family and got into the car. She pulled out of the driveway and the girls waved. "I don't think my mum's shed a tear for me before – and I'm only going down the road," Sorayah said.

"Hmmm, it's a big move though. Might not be in terms of distance, but it's a big change."

"You're quite deep today, Miss Ali."

"I'm always deep. You usually don't listen cos you're too busy looking in the mirror."

Sorayah grinned, but felt secure her mother would

welcome her back if needed. She watched Yasmeen surreptitiously. Her friend looked centred. Ironically, it was because of Raheem. He sent Yasmeen flowers every Friday with brief notes. "You don't get a guy like that every day," Sorayah had said to her friend, feeling happy for her, and jealous at the same time. *I always get the Ravs and Haroons. Immy's right. I want stuff that isn't any good for me.* The difference this time was she hadn't promised herself that she wouldn't go for the wrong type. She had another dream in her life.

Later, in Sorayah's new flat behind the Curry Mile, they collapsed on the sofa. Sorayah sighed, exhausted.

Yasmeen broke the building silence. "I – I've been meaning to ask you something. You know that day when you came to my house when you spoke to Daddy in the front room?"

"Yes?"

"You didn't tell me everything."

"What do you mean? I told you about the money I'd borrowed."

"No. That isn't what I mean. You're not listening."

"I'm listening, Yasmeen. Honest."

"When I asked you what you'd spoken about you said 'nothing'."

"Did I?" Guilt pricked Sorayah.

"Yes."

"I didn't want to bore you with the details."

"You didn't want to share it with me. You abandoned me."

Sorayah turned to face Yasmeen. "No, Yaz. Honestly, that's not why I didn't tell you."

"Then why didn't you just tell me?"

"Because..." Sorayah hesitated.

"See, you don't even want to talk about it now," her friend accused. Yasmeen stood up.

"Don't go. Sit. I'll tell you."

Yasmeen sat down. "Go on."

"It's cos I didn't want you to think less of your father. He plays dirty." Sorayah felt elated that she was finally telling her friend the truth, but guilty, because she was enjoying it.

"You mean he's like your daddy?"

"Yes. I guess they're the same."

"Then why didn't you just tell me that? I would have understood. I grew up with you. I always knew they were the same!"

Sorayah nodded. "You're right. I was stupid. I should have told you."

"The truth is always best."

"But the truth hurts sometimes."

"Lies hurt too."

"Well, that's true too."

They grinned.

"Now," Sorayah said, "let's go and buy a kettle."

"We were broken into a few nights ago," Shokat told her on the phone that evening.

Sorayah's heart skipped a beat. "What happened?" she asked.

"They broke into Dad's office and tore the whole place up."

She wanted to ask if her abbu was okay, but couldn't find the words. She was too angry with him. A part of her felt it served her father right. *He probably cheated somebody.*

"Abbaji's okay. Looks a bit worn by it all, but you

172

know him. He's as strong as an ox."

She wanted to enquire more, find out if he really was okay, but she couldn't. She knew any sign of softness would be transmitted to her abbu by Shokat. Her abbu would then exploit the weakness.

"Are you at the Kohinoor?" she asked quickly. She didn't want her brother to suggest another meeting with their father.

"No, I'm out. Looking for a new supplier for the rice. Got this great lead in Keighley. Going to check it out. Hey, guess who's working at the Kohinoor?"

She didn't want to discuss the Kohinoor or her father. She wondered if her brother was cleverly trying to get her to make up with abbu. *But Paijaan isn't like that.* She hated herself for being so cynical. "Who?" she sighed.

"Uncle Kashif!"

"Really?" She couldn't believe it. She hadn't seen him for years. She'd last heard he was working at the Curry King in Bradford. He'd been her father's senior chef for almost twenty years. *The Kohinoor must be doing worse than I thought.* Sorayah learnt to cook from Kashif. He'd drilled lessons into her that lingered beyond childhood. He taught her that that the real mark of a good curry house wasn't the money that they were making at the till, but whether or not the chef truly loved his work and Sorayah had always known Kashif was her father's secret weapon. Her abbu was lucky that Kashif didn't care about the money, he loved his food and his ample belly proved it. "When did he get back?"

"Yesterday. You going to go and see him?"

Sorayah hesitated. She didn't want her abbu to think she had capitulated and was crawling back. *Why do I flipping care what abbu thinks? Am I afraid of him?* "Yes, I'll go and see him."

It was a five - minute walk from her flat to the Kohinoor. Although it was still early, Wilmslow Road was as busy as ever with students, commuters, buses, cars, the homeless and Muslim missionaries seeking donations for their respective mosques. She entered the Kohinoor and met Saleem. She asked him where Kashif was. He pointed to the kitchen. On entering, she heard a familiar voice booming in machine - gun Punjabi, "No, you idiot, what are you doing? Why does Ajmal give me these fools!" He then turned and noticed her standing in the doorway. "Sorayah!" Kashif boomed and switched to English, beckoning her to approach.

"How are you, Uncle?" she asked, smiling.

He touched her briefly on the head in welcome. "There was a time, little girl, when only gorays couldn't tell the difference between a good curry and a bad one. But even our own people can't tell the difference any more! I hate them! I'll kill them!"

"Why, Uncle? Why do you hate them?" she grinned.

"Because food is culture. Food is more than something that fills my belly," Kashif said pummelling his waist. "Your father wants me to cook faster. He tells me quality matters. I know he doesn't give a kajoor about quality!" he said, raising his voice and pointing upwards indicating her father's office. "But it matters to me. I'm a proud man. I've created dishes, great ones, but nobody appreciates them."

"I do."

"How?"

"I know how good you are."

He sniffed. "You've been away from the kitchen a

long time. What do you remember?"

"I remember," she said quietly, "that it's all about the aroma."

She remembered asking Uncle Kashif as a child when a curry was ready. "The aroma," he'd whispered, as if he feared someone might overhear. "The nose is the most sensitive organ in the body. I might be a cook, but I studied zoology in Lahore and I can tell you a thing or two about the nose. It's about the blend of chemicals, yes, spices are chemicals and they are delicate, beautiful things. Look at the colours, see them mingle and change, and smell them. Yes, smell them."

Uncle Kashif smiled now. "Ah yes, you remember after all." He chortled in delight, rubbing his belly. "You were always my best student."

"Make me something," she said.

"Of course, then you can show me how much you really appreciate my food!"

Home-made curries can take hours to cook, but even a top - notch restaurant's curry takes a few minutes with most elements pre-cooked. Kashif pointed out a badly cooked shish kebab. "Now you think this is good, yes?" He didn't wait for a reply. "The meat is burnt."

"It's meant to be like that, isn't it?" she said, playing along.

"Silly girl! No, it's not. It should be cooked delicately. See the lamb in the Karahi, yes? Same meat. Why's that soft? This isn't."

"Cooked too fast?"

"Yes, good girl! The idiots burn half of it and those goray eat it any way thinking that's how it's meant to be. Charcoal. Silly people. Anybody can cook things fast. Doing it properly and fast, now that's an art!"

Uncle Kashif shouted at his staff as he readied himself to prepare a curry for Sorayah.

Then she heard her father's voice. He was standing in the doorway, fuming. She stiffened, anticipating a tongue-lashing, but it never came. Normally, her father looked immaculate, but today he looked tired, drained, bags under his yes. She felt sorry for him, but she stopped herself from showing any remorse. *He doesn't care whether I exist or not! Why should I care for him?*

"What now, Ajmal?" Kashif bellowed in Punjabi. "You want it faster again? You're always in a hurry."

Ajmal looked at Sorayah. "I'll speak to you later," he muttered and turned on his heel. Sorayah smiled inwardly.

"Why does my father want you to cook faster?" Sorayah asked curious.

"Jafar, your dad's best friend, is advertising he's got the fastest curry in town."

Sorayah had to smile. Kashif loved goading her father. Calling Jafar her father's 'best friend' would be galling to her father. "Your dad doesn't want to be outdone by him. Sometimes, I think your father behaves like a child."

Sorayah agreed, but kept silent. Even if she was angry with her father, she would never reveal the fact to anyone other than her closest friends. She asked, "This claim of Uncle Jafar's, did someone actually time his curry making?"

"Probably not! Most of the ingredients are pre-cooked anyway. It's a stupid concept! When do you start counting, eh? When you slaughter the animal?" Kashif chortled. "You can't cook anything faster than it's meant to be cooked, because you'll burn it. Then nobody will want our curries." He frowned and motioned for Sorayah to come closer. He whispered, "He doesn't understand it's not my fault if the Kohinoor isn't doing as well as he needs it to." *Ah, so that's why abbu's so stressed.*

"Uncle, you've worked for abbu for many years. You know he's not a bad man, he's a businessman. If the business is suffering he's got to do something about it."

"There's nothing wrong with the food."

"Then what's wrong with the business? The business *is* the food."

"I don't know. I've discussed it with your brother Shokat and we can't work it out. The Kohinoor shouldn't be doing any worse than any other restaurant."

Sorayah nodded, her mind whirling. "I have to get going. Got to buy a few things for the flat."

Kashif smiled. "You're always in a hurry." He switched to English, "but you shouldn't hurry a curry!" He laughed at his own English rhyme.

"Uncle," she said, "I might need your help."

"What, puttar? You don't even have to ask."

She'd thought hard about finding a place on the Mile, but it was incredibly competitive. There were more Indian restaurants and takeaways on the Curry Mile than anywhere else in the country. Intuitively she knew that the only place that would be successful was Wilmslow Road. She needed information. She refused to depend on Uncle Jafar to find a location. She needed to prove to herself that she could do it without him. "I want to set up a restaurant."

Two weeks later Uncle Kashif phoned her with good news. "A contact has told me one of the Arab places is facing closure. They're in debt. You can do a sweet deal before it comes onto the market."

"Thanks, Uncle – I owe you a curry."

"No, I'll make a curry for you, your cooking is good, but it isn't as good as mine!" Sorayah laughed.

She phoned Uncle Jafar.

"How did you hear about this?" he snapped. "Nobody's mentioned this to me."

Sorayah smiled. "Look, it doesn't matter where I got the info from. If we're going to work together you'll just have to respect that I've got my own contacts."

She arrived at the Golden Scimitar as agreed with Uncle Jafar. He was already there, looking resplendent. The Arab who shook her hand had circles under his eyes and three days of stubble.

"This is my partner," Jafar Ali began, gesturing towards Sorayah. She felt warmth flow into her. *Abbu would never have called me his partner.* "She's got lots of experience and I'm not making any decision without her." Sorayah couldn't hide the smile.

They had mint tea, baklava and shisha which made Sorayah reminisce about London. Uncle Jafar raised an eyebrow, but didn't make any remarks.

"I need cash, hard cash," Mohammed Al-Bustani told them, "or else I will have to put the restaurant on the market. Ya'nee, if you want to do business with me, alhamdolillah, otherwise I have other interested people."

"I don't know if this is in the right location," Sorayah said, looking towards her new business partner.

Uncle Jafar nodded, "You could be right, Sorayah."

"It is a good restaurant!" the Arab insisted. "It is amongst the best in the whole of Manchester. Wallahi, it is amongst the best in the whole of England."

"The restaurant or the location?" Sorayah asked, sipping her mint tea.

"The location. Please, have a look around. It is good. Come, we have a new kitchen, come!" He insisted on showing them around. It wasn't as large as the Kohinoor, largest restaurant on the Mile, but it would do nicely for starters.

Sorayah caught Jafar's eye. They had pre-negotiated a fee with the clear understanding that they would be equal partners. Uncle Jafar would put up the capital, and Sorayah would run it with no interference.

Later, in the Shandaar, Uncle Jafar toasted her. "You're a remarkable young lady. It's a good job you're on my side!"

Sorayah was quiet. Uncle Jafar's core team were in the office: Bilal, Samri and Atif. She'd quickly learnt that Uncle Jafar ran his shop differently from her father. Far more openly. She'd finally understood that during the lean years when her father had the upper hand, Uncle Jafar had had no choice but to adapt and learn new ways.

"I've got an excellent interior designer who's ready to meet us in the morning," Jafar began. He was sipping mango lassi and smiling from kan to kan.

Sorayah's eyes narrowed. "We had a deal. Your money, my know-how. We're going to do it my way."

Jafar's smile faded a notch, but didn't disappear. "It was only a suggestion, daughter. Nothing else. Of course, you don't have to see the designer if you don't want to."

In her peripheral vision, she saw the other men scrutinising her. "We haven't even bought the restaurant yet," she said.

"It's just a formality, I'm sure," Jafar Ali replied, his smile growing again.

"I respect you a lot, Uncle, but the design will be mine. If you don't like it then…" she let the warning hang in the air.

Silence grew between them. Then Jafar Ali laughed. "See, what did I tell you, men. She's even better than her father!" The men laughed. Sorayah's smile was brittle, but she held Jafar's gaze.

When the team had left, Uncle Jafar became serious. "Sorayah, I want to thank you."

"What for?"

"For helping my daughter. No, don't say anything. I know that you're best friends and whatever has happened has happened. I'd rather lose a groom than my daughter. If you hadn't been there for her, well, there's nothing else I can say."

"She's like a sister to me."

"And you're like a daughter to me."

Sorayah felt a lump in her throat. "Thanks, Uncle."

Al-Bustani phoned the next day.

"I'm afraid I have a better offer from another gentleman," he began.

"You won't get a better deal than ours," Sorayah told him.

"I would beg to differ, I have a potential buyer who is willing to sign immediately."

"How much more do you want?"

"How much do you have to offer?"

He was obviously lying. "Let me speak to my partner and I'll get back to you."

She sat in her flat and pondered what she could do.

She took out her journal and wrote down the different options facing her. She was stuck. Finally, she phoned Shokat. "Paijaan, I need your help."

"Is everything okay?" Shokat said in his slow voice.

"I'm negotiating for a restaurant on the Mile. The guy I'm dealing with is slowing things down and we need to push him."

"I dunno, Sorayah. Abbaji won't be happy if he finds out I've helped and to be honest, I don't know how I can speed things up for you."

"What about those bailiff type companies?" Large business customers, usually companies that spent thousands on an evening's entertainment, were sometimes hesitant in settling their account and a nudge worked wonders. From Al-Bustani's unkempt appearance she'd surmised he needed to raise cash quickly to pay his creditors.

"That'll scare him a little. But I don't know, Sorayah, abbaji told me not to help you."

"Look, I really need this. I don't want to do it, but I don't have a choice. I know that abbu uses bailiffs all the time. Couldn't you ask for a favour? I need you, Paijaan. I don't want to ask Uncle Jafar for his help."

"Okay," Shokat said reluctantly, "let me make a few phone calls. I'll let you know when it's in place."

He called her late in the afternoon.

"It's done. I think he's been rattled a little bit. Try calling him in the morning. He'll be even more rattled."

"Why?"

"People always are when they haven't slept."

Sorayah didn't laugh. It was a cruel thing to do to anyone. *But he was lying to me, trying to get more money out of me. He assumed I'd cave in cos I'm a woman.* She'd always hated the way men took advantage of women when it suited them.

She rang Mohammed Al-Bustani in the morning. "We're going to let the other party take it," she told him.

"No, no," Al-Bustani insisted. He laughed awkwardly. "Maybe there was a misunderstanding. I just was checking your desire to buy the place. I just wanted the best owners to take it, wallahi."

"I'm afraid we don't have as much money as we did a few days ago."

"What? What is this?"

"Yesterday, when you said you had another buyer we went and bought a lot of stock after deciding it wasn't for us. But if you say that it's still up for grabs then we'll do it, but no more back-tracking."

"Why don't you and your partner come and see me today? We can arrange everything, inshallah. We can do it today."

Back in her flat, Sorayah sat at the kitchen table, her notebooks and documents everywhere. She slowly sipped a cup of coffee and felt she'd sold her soul to Satan.

Her phone beeped twice. It was a text message. She scanned it briefly. *Javed.* She grimaced. After she'd changed her phone number, the text messages from Ravinder and Haroon had dropped to zero. Javed replaced them, as if a baton had been passed between the men. *Well, I'm not going to be tossed from one guy to the next.* She wanted to shout at Yasmeen for giving her new number to Javed, but couldn't.

She walked down to Wilmslow Road. It was cloudy overhead. The traffic was busy, but the world seemed subdued, quieter, more distant somehow. She passed a queue of students waiting for a bus a few doors away from the Golden Scimitar. Nobody glanced her way. *Well, my market value must have hit the floor.* She smiled. She continued walking and stopped outside the Golden Scimitar, searching its empty dark windows for signs of future life.

Please God, make this happen. Please.

15

Ajmal Butt's eyelids were drooping. He had spent the day touring his Yorkshire factories in Wakefield, Kirklees and Keighley weighing up their selling price. Now he was returning to Manchester. He turned up the volume on his CD player. Nusrat Ali Khan filled the void in his breast as he pointed the car away from Yorkshire and back home.

If only Shokat were half as fast as Sorayah is. He had to do something about his eldest son and soon. *They'll eat him and my business alive once I'm gone.*

He stopped at red lights. He was a few minutes away from his beloved Kohinoor. His eyes closed. The honking of horns woke him. "Bastards," he muttered and hit the accelerator.

He hadn't seen Basharat for a month. His youngest had disappeared, but reports from Mumtaz informed him he was still around. His son had kept a low profile ever since the scuffle.

He wished his children had been more like him, passionate about the business, ready to fight tooth and mekh for the business. *But they're limp sheep.* Desperation and depression settled over him.

Sorayah's betrayal had been a great blow. Worse, he himself had pushed her into his enemy's restaurant. *I begged her and she didn't come back to me.* A few weeks ago, Sorayah raised his hopes of reconciliation when she'd visited the Kohinoor. He refused to say he was sorry. *I'm her father, damn it!* He was certain she was setting up a restaurant with Jafar and it would be a further nail in his coffin. *I have to do something to bring her back, I have to. Oh, God help me.*

Without realising, he directed his car to the south of Manchester. It was only when he'd parked outside the large detached house in Altrincham that he realised where he was. He'd returned to Pir Syed Ismaeel Barakullah.

He walked up the steps to the front door and rang the bell. A demure young woman wearing a white dapatta opened the door. She was a distant relative of the Pir, a delightfully quiet girl who gathered offerings made to his Holiness.

"Ajmal Saab," she said in Urdu, opening the door wide. He felt a thrill of pleasure at being recognised. It confirmed that he belonged to the Pir's inner circle. She gestured for him to enter.

"How are you, daughter?" he asked, switching to the Mogul tongue.

"I'm well, Ajmal Saab."

"Is the Pir busy with his disciples? Is he praying?"

"He's always in a state of remembrance of the One. Come in and he'll remember you too."

He followed her into the peaceful abode. He took off his shoes and was seated in the front room. It was decorated beautifully yet simply in white. A large photo of the Pir in deepest contemplation was perched on the mantelpiece. Ajmal felt his muscles unwind. He'd come to the Pir's home on many occasions. Each time he felt equally at peace, at one with himself.

"My brother," the Pir said, entering the room. A disciple followed and sat down quietly on the floor near the fireplace. Ajmal rose quickly and kissed the old man's ring.

"What brings you to my home? It has been too many days without my favourite friend."

Ajmal smiled. "The business has kept me busy, otherwise I would have come to you sooner. The world presses."

"Yes. Indeed it does. The world is a dangerous place. It makes us forget our true purpose. We must never forget that. Here, let me make a prayer for you, it's a prayer that came to me in a vision when I was near the Kaabaa."

Ajmal leaned forward and lowered his head as the Pir raised his hands in supplication and mouthed a silent prayer.

"She came back," Ajmal said, sipping tea. Another disciple had brought in chah for the two gentleman. It wasn't the nectar Sameena brewed, but it lubricated Ajmal's parched throat.

"I knew that it would happen so."

"But she's gone over to my enemy!"

"A friend so easily becomes an enemy, an enemy so easily a friend."

"What must I do?"

"I shall contemplate what the Lord sends me tonight. I will have a vision of what must be done."

"I need an answer quickly. My business – it – I need to have strong friends and family around me. They aren't there. I'm alone."

"Doesn't your son work for you?"

"Yes, but…"

"Doesn't he do a good job?"

"Yes, but he isn't me." There it was. The truth. He'd always wanted his children to be him, but they could never be. Inglastaan had diluted their blood. They would never have his Killer Instinct.

"Ajmal, my dear friend, none of your children can be

you," the Pir said quietly. There was a note of sadness in his voice. Ajmal had forgotten that the Pir, although married for many years, had no children. Embarrassed, Ajmal cleared his throat.

"I just want them to be the best they can be, that's all."

The Pir shook his head. "To find what you seek, there is a price."

"I'm willing to pay any price."

"Are you? Any price? Are you certain of this, my friend?"

Ajmal was silent. *Yes, any price.* But he didn't speak his thoughts aloud. His mind was set. He'd fight for the future.

"I removed the demon from your daughter through the power of my prayers," the Pir said.

"And I thank you for that. But, I need more. I need her by my side."

"She will be in time, but you must have patience, the patience of a saint." The Pir looked wistfully upwards, his long white beard swaying from side to side. "I have looked into the infinite depths of the seven heavens, I have seen great evil, evil that resides in the souls of men – and more so in women. It was difficult to remove the djinn from your daughter, but it may return and make my work more difficult. Jafar Ali has a streak of evil."

"Yes, I know! He's a vile man. I've had dealings with him."

"Yes, yes," the Pir said, nodding and stroking his beard. "What must be done, must be done well, but you must have patience. I shall make prayers and you must come to one of my seminaries. They are truly powerful. Doorways to God. What else can a believer ask for?"

Ajmal nodded, feeling his old exuberance return.

There was a spring in his step as he left the Pir's house.

He awoke refreshed. He felt joy as he did his tie in the bathroom. He sensed the Pir's prayers spinning in the background, and knew the saint's words rang true. When he arrived at the Kohinoor he phoned Shokat and asked him to come to the office immediately.

"Yes, abbaji," his son replied, irritating Ajmal. *He always sounds like a sad donkey.*

Shokat arrived within half an hour. Ajmal smelt fear on his son and frowned. "Have you seen Sorayah?" he asked.

Shokat eyes widened for a split second.

Ajmal cursed under his breath. "What are you hiding from me? What have you done?" *Why didn't you give me a lion, Lord? Why did you give me this sheep?*

"I haven't seen her, she hardly comes round."

What is it about Sorayah that make others open up to her? Kashif the chef was mesmerised by her and Shokat was under her thumb. *Her tentacles are everywhere. She's even more dangerous than that kanjar, Jafar.*

"You fool, I can tell you've been in touch with her. Did you tell her anything you shouldn't have?"

"Oh no, nothing like that."

"Then what? I'll break your legs if you don't tell me."

"Well, she needed some help, abbaji."

"What kind of help?"

"It was nothing really."

"If it was nothing, then you won't mind telling me, will you?"

"It was nothing serious."

"Let me be the judge of that."

"She needed help in buying a restaurant."

"What?" Ajmal couldn't believe it. Following his meeting with the Pir he'd been sure Sorayah would be returning to him soon. "And you didn't think to ask me first? You're not just a fool, you're a traitor." He wanted to shout at Shokat, but he couldn't find the energy. Curiosity got the better of him. "How did you help her?"

Shokat told him.

Ajmal smashed his fist on the desk. "How dare you? She's just like that Basharat. Useless, doing my besti, everywhere. And you go and help her? You're useless. Get out of my office, get out!"

Shokat left hurriedly.

Ajmal walked up to the window and pushed his bulbous nose against it. The cold calmed him a little as he watched the traffic flit by below. "Well, if she thinks she can rub my nose in it with that cunning bastard then I'll have to show her. I'll show her life can be made into hell."

He hadn't heard Shokat walk down the corridor and guessed his son was waiting there, contrite.

"Shokat, come back in," he shouted. A few moments later his son returned, looking nervous. "Son, start contacting our council people once she opens the restaurant. Complain about hygiene issues. You know the drill."

Shokat's eyes opened wide. *Well, if she wants to bat first she's going to have to work for it. She isn't going to beat this all-rounder.* "And don't you dare tell your sister or I'll kill you myself!"

Shokat shot off. Ajmal felt distracted, disheartened.

He paced up and down the room. He was irritated at his secretary's absence. Sameena was off ill with a virus. He couldn't even visit her. She'd told him it was quite bad. He missed her soothing presence.

Then he did something he never did. He phoned Imran.

"Imran puttar, this is your father," he said in Punjabi.

"What's up, Dad?" Imran answered in Punjabi, sounding surprised.

"Listen, puttar doctor, you know your sister?"

"You mean, Sorayah?"

"Tell her that if she wants to run a restaurant in Manchester, she's better off doing it with me. Or else I'll make life difficult for her."

After a few moments, Imran said, "Abbu, isn't this something you can work out between yourselves? Cos I'm off to the hospital in a moment."

"Puthar, she'll listen to you," Ajmal replied, switching to English. "You're education. She doesn't listen to the others."

"She will if you speak reasonably."

"What? Am I not her father? I know what's best for her. Tell her from me that she should leave that gunda, Jafar, and come and work for me. It'll be much better for everyone. You're a doctor – tell her it'll be good for her health."

"I'll let her know you rang me."

"Shabash puttar, I knew I could trust you."

16

"No, no, I want it over there," Sorayah told the workmen.

The Lithuanians gave her a sullen look and walked away. Sorayah sighed. She'd have to find the foreman, a stout Persian named Reza. She wanted the tapestries exactly in place before they left. The foreign workers were cheap, but their lack of English made communication tricky.

Despite the difficulties, they'd removed the Scimitar's veneer and the shell was fast becoming the restaurant Sorayah had always desired. The paperwork took three months. The renovations had taken another six, but soon she'd launch Maharani. Her old friend from London, Nazia, had designed the interior. "For you, honey, anything," Nazia had said.

Sorayah spent all her time at the restaurant and caught more than a baleful glare from her father whenever she saw him. She kept Uncle Jafar at a distance, but the pressure was constant. She had to open soon and with a bang. Maybe then, both Uncle Jafar and her father would relent.

The basement had become her office. She sat there in a rickety chair and took out her journal. The launch had to be spectacular, to get tongues wagging. *What would abbu do?* She considered phoning Shokat, but abbu was keeping constant tabs on him.

"He reckons I tell you everything," her brother had moaned.

"Of course you don't," she'd consoled him.

"I won't be able to let you know too much now."

"Don't worry about it, Paijaan. I'll manage."

"But if you need any help… "

Now something was bothering her; it was like a scratch between her shoulder blades that she couldn't reach.

She went for a walk down the Curry Mile. She enjoyed absorbing its warp and weft. It had changed so much since her childhood. There were Iranian, Arab, Jamaican restaurants fused into the predominantly Pakistani-owned businesses. She looked yearningly in the direction of the Kohinoor. She saw movement in her father's office. Quickly, she crossed the road so she wouldn't be seen.

She compared the menus of other restaurants. They were posted outside in glass cases or on small billboards. As she ambled past the Shandaar, she caught sight of a bright yellow banner beneath its name. "National Curry Award Winner – 2002."

"Of course," she said to herself. "We need to enter." The Awards were several months away. *It'll easily double the sales if I win. Even to get nominated will raise my profile.*

She raced back to Maharani.

Back at the restaurant, Shabnam was with the builders. "Yes, I'm her best friend. I taught her everything. She loves me totally. What do you think of my shoes. Oh, Sorayah, I didn't see you there!"

"Shabs, what are you doing here?"

Shabnam looked embarrassed. They hugged and Shabnam whispered, "I need a really big favour."

"What?"

"Can I borrow your car?"

"Sure. Why though?"

"I'm meeting *him*." Shabnam started giggling.

"You mean your Hrithik?"

"Hrithik? No, he's called Parvez. I didn't say he was called Hrithik, but he's got muscles, and not just in his arms."

Sorayah handed her the keys to the Mercedes.

Shabnam promised to update her, "Oh, I love you Sorayah. I'd do anything for you."

"Enough. Get out and let me do some work."

"I won't have an accident."

"Out, Shabs, before I change my mind."

Shabnam left in a hurry.

Back in her office, Sorayah phoned the National Curry Awards office and requested an application form.

"You say your restaurant is new? When did you open? I only ask that, as only existing restaurants trading in this financial year may apply."

"Oh, a few months," Sorayah lied.

"No new entry has ever won the award so it would be unwise to raise your hopes too high."

"I understand. I'd still like to enter, please."

"I'll send you the pack. It contains the entry requirements. You have until the end of this month. Unfortunately, if it is late then we cannot make an exception for you."

Sorayah put the phone down. *The restaurant will be open by the time the Awards come round, so it isn't really a lie.*

She went upstairs to check on the builders. Most of the work was complete, but the finishing touches were taking longer than anticipated. The extractor fan in the kitchen had broken. The previous owner, despite his claims that "It is state of art, wallahi," had never installed the proper equipment. The tables were polished and gleaming, but the chairs were yet to arrive.

There remained one big headache. Supplies. Uncle

Jafar was ready to link her into his suppliers, but Sorayah refused. She wanted to buy him out quickly and become independent. The first few meetings and phone calls had confirmed her suspicions.

"Oh yes, you're Butt's daughter, your father said you'd be coming. He says he'll supply you – we have a ten year relationship with your father. We will give you good rates through him. How much meat will you be needing?" Brailwee & Sons asked her. She'd grimaced and found the exit quickly, feigning a headache. *Abbu is blocking me everywhere. I knew he'd do something like this. Does he really think I'll go running to him and say 'abbu, forgive me, let me work for you'?. He's crazy.*

She phoned Imran and complained.

"What am I going to do?"

"Just tell abbu that it's not on."

"Can't you speak to him? You're his 'puttar doctor' after all."

"You know, sometimes I wish I'd become a taxi-driver. How's Yaz by the way?" he deftly twisted the subject. She realised after the call was over that he hadn't promised to help.

She was walking along the Mile when she noticed the Haji Khan & Sons sign. She'd avoided it since returning to Manchester, but now something inside nudged her. She stepped into the shop.

Haji Khans & Sons was a Mancunian landmark. Everyone who lived around Wilmslow Road was familiar with its lime façade. When Sorayah entered, it was surprisingly quiet. The veteran shopkeeper was sitting on a tall chair at the back of the store nursing a cup of tea in his hands. Haji Khan was stroking his long white beard. She used to play hide-and-seek in the shop when she was younger. She remembered him as having been very tall, but the weight of his years had bent his back until the tip of his beard touched the shop counter. She had sat with him for hours. He gave sweets to her and Yasmeen and told them the most wonderful stories about Solomon the Wise and Akbar the Great. Not having met any of her grandfathers, Haji Khan had a special place in her heart.

Sorayah spied Asif, a fat and balding man from Faisalabad, who helped customers with the heavier goods. Asif saw Sorayah. She waved at him. He smiled and waved back. She gestured with her head towards the Haji and Asif waved her away, ruefully shaking his shiny head. As she walked up the aisle towards the Haji, he looked up, confused. *Has he forgotten who I am?*

Then he smiled.

When Haji Khan had opened the first Asian grocers in Manchester thirty-five years before, it was a tiny affair clinging to one of Manchester's main thoroughfares. In those days, the road was simply Wilmslow Road. It would take a couple of decades before the appellation Curry Mile was coined. His meat business fuelled the Halal food trade, which was the essential driver for the creation of Manchester's restaurant empire. It took a generation of blood and spice before people brought families there on Eid.

Haji Khan once supplied meat to her father's restaurants. That was before the larger out-of-towners entered the game.

"My beti, Sorayah, it's been so long!" the old man said in Urdu and attempted to rise from his chair.

"It's okay, Uncle, you don't have to get up for me!" Sorayah said, replying in Urdu.

"No, you are like a guest here." The old man passed his hands over her head. When was the last time I saw you?" he asked.

"About two years ago."

"Yes, I remember now. You've grown so much. I remember the first time I saw you." She'd heard the story a thousand times. She was three years old and her father had come into the shop to arrange a delivery. While her father's back was turned, she began pocketing eclairs. The sweets tumbled out of her pockets as she'd walked out of the shop. Her abbu was furious. Haji Khan thought it was delightful.

"You were always so full of energy. Ah, I used to have so much energy. I had the heart of a lion."

Abbu says that as well. An old man entered the shop and shuffled from aisle to aisle. Sorayah knew the Haji had a mind like an encyclopaedia about his customers. In the days before market analysis and profiling, the Haji had already perfected the art. Sorayah wondered if it would be a useful piece of research to do. *BME Organic Profiling and Market Analysis Methodologies in Post-Modern Britain.*

"Hello, Mr. Johnston!"

"Hello, Haa Jee. How do? How do?" Mr. Johnston said. It took a moment for Sorayah to realise that the two words "Haa Jee" were meant to be Haji.

"I'm doing very well," Haji Khan replied in English.

"Good, good."

The pensioner left without noticing Sorayah.

"Do you want some tea?" the Haji asked.

"No, Uncle."

But he wasn't listening. He'd already fished out a teabag. "You'll have to use the yellow things."

"You mean the coasters?"

"Yes, is that what you call them? My granddaughter, Maryam, brought them. She says I make the counter all dirty and that customers don't like it! Maryam is such a thoughtful girl, a bit wayward, but she has a good heart." Then, "You know beti, I've had a full innings and my time's almost over."

"That's not true," said Sorayah, feeling awkward.

"And I'm waiting for my sons to take over completely, but you know, they don't have the drive I have. Oh hai, beti, I'm very happy to see you again after all this time. Your father was very upset. He told me about what happened in London." Sorayah stopped breathing. *How could he tell the Haji?* She's never felt so embarrassed in her life. She'd learnt over the last few months that her abbu had never mentioned Ravinder to her mother.

"Your father loves you very much. He loves you more than even his restaurants."

Yeah, whatever.

"I'm happy that you decided to return home. My family has seen much sorrow in England – also some success – but there is nothing better than the happiness that a good daughter brings."

He beamed at her and then continued, sipping on his tea between bursts of sound. "Your father mentioned you're working with Jafar Ali."

Sorayah felt a dull anger growing in her belly.

"You are more than a daughter to me. Your father loves you so much, why don't you work for your father?"

She regretted setting foot in the shop. Her father had obviously anticipated that she'd visit Haji Khan and spoken to him in advance. She looked away towards the shop entrance.

"If I had one of you in my family I would have no worries for the future."

Sorayah turned to look back at the Haji. "Thank you, Uncle. But you don't understand. My father has never seen me as an equal, I'm just a girl to him. He'd never trusted me, not like you do."

The Haji was silent. "You're a good girl, like my Maryam."

Don't tell me, wayward, but with a good heart?

Sorayah wasn't sure if she should ask him, but a part of her wanted to. "Uncle, I need your help."

"Name it and it is yours. Whatever you need."

She told him about getting suppliers to deal with her, without going through her father. The old man stroked his beard thoughtfully.

"They will help you if I ask them to, but I'll have to speak to your father. He won't be happy."

That was the last thing she wanted the Haji to do.

"I can see that there may be trouble, but your father respects me. I'm an old man, what will he do to me?"

There was a commotion at the front as customers entered the shop.

Sorayah said, "It looks like it's getting busy, I should make a move, I'm decorating the new place. And – thank you."

The Haji nodded. "Come back in a few days and I'll let you know what the suppliers said. If worse comes to worse, I'll supply you directly myself. And Sorayah, don't be embarrassed by what an old man says, my mind is on the next world and I don't mean to offend you so forgive me if I've said anything."

"There's nothing to forgive."

Back in her office, Sorayah could sense the business beating in her heart, felt the links and lines and relationships tying one business to another. *The restaurant bone connected to the Haji Khan bone, the Haji Khan bone connected to the Ali bone.* The network went on and on and never stopped. She understood then that trade was locked in her blood, the only thing holding her together. *Or am I looking for something to fill the emptiness I feel?* She'd come to terms with loss of Ravinder and she felt a new vigour for life that she hadn't felt in a long time.

She felt anew the embarrassment of the Haji knowing about Ravinder. *There aren't many people abbu would have trusted. Why did he tell him?* She turned on the CD player and listened to Shabnam's freshly burned Juggy D hits. She turned up the volume.

The next few weeks passed in a blink. Sorayah scrambled around checking the menus were printed, made deals with the local Asian papers (again her abbu had beaten her to it and she was forced to ask Uncle Jafar for help, a blow to her). Despite the trials and tribulations, Maharani inexorably neared completion. She abandoned the flat and slept in her restaurant.

Imran visited. Shokat was more circumspect, but he popped round when abbu was out of Manchester. Baji Shazia had got a job, but dropped in occasionally. Basharat never came. She tried contacting him. He never answered her calls.

Her mother visited to her great surprise. Shabnam (who'd adopted the restaurant as her "chill out place before I get, you know, hitched,") ran upstairs, breathless. Sorayah had moved her office to the first floor.

"It's your mum, oh my God! What are we going to do? Should we hide?"

"Don't be so silly, Shabs. It's only my ammi." Slowly, she went downstairs. Her mother was standing in the entrance wearing a long beige coat cinched a little too tightly. Her mother's cream dapatta was rain splashed.

"Ammi, please take a seat," she said in Punjabi. "Can I get you something to eat? To drink?"

"No, puttar," her mother said, dutifully sitting down. She didn't seem well. "Puttar," she said finally, "you have to get married, you know. People are talking. Every time I go to people's homes they're talking about you. Only you. Sorayah this, Sorayah that. Sorayah's restaurant. I don't know what to say to them any more."

Sorayah wasn't surprised, but she didn't hear the needling tone from her mum, the one she'd constantly heard in her teenage years.

"I will ammi, I promise I will, let me get this restaurant launched first."

"You're so much like your father. That's probably why."

"Probably why?"

"Your father never really had time for the family. The restaurant was always his real family." Then, "Sorayah, will you remember me when I'm gone?"

"Ammi. Don't talk like that."

"My time is coming, I can feel it. I can feel the hands of the Death."

"You've got a long time to go yet, Mum. Women live till ninety in this country."

"But they don't have the worries that I have. Basharat, Shokat, Shazia, my grandchildren. And you're not happy. None of my children are happy. Why aren't you happy?"

Sorayah couldn't answer that.

"Let me show you the restaurant," Sorayah said brightly and stood up.

Her mother hesitated then stood up and followed her. Shabnam followed, a goofy smile on her face.

"You know," her mother said at one point, "your father never showed me any of his restaurants. We've been married thirty-seven years and he never showed me one. What kind of life did I live?"

"Come on, ammi, your life isn't over. There's lots still to do."

"And why didn't your father get servants like others? He has enough money. Why do I have to do so much work? I'm tired of it, Sorayah. Doing everything. My daughter-in-law is useless. She doesn't do any of the work any more. She thinks she's a queen. And Imran and Basharat won't get married."

They were in the kitchen, thankfully empty of people. Sorayah had never known her mother to be so open with her.

"You could go on holiday somewhere," Sorayah offered.

"Holiday? I visited your Auntie Reshma last year. I can't have another holiday."

"That wasn't a real holiday. I mean why don't you go shopping with some of your friends?"

"Where would we go? I don't need any clothes. Your father promised me he'd buy me some bracelets. He hasn't even done that."

"Why don't you take his credit card and go shopping? I'm sure he wouldn't mind."

"I couldn't do that. I've never done that. He only gives me what he says I need. He knows best."

"His money's yours as well, you know. After all, he works for the family, so why can't you use it? It isn't as though you'd buy useless things, would you?"

Her mother looked thoughtful. "Well, maybe you're right. I know where he keeps them. I'll speak to your Auntie Gulshan. She knows where we can get the best bargains."

She continued the tour of the restaurant. Shabnam had disappeared. Sorayah sighed. Shabnam was probably hiding in a corner on the mobile phone to her Mr Hrithik. Upstairs in the office, she made her mother a cup of tea. They sat in amiable silence for half an hour. Shabnam interrupted them. She was out of breath, her face was wet and she was holding a plastic bag.

"Hello Auntie, I got you some sweets!" she said in Urdu, revealing a box of Asian sweets.

"Why daughter? You didn't have to do that for me."

"It's the first time you came to the restaurant and that's the most important thing that's happened to us — isn't it, Sorayah?"

"Oh yes," said Sorayah, surprised and thankful for Shabnam's gift.

After her mother had gone, Sorayah said to Shabnam, "You know, that's the nicest thing you've ever done."

Shabnam beamed. "I did it cos I love you. And you love me." She wrapped her arms around Sorayah. "Now can I borrow your car?"

Sorayah received a terse letter from the National Curry

Awards panel.

```
Your application for entry has
been rejected. It has come to
our  attention  that  you  are
currently  not  trading  and
therefore cannot be considered
for  entry  into  this  year's
competition.
```

She sat down hard on the office chair.

"What's the matter?" Shabnam asked her.

Her mind was working furiously. She'd told Shokat she was entering. She surmised their father had driven it out of him and contacted the panel. She was angry enough to phone her abbu, but she controlled herself. *Come on Sorayah. There has to be a way round this. There's got to be. If I can win this competition I'll break even inside a year and I can buy Uncle Jafar out.*

She explained to Shabnam what had happened.

"Oh my God! What are we going to do?" Then, "Is this serious, Sorayah?"

Sorayah nodded.

Abbu used to say gorays are sticklers for rules and regulations. You only have to know how to tweak them. She opened the filing cabinet and heaved everything onto the floor. Immediately, she spotted the saffron coloured 'Guidebook for Entrants'. Sure enough Rule 2 stated: 'All contestants must be trading to be eligible for entry'. Undeterred, she continued reading. Rule 16 read: 'Market research, in some instances, may be deemed as trading if the consumption of food is involved'. It was all she needed.

Sorayah phoned Yasmeen, Dina, Farzana and Tayiba

and asked them to come to the restaurant. She cooked a meal herself and Shabnam decorated the kitchen for a party.

"What are we celebrating?" Yasmeen asked.

"Survival!" Sorayah said.

They thoroughly enjoyed the food and she took lots of photos. She even took them standing inside against the restaurant logo. Then she phoned the National Curry Awards.

"We're sorry, but we cannot reconsider."

"In your Guidebook for Entrants, Rule 16 says that market research involving the consumption of food is deemed as trading. I've tried out the food with the locals – particularly students." That was true enough. *We're all students in the University of Life.*

There was a long pause. Then finally, "Do you have evidence?"

"I've got completed questionnaires and I – we carried out further research and produced a report."

"If you can get that to me, we can place it for the panel's consideration. But I must stress that this is highly unusual."

"Rule 16 says that market research if involving… "

"Yes, I'm aware of that now, Miss Butt."

"I'll be sending it by recorded delivery." Her abbu always said to keep the pressure on.

"Yes, Miss Butt."

She didn't inform Uncle Jafar about the problems with the panel and decided to wait a week before chasing for a verdict.

The girls started visiting her more often, making a den out of her office. Sorayah enjoyed the company. She hadn't realised how lonely she'd been. Yasmeen visited her every day. One day, she pulled the reluctant Sorayah out of the Maharani and into the TC, the Trafford Centre. They sat in a small café and watched people.

After a lull in the conversation, Yasmeen asked, "What's the matter?"

"I didn't want it to be this way," Sorayah replied.

"Going against your father?"

"Yes. He made it impossible for me to do it any other way."

"That's dads for you."

"At least yours saw sense."

"Yes. Finally. Javed and Parveen have really helped. I'm surprised though."

"Why?"

"Well, I should be a pariah. I messed up everyone's plans."

Sorayah could see it was painful for her friend to speak about the suicide attempt. She squeezed her hand. "We all learn from life. We gotta move on. Move forward."

"Hmmm, yeah. I suppose so."

"Are you going to reconsider? Raheem's totally in love with you."

"I think he truly does love me. He's been so understanding. I don't think I really knew him before. I think his heart was set on me, but you know, I just didn't know that. I thought – I thought too many things. Hmmm? What's to do? I don't know."

They sat and watched the people fade in and out of the Trafford Centre. Sorayah realised that being boyfriendless, sleepless and not knowing how the restaurant would fare, actually made her content.

Happiness wasn't important any more. She preferred contentment. All the running around, dressing up, chasing and being chased were meaningless to her now.

"What you smiling at?" Yasmeen asked.

"I think I finally found what I was looking for."

"And what's that?"

"To just be. What a cliché, eh?"

"Just be?' Wasn't that Calvin Klein?" Yasmeen said, and Sorayah laughed.

Sorayah's phone beeped. She smiled. She didn't check who it was from and Yasmeen didn't ask. Both of them knew it was Javed. It was an open secret between them.

She received a call from the National Curry Awards panel two days later.

"Miss Butt?"

"Yes?"

"The board has reconsidered. You will be allowed entry."

She bought a greeting card and wrote, 'I'll see you at the National Curry Awards'. She walked across the road and handed it to the Kohinoor's manager. She smiled at him and said, "Abbu will want to see it as soon as possible."

She walked out of the restaurant, still smiling.

17

"Oh my Lord, what am I to do?" Ajmal muttered, rubbing his eyes. He wanted to end the meeting with the accountant: Mudassir Shareef's words were an incoherent babble. He licked his lips and grimly persevered. "I've told you a hundred times already. I want the tax reduced. Why are you giving me this headache?"

"I'm doing the best that I can, Mr Butt, sir," Mudassir replied.

Ajmal grimaced. His accountant was trembling – his nervous temperament had had him thrown out of the Pakistani army.

"I have tried everything I can, sir. You can't hide all the income. You've got to give the Revenue something or they'll eat you alive."

Sameena entered the office with a tray laden with tea and biscuits and the accountant was momentarily distracted. Sameena put the tray down and left.

"The Kohinoor needs more funding," Ajmal insisted.

"Yes, Mr Butt, sir, but wouldn't it be better to sell… ?"

"How dare you? I've already told you not to raise that subject again. I'm never, and I swear by my mother's name, that I'll never sell the Kohinoor. I want my factories sold."

The accountant relaxed visibly. "They'll get a good price, sir, I'm sure of it. But I'm not sure it'll be enough."

"Mudassir," Ajmal began, his voice low and feral, "if you raise the issue of the Kohinoor again I'll throw you out of the office window. Do you hear me?"

"Yes, sir. I understand your position more than clearly. It's like the waters of the Jamna. Crystal clear, sir."

"No, I don't think you do understand so let me make it clearer for you. If the Kohinoor goes down, I go down with it. I've put too much of my own blood into this to let go of it now." Then he relented, "Mudassir, my friend. We've been through tough times before. What you say is probably the best thing for me to do, but it wouldn't work in the long term. I've put my reputation into this restaurant. If it collapses then my entire empire collapses. So it has to succeed."

Ajmal watched Mudassir soak in the information. Mudassir nodded, but didn't say anything else.

"Now drink your tea and give me a résumé of last month's income and expenditure."

At one point, Mudassir pursed his lips and said, "There is a discrepancy with one of your credit cards. You appear to be buying a lot of Asian women's clothes. Are you preparing for your daughter's wedding, sir?"

Ajmal almost hit him.

That evening, as Ajmal drove BUTT1 away from the Kohinoor, he passed Sorayah's restaurant-to-be. He grunted. The restaurant windows were boarded up. Only the door was visible. "Manchester's Maharani Restaurant: Coming Soon" was emblazoned across it in garish red. He noticed passers-by and drivers glancing at it. He was tempted to pay some of the young men he occasionally used to graffiti the building.

He drove to Alexandra Park and turned into a side street. It was dark. A car pulled up shortly behind his Mercedes and cut its headlights. He heard a door open and close and a shadow appeared next to his car. The passenger side door opened and a man got in. It was Atif Qurban, one of Jafar's closest workers. He worked at the Shandaar and was privy to all of Jafar's secrets.

"What news do you have?" Ajmal said quietly.

Atif Qurban didn't say a word. Ajmal reached into his inside pocket and brought out an envelope. He handed it to Qurban. It disappeared immediately.

"The development of the new restaurant is proceeding very quickly," Qurban said in Urdu. "They'll be open in a few weeks."

Ajmal hissed. The last report stated that Sorayah was facing difficulties fitting extractor fans. She had made progress. "I want an exact date. I pay you enough, don't I?"

Qurban looked ahead. He hadn't looked at Ajmal once during their conversation. "Provisionally, the end of next month."

"That bastard is doing everything to make sure this is a success."

"They're preparing for the National Curry Awards. Your daughter has entered."

"What? I phoned them. I know their Chief Executive personally – John's eaten with me many times! He promised me he'd get the – the restaurant isn't even open yet! How did she…?" Then he understood the card she had sent. He cursed under his breath, but he couldn't help feeling pride that his daughter had outsmarted him. He smiled momentarily. "Have you found out where he's getting his funds from yet?" He'd been trying to determine Jafar's financial source for several years.

"Nobody knows and if I ask too many

questions people will become suspicious."

"I want answers, not excuses. Don't you understand, I'm the Curry King here, not Jafar Shafar or anyone else."

"I'll do the best I can."

"You'd better do better than that or I won't need your services any more."

"I have heard something, but I haven't been able to check it fully."

"Stop stalling and tell me something useful."

"A few workers think he has something going on in London. He spends a lot of time there. A few days every month."

"What's that got to do with anything? He's got three restaurants there."

"Yes, but he doesn't spend much time at the restaurants when he's there."

"That could mean many things." Ajmal thought about it for a moment. Then said, "Find out what, and do it quickly. I pay you enough to spy." Ajmal suspected that Qurban threw him titbits, because if he gave Ajmal the full curry he wouldn't be needed any longer, so only droplets of information were his offerings. Ajmal despised him. He would love to have taken a cleaver to him and make him into human keema.

Qurban left as silently as he'd come. Ajmal wondered for the hundredth time if Qurban was passing information both ways. He doubted it, but he suspected one of his own workers was feeding Jafar information. That was life in the jungle. It was the only way he could explain how Jafar was always one step ahead. Somehow, Jafar Ali was able to maintain good internal defences so men like Qurban could only supply him with late, out-of-date information.

He felt infinitely alone. *Why didn't my children turn out the way I wanted them to? If Shokat had half of my Killer Instinct he'd be invincible.* Ajmal had been so proud of his catch of three sons when he was younger. *Maybe this is the price I've paid for bragging about them to my brothers when they were children.* The one he'd never considered to run his business had outdone them all. Sorayah. She was like a shining star. *What did I do wrong?* Basharat had the fire in him, but he was impossible to get hold of. He'd started missing Juma prayers, something he'd never done before. Ajmal sighed.

He made his way home. It was silent when he arrived. Hardly any of the children called round any longer and they didn't have the visitors they used to. *I have a palace and nobody comes to it.* He felt depressed and dejected. Without Sameena he didn't know what he would do. He entered the kitchen and found his wife wasn't there. A message in Urdu had been left on the fridge. "Gone shopping." He understood then who'd been using his credit card and he knew without asking a single question whose influence was behind it. He stormed out of the house.

That evening he ate in the Kohinoor. The chicken tikka masala was tasteless. He mulled the future. As the evening wore on the restaurant became busier and his optimism returned. He went downstairs to do his 'rounds'. He loved this aspect of his job. It allowed him to revel in his own glory and greet people. He shook hands, "Curry bringing people together" flowed from his lips, and he felt at ease again, eager and ready to seize any opportunity.

Waseem Kareem, a local councillor and old friend

from the early days of working in the restaurant business, arrived with his wife and three children.

"It's good to see you, Councillor Saab!" Ajmal said in English.

"I've come for your vote tonight – but good food will do if you don't have it."

Both men laughed and Ajmal led them upstairs to the more elite tables.

"I've heard good things about your daughter," Waseem said. Ajmal kept his face blank. "You've done a good job with her. Allowing your daughter full reins. That inspires me for the future." He turned to his daughters, "See how your uncle is allowing his daughter freedom?" Then he turned back to Ajmal and leaned forward, lowering his voice, "but at least she earns her way instead of taking all the time."

"Yes, she works very hard," Ajmal agreed. *So he knows something, but not everything.* Over the last few weeks, he'd heard similar comments. Everyone thought he was behind his daughter's restaurant venture. *How come more people know about her restaurant than me? What is it that she's doing that's getting everyone interested? Is it because she's a girl?*

He was glad Haji Khan had spoken to him and told him he'd be supplying Sorayah with meat. Ajmal didn't want to get into an argument with the old man. He deeply regretted pushing her away, but he couldn't apologise. He knew she'd have returned to him in the time it takes bails to fall from a stumped wicket like she did when she was a child. *But a lion doesn't apologise, he takes and gives the pieces that are left to whom he wills.*

"I'll definitely try out her restaurant when it opens. I'm sure it'll be better than the Kohinoor," the councillor said. Ajmal forced a smile and departed.

Mudassir Shareef followed Ajmal's order to the letter and the factories were up for sale within days of the decision. The Wakefield textile factory secured an eager buyer, a Mirpuri from Bradford. *Too much money for his own good.* Ajmal disliked dealing with Mirpuris in general and was uncomfortable with the Punjabi spoken in the mountains; but money spoke louder than words.

Ajmal kept his eldest appraised of the sale. "And don't say anything to Sorayah or I'll chop your ears off." Shokat had confessed that Sorayah had been hounding him for days about why abbaji was selling the factories. Ajmal feared she'd guessed the truth. The last thing he needed was for Sorayah to start spouting off and influencing Shokat.

There was still the small matter of David Mirza, which remained to be settled. Shokat had commented on the appearance of a large bouncer at the doors of the Kohinoor, but Ajmal told him it was for the protection of clientele. The boy hadn't questioned him further.

Dilawar urged him to forget the path of vengeance. "Leave Mirza, he's not worth it. He's a killer."

"Have you ever known me to turn away from such a challenge?"

Dilawar shook his head and pressed his mosque hat tighter onto his head. "No, yaar, he's scum, you'll end up getting yourself too deep. You don't want to be dealing with people like that, God knows I'm right!"

"Leave it to me, I'll find him some day."

He drove to Wakefield with his accountant to finalise the deal with the Bradford entrepreneur, Zia Chaudhry. The businessman's hair was greasy and his stubby beard made Ajmal think he was dealing with a homeless bum, but he kept his feelings at bay, praying the Mirpuri would sign.

At one point the man said, "I've heard that your daughter is soon entering the restaurant trade." Ajmal's breath caught in his throat. *They've even heard about her here.* "My friends tell me she will be quite remarkable, being your daughter and all. In fact, I hear that this new restaurant will open soon and it will be very, very successful."

Ajmal imagined the Kohinoor sinking like the *Titanic* and his daughter's restaurant rising from the depths to take its place. He cursed under his breath.

"I'll tell you what, Ajmal, I like doing business with successful men like you. I'd consider investing more in your businesses if I can have a potential stake in anything your daughter might do. It might be a little too late with this venture, but perhaps the next. I'll make it worthwhile for you."

Reluctantly, Ajmal agreed to ask his daughter.

It took him two days to build up the courage to phone Sorayah. He finally gritted his teeth and dialled her number. She was surprised to hear his voice.

"What do you want?" she asked sharply in English.

He bit back a harsh reply. "Oh, how is the restaurant doing?"

"What you on about, abbu? It's not even open yet. I'm sure your spies have kept you informed. How is the sale of the factories going?"

He was glad they weren't sitting facing each other, otherwise his facial expression would have revealed his thoughts. "Oh, all fine. I was ringing to see if you were okay."

"I don't believe you, abbu. What do you want?"

She had him in a vice. He stood up and marched to the window overlooking the road. He looked down the Mile at Maharani, two hundred yards away. He imagined her sitting, gloating.

He cleared his throat. "I've met with a financier," he said, "he's got a lot of money. He wants me to go into a new partnership together. It could be massive. The biggest thing I've ever done."

"Why are you telling me this? What's it got to do with me?"

He loathed her insolent tone, but he'd started this journey and he had to continue. "Well, you see, puttar, he wants to invest in your business too."

"Why would I consider this, abbu? You've done everything to stop me."

"I've done no such thing."

"I know about the National Curry Awards. And you tried to stop people supplying me."

"I let Haji supply you. I wouldn't have done that if I wanted to stop you. You could have got good rates through me."

Sorayah didn't reply immediately. "I know what you're like, abbu. You need the money, that's why you're doing this."

Ajmal was knocked for a six. Shokat had never understood and there in one breath, one conversation, his daughter had figured it out.

"No, I'm doing it for you."

"The answer is no. In capital letters. Shall I spell it for you?" She ended the call without saying goodbye.

The rage didn't come immediately. *I knew she'd turn me down, but I went to her like a fool anyway!*

Angrily, he rang Imran, but it went straight to

18

Sorayah was in the office finalising the launch invitation list when Yasmeen rang.

"Listen, Sorayah," Yasmeen said, "I've got to speak to you, it's important. Can you leave the restaurant?"

"Sure. But can you come here?" The launch was three days away.

"I can't. I wouldn't ask you if it weren't important."

Guilt forced Sorayah's hand. "OK. Where are you?"

Shabnam agreed to cover for her. Sorayah drove at breakneck speed to Yasmeen's house wondering what her friend needed to talk about. *I hope everything's okay.*

She parked in the Ali driveway, butterflies in her stomach. She recalled the derailed wedding and attempted suicide. Then there was Sorayah's partnership with Jafar and Javed's feelings for her. She felt a tandoori mix of emotions as she walked up the path. But nothing would obstruct her friendship with Yasmeen.

She rang the doorbell and a breathless Yasmeen opened it.

"What's happened?"

"Come upstairs."

Sorayah followed. She could hear the sounds of television coming from the living room.

"Who is it?" she heard Yasmeen's mother shout in Urdu.

"It's Sorayah, Mother," Yasmeen shouted back.

Sorayah was bundled into her friend's bedroom.

"Okay," Sorayah said, sitting down on the bed, "what's going on?"

"We needed to have a long chat and you're stuck in that restaurant of yours."

Sorayah sighed. She guessed Yasmeen was feeling insecure.

"I know we haven't met up much lately, but the launch is only a few days away. I've got to get back… "

"You don't. Shabnam's there. I was there yesterday and it looked pretty much ready then."

"But it has to be perfect."

"Hmmm, no more time for your friends?"

"Hey, it's not like that, I'm here aren't I?"

"Good? Tea?" Sorayah sighed and nodded, but her mind was restless. *Napkins. Forks. Paint has come off the bar. Need that varnishing…*

"Sorayah?"

"Er, what?"

"Are you here in this room or still in that restaurant of yours?"

"I'm here. Honest."

"Then you won't mind doing my hair will you?"

Sorayah felt instantly guilty. Normally she wouldn't think twice about combing her friend's hair. *I'm becoming just like abbu.* "I'm really sorry. I guess I've become obsessed with the restaurant."

"As Parv would say, acknowledging the problem is the beginning of the road to a cure."

"So what's the cure for it?" Sorayah laughed, grabbing a brush from the dressing table.

"Well, it's either shopping or boys."

"Shopping's cool, but I'm off boys." Sorayah began brushing Yasmeen's hair. She expected Yasmeen to mention Javed, but she didn't. Slowly, as the minutes passed Sorayah found herself unwinding.

"Sorayah?" Yasmeen said in a little voice. "Don't become like our fathers."

She stopped brushing. "I don't want to either. But it makes you like that."

"There's a way you can stop becoming like them." Sorayah smiled sadly. "What? Shopping and boys?"

"No. Don't cut yourself off. You need people around you."

"Who can I rely on? I'm in this alone. Anyway, your dad's pretty open with his team."

"Daddy isn't as open you think. He keeps most things to himself. Hmm, I should know. And you can't say that you've got nobody – Shabs has been there for you, hasn't she?"

"Yeah, I know. She's been great. I don't think I'd have come this far without her – I can't believe I'm saying that!"

"Why don't you get the girls involved?"

"Everyone's busy. I can't ask them to leave their lives and come into mine."

"You'd be surprised."

"And what about you?" Sorayah asked.

"Me too," said Yasmeen, "I can get stuck in."

"Well, it would be nice to have people involved, but I don't think it's really practical."

"You're doing it already."

"Doing what?"

"Discounting us. Putting the wall up."

"I'm not. I've just got loads to do. The launch–…"

"Is only three days away. Yes, I know that. But we can help."

Sorayah sat down and squeezed her friend's hand. "I really appreciate what you're saying, but this isn't a party we're organising. It's a business."

"I know that, Sorayah. I grew up in the trade just like

you. I know what it does to people. I've watched my daddy all his life grow further and further away from us. He has no idea how Parveen feels about Imran or how Javed feels about you."

Sorayah felt herself stiffen.

"Anyway," Yasmeen said, "if you don't learn a coping strategy now you'll make the same mistakes.. You'll lose everything you have. I know what it feels like losing everything. Life included. Don't do this."

"I've got to finish it."

"I'm not saying don't do it, I'm saying bring us in. Use us. Let us belong."

"Okay, okay, oh wise one, in what way do you want to be involved?"

Yasmeen looked at her watch. "Well, why don't I come back with you to the restaurant and we'll talk about that?"

"Sure," Sorayah said, eager to be back at Maharani.

"I need to change first. Help me choose something?"

They chatted in the car. Sorayah felt oddly excited about Yasmeen returning to the restaurant with her.

"Daddy's going to hate this," Yasmeen confessed.

"Why? What's wrong with you helping out? Your father and I are partners."

"You think so, Sorayah?"

"Yes, of course."

"I don't know if I should tell you this. Oh, what the hell. Javed told me something yesterday and I know he wanted me to tell you."

"If this is about Javed– "

"Don't get your knickers in a twist, it's nothing to do with Jav, it's to do with the restaurant. You know the Arab guy who you bought the restaurant off?"

"Yes?"

"He wasn't the owner."

"Eh? I saw the papers."

"Hmmm. I'm sure you did. Javed, you see, helps Daddy out with the accounts and he realised you didn't know so he told me. The restaurant was already owned by Daddy. He'd leased it to the Arab. He went through an intermediary and the Arab guy didn't even know he was leasing it off him."

"So who owns it?"

"Haven't you guessed?"

It dawned on her. "Javed?"

"That's right. Daddy doesn't put all the restaurants in his name. The building you're in is owned by Javed."

"Oh my God!" Sorayah was horrified, her mind in overdrive. *He's played me all this time.* They were nearing the Mile. "If your father finds out Javed let the cat out of the bag…"

"Exactly. So keep it close to your chest until you need it," Yasmeen said.

They drove in silence.

"Why did you tell me?" Sorayah asked.

"It's not why I told you. I'd have told you sooner or later. The question is why Javed told me to tell you."

Sorayah pursed her lips. "Your father will skin him alive."

"Oh yes, you better believe it."

They parked on Wilmslow Road, in a parking space a few doors away from the restaurant. Sorayah got out, but Yasmeen lagged behind. Sorayah turned back. "Are you okay, Yaz?"

"Oh yes, of course, go on, go in, I'll catch up."

Confused, Sorayah opened the door of the

restaurant. She was greeted by a room full of people shouting "Surprise!" Then Shabnam was pulling her in.

"We thought we'd do something special before the launch – just for you."

Dina, Farzana, Ghazala and Tayiba – all the girls – were hugging her. And Imran was there. "Immy, I can't believe it!" She hugged her brother.

"Well," he quipped, "Yasmeen did my head in and I tell you, there's nothing worse than getting your ear done in by an Ali."

Shazia had come with her kids. Nazia had come up with her London posse, including Nazia, Rubeena, Priya, Kulbinder, Anita, Aminah and Tanzeela. Sorayah started to cry. Then Varinder Singh brought out a cake for her. She hugged him and he said, "I specially had this made for you, sohniye."

Shabnam lit the candles and they shouted, "Make a wish, Saz!" She blew out the candle and thanked them.

"You're a real cow," Sorayah told Yasmeen, after she'd cut the cake.

"Hmmm, I know."

"You lured me away so that they could set this up?"

"Yes, sorry."

"Were you serious about helping out?"

"I've never been so serious in my life."

Later, Sorayah gathered everyone around her. There were over thirty people. She felt warm and tingly. "I wanted to thank you all for coming. Yasmeen has told me that a few of you want to help out and I really appreciate that. The launch is three days away and I could use it."

Imran cornered her when they started cleaning up. He had a particular look on his face.

"I can guess, Abbu phoned you," Sorayah said. It was becoming a habit. Abbu was using Imran as leverage. "What am I meant to have done this time?"

Imran mentioned the business deal she'd turned down.

"Tell me Immy, how can I go and do a deal with someone else when I'm already in a contract with Uncle Jafar? It's not my call. I have to sit down with Uncle Jafar and discuss it first."

"He said that you put the phone down on him."

"He got what he deserved. He was lying to me, using me."

"You know he loves you, though?"

"Does he? The only reason abbu rang me was cos he needs the money. It's that simple. Immy, you're bright enough to know that. Our dad's only got one thing he cares about: himself."

"I'm just an innocent bystander in this, little sis. I just want you guys to get on with each other."

"If he were straight with me then I might help him out, but first I want him to say he's sorry for saying all the horrible things he said to me."

"Oh, Sorayah. You know he isn't going to do that. He's our dad. He won't say sorry. He never says sorry to anyone."

"Well, he better start learning soon, cos I'm not going begging to him."

"So it's true. You've turned your back on him. He said you've rejected him."

"Whose side are you on, big brother? He rejected me, for your information! If he needed help he should have just asked. He should grow up."

"You guys gotta sort this out, otherwise this will just

go on and on."

"Doing your head in, is it?"

"Very much so."

"Welcome to the club."

"Well, what do you say?" Imran pressed.

"I'm not going to see him. He can get lost."

"Sorayah."

"Immy, I love you, you're my brother. And despite what he's done and said I still love abbu, but you must be crazy if you think I'm going to go meekly to him and beg to be forgiven."

"Listen, he's our father. That'll never change no matter what we do."

"I'm not interested, Imran." Sorayah frowned. "Is this why you came back to Manchester?"

"No! I came back for you."

"You're not lying to me, are you?"

"I've never lied to you, Sorayah," Imran said. He never called her Sorayah unless he was very serious.

She relented. "I'll meet him, but only if you're there and if he comes to my restaurant."

Imran looked thoughtful. "Of course I'll be there, but why don't we go for neutral territory?

"Like what?"

"Home?"

"That's neutral?"

"If I'm there it is."

She pondered meeting her father again. She did and didn't want to see him. Then she decided that as long as they met as equals it would be okay.

"Okay," she said finally, "but I'm only doing it for you."

Imran hugged her quickly. "I'll find Dad."

The meeting went ahead in the family home later that evening. Their mother was staying at Shazia's and Imran and Sorayah waited for their father to arrive. Imran paced up and down the living room like a caged beast. Their father arrived late, looking flustered.

"Why won't you work for me, instead of that harami?" Ajmal said.

Sorayah glanced at her brother and opened her eyes wide as if to say 'told you so'.

"This isn't about Jafar Ali. It's about us," Sorayah told him.

"I offered you a great opportunity the other day and you turned me down flat. How do you think I should react?" Ajmal asked.

"If you hadn't noticed," she said, "I don't work for you. You have no right to tell others that I'll go into partnership with them. And on top of that you've done your damndest to ruin me!"

"I haven't done anything wrong," Ajmal claimed.

"Well, if you're going to lie then I'm leaving," Sorayah said, standing up.

"Come on, everyone," Imran said placatingly. "Dad, listen to what she's saying."

"Okay, puttar doctor, but tell her not to be so rude."

Sorayah sat down. "What do you want? I've got a restaurant to launch and I haven't got time to have a nice long chat with you."

"I want you to leave Jafar Ali and come and work for me."

"You must be kidding," Sorayah said, laughing. "After all you've done? The cheek of it. Immy, he tried to get me kicked out of the National Curry Awards and

I wouldn't be surprised if he's been doing other things behind my back as well."

"How dare you?" Ajmal said, "I only did what was good for the business."

"That's all you've ever cared about," hissed Sorayah. "You never cared for us. And you never will."

She could see the rage building in her father's eyes, but she refused to cave in.

"If you don't leave that bastard and come back to me I'll make you struggle every day of your life," Ajmal declared.

Sorayah looked at her father, matched his gaze and said slowly, "if that's what you want, then fine. I'll manage without you. I'm doing fine without you already. I'll send you a special invitation to the launch and you can come and taste the kind of food your restaurants will never serve."

Her father stormed out.

Imran shook his head.

"I knew this wasn't going to do any good," Sorayah said.

"Looking on the bright side, it wasn't as bad as it could have been."

"Could it have been any worse, Immy?"

"It can always be worse, sister, you know that."

"He didn't ask me to go into business with him. Did you notice that?"

"No, I guess he didn't."

They sat there in silence. She'd noticed that her abbu had lost weight. She knew she could never work for her father and that they would probably never have a civil conversation again, but she still loved him. She sighed. She got up to leave and stopped at the living-room door.

"He's pushing himself too hard, Immy. He'll do himself an injury. You're his puttar doctor. Tell him to take it easy."

19

Ajmal Butt licked his lips and rubbed his hands together in glee. 'Eat a Curry For a Good Cause' was stencilled on a large laminated poster outside the Kohinoor. *If Sorayah can pick up customers with silly notices then so can I. Khudaya, these gorays are so stupid.* He beamed and scanned the growing queue by the entrance. Sikander Riaz, his manager at the Lazeez, had reported an equally brisk trade.

The 'Charity Meals' were inspired by Dilawar. "What, my dear yaars, is the one thing the English do better than anyone else?" Dilawar had asked at one of their get-togethers in Bradford the previous summer. It had been lunchtime and Ajmal was enjoying Kashif's curries with his inner circle of friends. Umar Miah, Ikram Haq and Waseem Nazir were old colleagues of Ajmal's, men he'd worked with in the Manchester markets before entering the world of spice. None of the men was a direct rival, none had entered the curry trade and so they'd remained friends.

"I think, Dilawar Saab, they know how to lose in cricket," Waseem quipped, his toolbar moustache shaking with mirth. Ikram smacked him on the back.

"Everybody hates them for doing the exact opposite of everyone else?" Ikram suggested.

"They strip off fastest when they see a ray of sunshine? Pagal de puttar!" Umar chortled.

"They're more racist than anyone else?" Ajmal hazarded.

"No, you're all buffoons," Dilawar cried, "It's charities – they're brilliant at charities!"

"Charities?" Ajmal asked, surprised. *Of course.* The

friends looked at each other.

"Yes, the English can create a charity in a heartbeat. I'm telling you my friends, they probably give more to charity than any other country. You only have to suggest the mere possibility of giving some of your money to charity and they'd be kissing your feet!"

The friends hadn't believed Dilawar, but he'd insisted, "You don't believe me, but I'm not wrong here, God knows I'm right!"

Ajmal had forgotten Dilawar's words, but they had sunk like hidden treasure in his dark mind. He'd watched builders entering Sorayah's restaurant-to-be, his desperation growing. Maharani's launch date was only a day or two away. He refused to be beaten by his daughter. *I'm her father, damn it, I know this trade better than anyone.*

The idea for the Charity Meals came to him in the middle of a sweat-drenched night. The concept came fully clothed. *One day in the week given over to a charity.* And the dream had become a reality. He wanted to dance in joy. *This'll show Sorayah. Dilawar was right – we are bewaquf sometimes – and the angrez are even bigger bewaqufs.*

Ajmal laughed. He was charging customers extra for eating the Charity Meals, but still they came. Even more wonderful was that students made the bulk of the crowd. They entered in class-size bunches wearing 'Stop the War' T-shirts. *They bring ready cash, but they're as fickle as British weather.*

Saleem approached him. "All the restaurants are busy. Totally full, boss."

"Excellent!" Ajmal replied in English.

He had taken the unprecedented step of arranging for all six of his restaurants on Wilmslow Road to serve the same 'Charity Menu'. The print run could have dented his scheme, but twisting the arm of the printers was much cheaper than anticipated and had provided a hidden marketing opportunity. Three hundred boxes of Asian sweets emblazoned with the Kohinoor's golden crown had exchanged hands. Shoaib Karim, the proprietor of Karim & Sons Printers, was in an expansive mood following the birth of his first grandson.

The real coup was persuading the Lord Mayor to preside over the event. Patrick Boyle, a broad ex-Union chief, had risen to the occasion. Ajmal didn't need to brief the Mayor on what to say, Patrick was an old fox. "Anything for an old mate, eh?" Patrick had said to him, patting him on the shoulder.

Ajmal had winked and said, "Please be sure to bring your wife and children whenever you want. All drinks on the house."

The opening speech had nabbed the punters. "Manchester's Curry King has kindly asked me to ask you, most-esteemed food tasters, to nibble your way to helping others." The audience laughed appreciatively.

Ajmal sighed in delight while sitting at the banquet table on the stage hastily constructed an hour before the doors opened. The words 'Curry King' aroused an emotion in him that nothing else did: no Indian movie, cricket match, Sameena's embrace or puff of a cigarette come close to the exquisite pleasure those two words engendered in him. He beamed. He imagined Jafar Ali squirming. *He'll want to copy this idea when he hears about it.* He reminded himself to buy a special gift for Sameena. She'd put in a lot of extra work to get the leaflets distributed to the local universities, colleges, clubs and pubs. He whispered a thanks to Dilawar for pushing her his way.

He went downstairs to check on Shokat's progress. He normally welcomed the clientele himself, but today was different. The Charity Meal was a new scheme and despite the risks, Shokat was at the entrance of the Kohinoor. For the very first time in his life, Shokat was greeting customers as they entered. Today was a choti revolution. It could have gone horribly wrong, but Ajmal was certain as England losing the next Ashes that Shokat had to be ready to take over from him. *I can beat Shokat into shape. He'll either become what I need or I'll kill him trying.*

He watched his son from the top of the stairs. *Our talk did do some good.* Earlier, Shokat had looked uncomfortable in the new black suit and red tie Ajmal had selected for him. Now he looked relaxed, he'd uncrossed his arms and was smiling openly. *Maybe he'll be my lion after all.*

Ajmal had cleared his diary five days ago, cancelling a meeting with a local MP. He ordered Shokat to come to his office at tea time. He'd asked Sameena to go home, "So you can spend more time with your daughter," but that was bakwaas. Ajmal didn't care two pakoras about Sameena's daughter, he hated the sight of the girl. He didn't want any distractions while he had his private chat with Shokat.

"Are you getting rid of me, Ajmal?" Sameena had asked in her squeaky voice.

"No, of course not. I'm having a private meeting, that's all." She'd left reluctantly.

As he waited for his eldest son to arrive, he peered

over the latest bank statements and did some quick sums in his head. He readjusted the figures to incorporate his various cash deposits and overseas accounts in Pakistan and smiled to himself. Then frowned. *If I can only get the insurers to pay quickly I might still have a chance.* They were truculent, delaying payment. He doubted they'd meet his claim for a million. Even a portion of the claim would inject life-saving cash into his business and repay Abdullah. After Mirza had ransacked his safe, he was desperate to balance his books. If he didn't, the Kohinoor would haemorrhage and take his entire business with it.

Shokat arrived early, smelling strongly of curry. Ajmal could taste the garam masala on his tongue. He motioned impatiently for his son to sit down.

"Abbaji, you wanted to discuss increasing the workers' wages?" Shokat said in his slow voice.

"What are you talking about?" asked Ajmal in alarm.

"Isn't that what you wanted to talk about?" replied Shokat, looking surprised.

"They don't deserve an extra penny. If they don't like the money they can get out."

"But abbaji, we should be treating them better."

What's wrong with the dunce? "Puttar, you don't understand… " he was going to say 'business', but stopped, after all the meeting was about remoulding Shokat. *Khudhaya, I need a cigarette.* He squeezed his temples with the thumb and index fingers. "Things are quite delicate at the moment. I know you normally deal with the logistics of the business, but I want you to start developing in a different area." Ajmal cleared his throat. "One day even a bowler has to go to the crease, so I have something else in mind for you."

"What, abbaji?" Shokat asked eagerly. Ajmal almost sighed. *I wish he wasn't so damned polite and loyal. Why did my firstborn have to be a lamb?*

"Why don't you start welcoming guests a bit more, you know, talking to them, getting to know them?"

Shokat blinked. "But I already talk to them, abbaji, I talk to them every day."

This was leading nowhere. He then hit on a brainwave. "You know when I'm with customers?"

"Yes?"

"How am I different to you?"

"Well, you talk to them like your friends, you make it seem like they're guests."

"Exactly. That's what I want you to do. I want you to spend more time with them, treat them like they're guests at home, like they're your friends. Pretend they are Arif and Tanveer, your friends from school days. Just be friendly. Like me."

"OK," Shokat agreed nodding slowly. Then, "How do I do it?"

Ajmal gritted his teeth, "Well, you need to spend more time around the bar. Just go around and say 'hello' to people and smile like this," he bared his teeth and Shokat tried to copy, but he looked more hyena than human. "That's enough. Just walk around, smile at them, nod your head so…" Ajmal spent an hour telling his son the kinds of things he could say to 'break the ice' and remember things about people. "Remember, puttar, that a person's name is the most precious thing in the world to them, so try and remember that. OK?"

"Yes abbaji."

At the end of the first grooming session, he'd spent more time with Shokat then he'd ever done before.

Shokat looked dazed, but Ajmal's confidence throbbed in his temples when his son left the office. *Yes, he has the makings of a lion. A small one, but a lion nevertheless.* Ajmal's optimism didn't last more than a few hours. That evening, his eldest had hogged the bar, looking out of place, with his hands in his pocket, robotically saying "Hello" to every customer who happened to be there. Ajmal picked up from customers' glances that they thought Shokat was retarded.

He walked over to his son and gently said, "It's better if you return to your normal duties – just for tonight. We'll try something else tomorrow." Shokat had looked relieved and rushed off as if desperate to go to the toilet. *I'll have to think of something else. He just needs to get started, then he'll be fine.* Ajmal didn't believe himself.

Now Shokat was standing to the side at the entrance. Despite Ajmal's previous reservations, his son looked relaxed. Ajmal watched him, observing each movement, smile, nod: he counted each failure and measured each point of success. *He's so different from Monday night. What's happened to him?*

The clientele increased as the afternoon wore on. Ajmal drifted around the restaurant, dealing with Shokat's normal duties. Later, he stopped near the Kohinoor's entrance. He leaned forward to catch what his son was saying to customers as they entered.

"Welcome to the greatest restaurant in Manchester."

Did I just hear that? Ajmal's eyes opened wide. *Is my son bragging about the restaurant?*

Incredulous, he inched forward to hear more.

"We're known throughout the world and this charity event is giving something back to the community."

He felt a surge of pride in his breast. His son continued. "Welcome to the Kohinoor. Are you here for the Charity Meal? Proceeds are going towards charity. The restaurants in the Ajmal & Sons International Chain are funding this event." He had to admit Shokat was really getting quite good at greeting customers.

Ajmal grinned at punters as they passed and he dropped the odd comment, "Wonderful to see you," "That's a beautiful dress, my wife would be so jealous", and other lies to lubricate the ears of customers with. He heard a customer whisper, "That's the Curry King," and it sent him into seventh heaven. To add to his joy, the restaurant was full. It was highly unusual for a daytime on a weekday. *Today's going to bring extra profit. Good. Good.* The waiters were flitting at a hundred knots. It made him happy to see his staff busy. Idleness meant wasted money.

The queue had come to a standstill and punters waited for people to leave to make way for more. He seized the chance to have a quick chat with his son.

"How are you finding it, puttar?"

"I think I'm getting it, it's quite enjoyable once you get into the swing of things. Sorayah said…"

Ajmal's blood went tanda. "Sorayah what? I told you not to discuss anything with her."

"Well, abbaji, she phoned me last night and asked me if everything was okay. I…I ended up telling her you wanted me to do this…welcoming. I'm sorry, abbaji."

"Haramazada, I told you not to speak to her." Ajmal was speechless with anger. *Sorayah's always so eager to interfere.* "What did she say to you?" Ajmal asked reluctantly.

"She said that I had to dramatise it all, make it sound

235

like the most thrilling event in the world. I told her that I wasn't sure I could do it, but she told me that if you go through the motions you actually start to believe it yourself. She told me to just try it ten times and I would get into the flow."

Ajmal nodded to himself. He wasn't surprised in the least by Sorayah's words. *She always had a knack with people. Well, if the besharam girl can't work for me she's being useful by helping Shokat. Maybe I should allow her to be more involved in the restaurant. But she already turned me down.*

As the clientele left, Ajmal gave an interview to a journalist from the local radio station, Key 103.

"Mister Ajmal Butt, what would you say your food's about?"

"Yes, the good food here is about bringing world together. It helps to bring divided communities under one roof. This is most delicious cuisine in world. Why do you think there are more Asian restaurants on this one road than any other in whole of Britain? You know, I'm from Pakistan and even in Karachi there are not this many Asian restaurants on one road. I'm telling you this place is special and it's because the food is special."

"Do you really think that Asian food can help bring communities together?"

"Listen, you won't get BNP making trouble here, not ever. This is where we see fruits of Asian culture mixing with the local white people. It's the wonderful world we live in when we can respect each other's culture. You know, my children they eat the fish'n chips just like their white friends, but they also love to eat curry, just like their white friends, so tell me are we any different from each other? How can we be different if we have the same taste in the wonderful food?"

The journalist then asked Ajmal's favourite question. "Why are you called the Curry King?"

"I don't deserve that title, but it was given to me. Some people say I'm Curry King because I own so many restaurants, I've got six on Wilmslow Road, but maybe it's because I've been in trade for so long and developed such new and exciting cuisine. Maybe because I've won 'National Curry Award' many times. I don't know. There are lots of restaurants here and everywhere in the UK. All I know is my customers love the food and keep coming back for more. As we often say, the proof is in the pudding, but here it's in the curry!"

"One final question: I've heard that your daughter is shortly going to be opening her own restaurant. Can you substantiate this?"

Ajmal's mind raced. "Oh yes, it's part of the family business. My children love the business as much as I do."

"You must be putting a lot of finance into this new venture."

"Well, she's my daughter. How can I deny her anything?" Ajmal Butt felt hot under his collar. The lie had been forced on him. He quickly engineered an end to the conversation: "Why don't I let the waiters serve you one of dishes – on the house of course and you can find out for yourself what our food is like?" The journalist agreed.

Ajmal returned to the first floor bar and contemplated his customers, troubled that Sorayah had taken the media limelight away from him at the final moment. *Maybe it's better if people think her restaurant is mine. Yes, that would be perfect.*

That evening, and with the launch of the Charity Meal behind him, Ajmal's thoughts returned to Sameena. On his way to her flat, he remembered how upset she'd been the day he'd called Shokat into the office to begin the grooming programme. That night, after the Kohinoor had closed he'd gone to her flat with a box of chocolates.

"I'm pregnant, Ajmal," she had told him tearfully.

Desire had left him instantly. He sat down heavily on her sofa. "How do I know it's mine?"

"Ajmal! I don't sleep with every guy who comes my way!"

"I know you, you want my money. Haven't I given you enough already?"

"I can prove it's yours."

"How? How?"

"I can have a DNA test that'll prove you're the father."

"What's this UN test?"

"It's a medical test that'll prove it one way or the other, but I know it's yours. You're the only one I've been with."

"Well, get rid of it. I don't want it," he hissed. "I have enough children and they're all crazy!"

"I can't get rid of it!"

"Why not?"

"It's my baby!"

Ajmal had then panicked. "I'll pay you, I'll give you the money. Just get rid of it."

"How much? How much will you give me? I need at least fifty thousand. Or I'm keeping it."

She had him against a wall. He felt himself

suffocating. "Okay," he'd agreed. "But I want it done first."

"I'll book an appointment straight away."

She took the next day off work and phoned him that afternoon. "It's done. I need the money."

"Then why do I need to pay you?" He almost laughed at her stupidity.

"I didn't say I had it done. I've only booked the appointment. I knew you'd double-cross me. I knew you'd kill your own child so that you don't have to hand over money. You're disgusting. But I knew you might try and cheat me so I want to be paid first, before I get rid of it."

Ajmal was trapped. *Damn her.* He reluctantly withdrew the money from his secret safe and delivered it to her door. Sameena promised she'd have the procedure done the following day. There were no recriminations, but he hadn't stayed long, preferring the cold of the Mancunian night to her hot embrace.

Now Ajmal raced to her flat, stopping at florists to buy her a bunch of roses. He tried phoning her. There was a single tone. *Has her phoned been disconnected?* Sameena hadn't come into work and he'd assumed she was still recovering from the procedure. Her mobile phone had a message stating, 'This number is no longer valid'.

Fear leapt into his mouth. He drove madly. He pulled up outside her flat. There were no lights on. He parked the car and charged up the stairs leading to the first floor and slammed his fist into the door, again and again. *Where is the bitch? Where is she?*

The neighbour's door opened and an old man stuck his head out, rheumy eyes peering at him above a golden security chain. "Keep the racket down! If you're looking for Sammy, you're a bit too late. She left two hours ago. She said someone might come looking for her. An old bastard, she said. I think she meant you. So fuck off now or I'll call the police!"

Ajmal was furious. "*Old bastard*"! *The bitch*. He trusted her with everything. He didn't know whether to laugh or weep. Numbed by her betrayal, he nodded to the old man then turned and retraced his steps to his car.

Back home, he stood lost in the darkened hallway. He remained there contemplating the future, the past and the present and discovered he hated all three in equal measure. Finally, he took off his blazer and shuffled into the living room, turned on the television and jabbed the remote control. The TV blinked on and he watched PTV Prime. A few minutes later, his wife came downstairs and slowly opened the door. He heard her walk up to his side.

"You're home early. Why are you here? What has happened?" He could hear the worry in her voice, but he couldn't explain to her, he couldn't look at her.

"Bring me some tea, I have a headache," he told her. She went away instantly. He sat in his favourite chair contemplating his loss. His wife returned within minutes and put down a hot cup on the table before him. He didn't look up.

"Mumtaz," he said, as she turned to leave.

"Yes?"

"You're a good woman."

She didn't respond immediately. He looked up, the television a blur ahead of him.

"If you need anything, Ajmal, you only have to ask."

"I know," he replied. She left.

He sat and watched the TV without focusing. His thoughts spun round and round, faster and faster, images of Mirza fusing with Shokat, and then with Jafar Ali, Bilal and the million other haramzadas who'd ruined his life. And through all the images, the intoxicating, beautiful, wraith-like Sameena wove a potent motif. *Where do the dishonoured go?* The only place he could think of was hell.

20

Rain greeted the morning of the launch. A bleary eyed Sorayah gazed out of her flat window at the grey sky. "Flippin' hell." She showered and dressed. She'd bought a beige suit for the occasion and inspected herself for several minutes in front of the mirror. "Come on, Sorayah, you can do this," she told herself. She checked her reflection one last time. Then she nodded to herself, grabbed her mobile phone, her car keys and purse and made her way downstairs.

Shabnam was shuffling outside the restaurant in the rain when Sorayah arrived. They hugged.

"Why didn't you go in?" Sorayah asked.

"Oh, I couldn't!" Shabnam replied, "it's the opening day and you have to go in first, otherwise the roof might fall down or something!"

"Everything will be fine."

"Don't say things like that! You'll get nazar on you!"

"Okay, but don't worry."

A reproachful look from Shabnam silenced her and she dutifully took out the keys. They pulled up the shutters. Sorayah made an omelette for both of them. She took her time, fried the onions until they were brown and tender. Shabnam moaned, "I'm going to die of starvation." She nicked the eggs expertly on the edge of frying pan. They cracked, spilling their contents into the pan, and she threw the shells into the large bin without looking. Salt and garam masala followed, then chillies to give it pizzazz. Simultaneously, she baked the paratas on another hob. The delicate aroma of readiness jolted her into action. Sorayah placed the sizzling omelette and paratas on the improvised breakfast table.

Shabnam didn't wait for Sorayah.

"Don't eat so fast, you might swallow your tongue," Sorayah cautioned, smiling. Shabnam didn't hear her.

"You know," Shabnam said, sipping the desi tea, "if I were a guy, I'd marry you."

Sorayah laughed. "No you wouldn't."

"Oh yes, you don't believe me – I love you anyway, you know that Sorayah, but you cook better than my mummy and that's saying a lot."

"You're too kind."

There was a knock on the front door. "They're here," Shabnam said. She carried the dishes to the sink and began washing up. Sorayah made her way to the entrance.

The gang had arrived: Yasmeen, Dina, Farzana and Tayiba. There were hugs, smiles and kisses all round. There was a further polite knock at the door. It was Javed. Sorayah kept her face neutral. "I suppose we could do with a guy. We need to take the 'Coming Soon' sign down. Jav, do you want to do that?"

The friends continued from where they'd left off the day before, decorating the restaurant. The chef would arrive soon and the preparations for the evening launch would begin. "Yaz," Sorayah said to Yasmeen when they were alone, "how come Jav's here?"

"He wanted to be here, he knew it was important. I had trouble keeping Raheem away. I tell you, everyone wanted to come. If you're really uncomfortable, I'll ask him to go."

"No, it's okay. Don't worry about it."

The girls got to work and Javed hammered out the supports holding up the sign. Shabnam passed cups of tea round.

Time was whizzing past and it was only at eleven o'clock that Sorayah realised the chef still hadn't arrived. "Where the hell is he?" She rang his mobile number. It went straight to voicemail. She left a message. She tried his house number. His wife didn't know where he was.

"Is everything okay?" Yasmeen asked.

"Yeah, just trying to get hold of the chef." She frowned. She phoned the chef's mobile phone several times. It was still switched off. *I should have made a contingency.*

She gathered everyone round. "Look, the chef isn't here yet and we've got to start cooking, otherwise we're going to be in serious trouble."

"Why don't you phone daddy and ask him?" Yasmeen suggested.

Sorayah shook her head. "We've got to find a way ourselves. I don't want to go to my father or anyone's father for help."

"But the launch is just under six hours," Dina said. "What are you going do? Cook everything yourself?"

Sorayah closed her eyes for a moment, panic nestling in her belly. "We'll have to start the ball rolling," she said. Everyone was staring at her as if she were crazy. "Okay guys, I'll phone around and see if I can get a replacement."

There was a collective sigh of relief.

She ran upstairs to her office to think. *What do I do? Why isn't he here?* She picked up the phone to call Uncle Jafar. He had a whole fleet of chefs who he'd ship over to Maharani at the drop of a nan. She put the phone back down. *There has to be a way.* She had to make sure that the launch was perfect.

By midday she hadn't made a single call and she felt

the tears about to spill. *I don't have a choice.* She began searching through her phone's address book for Uncle Jafar. Below Jafar's entry she saw Uncle Kashif. *That's it!* She dialled the number immediately.

"Who's this?" boomed Uncle Kashif in Punjabi.

"It's me, Uncle. Sorayah."

"Sorayah! How nice of you to call me! Are you coming for a curry? I'll cook you one really special. You didn't eat last time you came!"

"That's kind of why I'm calling." She explained what had happened. "Abbu won't want you to come," she conceded. She suspected her father might have had a hand in ensuring the chef didn't turn up, "but I really need your help. Will you come?"

"Sorayah," the fat chef said, "you know that I don't make the fastest curries in Manchester."

"I know that. I don't want the fastest, I want the best."

"Then to hell with your dad! I'll be there in ten minutes!"

Uncle Kashif arrived like a storm, patted Sorayah and her friends on the head and squeezed Javed's hand so tight Sorayah swore his eyes almost fell out. He strode into the kitchen and started screaming. "Where are my helpers?"

Three men emerged from the shadows of the kitchen. "Well, what are you looking at? You, get the stock ready! Shall I whip you?"

Sorayah backed out of the kitchen and closed the door. She turned to her friends. "I think we're going to be okay."

The friends split up to place the napkins and cutlery

and ready themselves for the guests. The Lord Mayor would launch the restaurant by cutting a ribbon and she would accompany him and his wife to the first floor where the invited guests would eat. The ground floor would be open to the general public. Javed helped lay the tables on the first floor. Sorayah stopped by his side.

"Jav?"

"Yeah?" His doe-like eyes looked up. They were oddly disconcerting.

"Thanks for coming."

"You don't have to thank me."

"I do. You didn't have to do this."

"You helped my sister out when she needed you and I know you'd have done the same for her."

"That's not why you're here though, is it?"

Javed continued laying the tables, "I don't want anything from you, Sorayah. The only thing I ever wanted was for you to be happy."

"You did want something from me. Have you forgotten what you said to me at the hospital?"

He touched his cheek. Sorayah looked away. She'd forgotten she'd slapped him.

"I was in a state, Sorayah. I thought my sister was dying. I wasn't thinking."

"No, you don't think, do you?"

He continued laying the tables and Sorayah felt annoyed. *Why doesn't he stop and just talk to me like a normal guy?* She wanted to slap him again for good measure. *What's wrong with me, it's not as if I fancy him.*

"Honest, Sorayah, I don't want anything from you."

"You're just saying that."

"No, I'm not," he said and looked up. "You belong to Rav. You love him. But that's life. It's hard, but the one you want usually wants someone else."

"Javed," she said gently, "I don't love Rav. I did once, but not any more. But I don't think I'll ever love another guy again. All those feelings, they're finished. I'm a different person now."

Javed nodded. "Yeah. You've changed. You're not the same Sorayah I knew as a kid. Always had the bright ideas, always got us in trouble."

Sorayah smiled. "But we had fun right?"

"You'll always be fun."

They looked at each other in silence. "I don't love you, Javed."

"I know. That's why I don't want to marry you."

His words hurt even though they weren't meant to. She couldn't understand why.

They heard footsteps on the stairs. They both looked away guiltily, but the footsteps stopped and went back down again.

"I've loved you all my life, Sorayah and you've never felt the same. I know that. I knew that even in the hospital, but I'll never be your Ravinder. I'll never rock your world."

"You don't have to say this, Javed."

"If I thought you might feel this way one day then I might want you to marry me, but you won't. Love is blind, that's what they say, but I always had my eyes open. I didn't want to love you, I just did. I wished I didn't."

It was the cruellest and nicest thing anyone had said to her.

"If I were a different type of kuri, I'd marry you in a heartbeat."

Javed shook his head. "You don't get it. I thought I

was the gormless one, but you are. If you were different, I wouldn't love you. Do you think I'd say all these things if I really thought you'd ever feel the way that I do? No, of course not. That's why it doesn't matter. I just hope you'll find a guy who rocks your world and doesn't let you down. And I'll be his best man if he asks me."

"You'd do that for me?"

"That's what love means. Always to give and never to take."

"I wish I did love you Javed, but…"

"It's okay. We'll both survive without each other."

There were footsteps on the stairs. Yasmeen popped her head up. "The waiters have just arrived," she said and ran back down.

"Jav?"

"Yeah?"

"We're still friends, right?"

"We'll always be friends."

She nodded and headed downstairs.

Patrick Boyle, the Lord Mayor, was dazzling in his robes of office and his shining golden chain. His wife, a misty fifty-something, was at his side, her wet blonde hair complementing the gold at her throat.

"Ladies and gentleman, I hereby give you, Maharani!" Cameras flashed and camcorders rolled. The scissors cut through the ribbon and the crowd of media followed the Mayor in.

The first curry was served by Sorayah herself.

"Delicious!" the mayor exclaimed.

Sorayah felt as if a huge weight had been taken off her shoulders.

Granada TV was there and a reporter thrust a mic in

her face. The camera wobbled precariously. "Tell us about the Curry King," he said.

Sorayah forced a smile. "I learned everything I know from my father. But this is my own venture."

She sat with the Mayor for a long hour of light conversation.

Parveen had joined the group of helpers. She looked beautiful and Sorayah regretted Imran hadn't been able to make it. Uncle Jafar arrived briefly, but didn't try to snatch any of her glory. It had been a long journey to the opening day, and Jafar never went back on his deal that he wouldn't interfere. She now hoped she could buy him out.

She was overjoyed to see her mother. She arrived with Baji Shazia.

"We wouldn't have missed this for the world," Shazia said. Sorayah located seats near the front for them and laughed with her nephews and nieces. She knew Abbu would be upset with them for coming to the launch. Haji Khan arrived looking more stooped than ever, and Sorayah forced an entire table to move to accommodate him and his family.

Neither Basharat nor Shokat came. She only hoped they'd come one day and see the restaurant their sister built. Her sister-in-law was absent too.

Shabnam appeared by her side. "It's going really well. See, I told you that you had to be first one in. It would have been a tragedy if I'd come in first!"

"You were right," Sorayah said smiling. "Where are the others?"

Shabnam told her what the girls were doing.

"Uncle Kashif?"

"He's shouting his head off. You know, I think it

makes him happy to shout so much. He eats more than me as well, I can't believe how he eats. It made me sick! I swear I'll never eat again."

"And Javed?"

"I think he'll be leaving soon."

"Why?"

"I dunno, I just heard him ask Yasmeen where she'd put his coat."

Sorayah thanked Shabnam and asked her to look after her ammi and Shazia. She spotted Javed emerging from her office with his coat on.

"Are you leaving?" she asked.

"Yeah."

"Why? The party's only started."

"I just wanted to help out, make sure it was a success. You did good, Sorayah. You should be proud. Hey, I'm proud and I only helped for part of one day. I'm going home and…"

"Have you eaten?"

"I'm not hungry. Growing up in restaurants kind of kills your hunger. You'll be fine without me, Sorayah. We'll survive. I told you that." He smiled.

She didn't want him to go. He'd already let go of her and Sorayah didn't want him to.

"Stay, Jav."

He only hesitated for a moment. "I'm not much good at parties."

"You don't have to be. Just chill out!"

When everyone had gone all the friends came together. Shabnam, Parveen, Yasmeen, Dina, Farzana, Tayiba and Javed all sat around a table on the first floor. Sorayah thanked everyone. Uncle Kashif came in and she hugged him. He was taken aback.

"I couldn't have done it without you," she told him.

"Anything for you, my daughter."

On the way home she picked up a copy of the *Manchester Evening News* from a petrol station. She flicked through and saw on page five:

```
Curry King's Latest Dish.
```

It stated how her father had masterminded the creation of Maharani. The article contained the entire history of his restaurants with only a passing mention of Sorayah. She hissed and almost threw the newspaper in the bin. She shook her head ruefully and began laughing.

"What are you laughing at?" Shabnam asked, yawning.

"My abbu. He'll never change."

21

Son of a bitch. Ajmal Butt moaned and turned in his bed. Sleep eluded him and Basharat's stomping footsteps ruptured his thoughts. He wanted to slap his son. *But what good would it do?* He forced his eyes shut. He caught himself staring into the darkness. He stared for so long that the darkness became a spot of light and danced crazily before him.

A few days ago, Sorayah's much-vaunted restaurant had opened. He had ordered Mumtaz not to go and she had. She'd never disobeyed him before.

"She's my daughter. She's your daughter. We must support her. It doesn't matter if Jafar loaned her the money. Sorayah's told me she runs it. He doesn't. It's her restaurant," Mumtaz told him.

He had lost control of his family.

He barely saw Shazia. He used to enjoy playing with her children, he used to look forward to the summer holidays. Since her divorce she'd changed. She'd shocked him by letting him know she was going to study at university.

"University? What for? You've got three kids."

"I want to make something of my life. You've seen what Sorayah has achieved? I want to do something with my life too. I don't just want to be a mother."

Sorayah's dangerous. She influences them all. He wished he'd married Sorayah off at the age of sixteen, that way she wouldn't have caused any problems.

Shokat was the only one now who was totally loyal. Shokat's wife, whose helpful smile and polite way of saying "Abba jaan" endeared her to him. *Why can't my children learn from her?* She'd been badgering him lately to let her help out since Sameena's departure. He'd told his family and friends that his erstwhile secretary had to move back to Bradford for family reasons. Truthfully, he didn't know where she was. Ajmal considered allowing his daughter-in-law to work for him. *It might be cheaper than hiring someone.* But she didn't speak English. It was ironic that he'd always disliked Sameena speaking English to him, but he couldn't employ a secretary who didn't.

He was glad Imran was on holiday. It was good to have his puttar doctor at home although he wished everyone would stop taking Sorayah's side. It galled him that she had manipulated, influenced, coerced everyone, including Kashif the chef. He had screamed with anger when he'd heard his head chef was instrumental in Maharani's launch. *I got rid of her chef and then she poaches mine.*

"Who are you to tell me who I can and can't help?" the fat chef had shouted, meaty fists at his side. Ajmal loathed the fact he was shorter than Kashif.

"Why did you help her? She wouldn't have been able to open her stupid restaurant on time."

"Exactly. I helped her, because she asked me. She's like a daughter to me. I'll help her every day if I want to. How are you going to stop me, eh?"

"I'll eat you alive. I'll crush you, you'll never work in this city again," Ajmal threatened.

And Kashif had laughed in his face. "Well, you're full of empty air and promises. I don't need to work for you. I only worked for you out of loyalty. I can go anywhere." He calmly took off his apron and put on his large leather coat.

"Hey, where are you going?"

"None of your business. I don't work for you any more."

"I was only joking."

"I don't care. You shouldn't have been so disrespectful. I was helping your daughter after all. You should be thanking me, but you're not a real father. You've only got hatred in you."

That had silenced Ajmal. He could only hang his head, as his chef of over twenty years, left. He'd guessed correctly Kashif would go straight to Sorayah. *I couldn't have given her a better chef.*

His accountant had admonished him for giving out fifty thousand pounds without consulting him.

"You know the situation we're in. You can't just give people thousands of pounds, sir." Mudassir Shareef said, forgetting who was boss, yet Ajmal didn't berate him.

"I had to pay a friend some money back," was all he told Mudassir.

He'd lost Sameena. He couldn't understand why she'd betrayed him. *Why Sameena?* Sameena's departure had left a hole in him. He missed her imperfections: he missed her squeaky voice, he'd forgive her speaking English to him. He tried to locate her through his sources. He suspected she'd moved to London. She'd told him how much she despised Bradford. It had bad memories for her. She had always loved travelling to the capital. He had wanted to throw her to the kutte the evening she betrayed him, now he wished he hadn't been so harsh about the abortion. He couldn't stop thinking about her. He'd never met any of her friends. He realised he'd never been interested in them or her daughter.

Over the last few days, people had openly approached him to buy restaurants. Jafar had phoned him and asked how much he wanted for the Kohinoor.

"You're a clown, Jafar."

"You'll be the clown and everyone laughing at you when your business collapses," Jafar Ali had snarled. "And your daughter and me will pick up the pieces."

Ajmal threw the phone against the wall. The Kohinoor was sinking, and Jafar had the money to make it float. *Well, I'm not going to let him have it. Over my dead body.* He regretted not having trusted Sorayah. His enemy was celebrating her success. *It should have been me. Kashif was right, what kind of father am I?*

He was awake. Restless. He yearned for a cigarette to quench his lips. A vice was squeezing his head, the room boxing him in. He turned and the digital clock eyed him from the side. 4:13.

He blinked.

He couldn't believe how late it was. He moaned and decided to get up and go to work. He had done it often in the past, although it had been many years since he'd felt the need. He changed and stumbled through the darkness and found his keys.

Outside, the night air cleared his thoughts. He got into the Mercedes. He didn't check if Basharat had damaged it. He drove to the Kohinoor jumping red lights. It made him feel stronger. He drove down the Curry Mile at speed, oblivious to the city and the surroundings, he just wanted to set foot in his restaurant.

He parked on the Curry Mile and got out, tasting the air. He looked up and saw a light flash in his office. His mouth dropped open. "Harami," he cursed. He squinted. Yes, it was definitely, a light. He edged towards the shutter of the front door. He walked slowly round the building along the side street and into the alley between the car park and the back of the restaurant. The back door shutter was up. He quietly opened the back door leading into the kitchen. The alarm was off. He immediately knew it was an inside job, one of his key workers. *Who? Who could it be?* He crept up the stairs, finding a broom to use as a weapon. *Is it Bilal sent on an errand?* His breathing was ragged. He inched his way across the second floor. Each creak was a crack of thunder in his ears. As he neared his office, he saw a white light dancing beneath the lintel of the door. He put his eye against the keyhole. There was someone inside. His heart was thumping like wild elephants. Gently, he opened the door. He shut his eyes and turned on the light. There was a shout, a loud crash and a dull thud. He rushed the blur ahead of him and banged the man hard on the head with the broom head.

The man fell comatose on his front. Ajmal blinked rapidly and turned him around. It was Saleem Rasool, his restaurant manager. He slapped his manager awake.

"Who are you working for, you bastard?" he yelled, beating him with the broom. Saleem tried to cover his head, but to no avail. "Tell me or I'll kill you." The man shook his head in defiance. "I promise I'll let you go free if you tell me." Ajmal lifted the broom stick threateningly over his head.

"Mohammed Qureshi. I'm working for Qureshi!"

Ajmal lowered the stick. "Who the hell is Mohammed Qureshi?"

"The man who came to see you over a few months ago with the bodyguards."

David Mirza? What? His name's Qureshi? "Who's Mohammed Qureshi?"

"Jafar Ali's cousin. He lives in London. Please don't hurt me any more."

Saleem was forgotten. Ajmal threw down the stick and staggered to the window. The world was shrinking around him. He felt as if his entire chest was burning, flaring brighter with each breath. He felt a squeezing sensation behind the breastbone. A lancing hot pain sliced through his entire torso. He cried out and fell against the window.

He couldn't remember the journey to the hospital except that it was hot and claustrophobic in the ambulance, a black man hovered over his head, sirens wailed in the background and the pain, hot and constant, throbbed in his chest.

He imagined his doctor bending over him even as he clutched his chest with the words, "I told you so," on his lips. *You were right, kutta doctor. Does it make you happy to know that you were so useless in helping me?* A thousand images swirled in his head. *My business will collapse without me.*

"I need a cigarette," were the last words to spill out of his mouth before darkness snatched him.

22

Sorayah fumbled for her ringing phone in the fog of sleep. She picked it up from behind the digital alarm clock. One eye opened. 6:15. She cursed. The mobile's screen was flashing 'Imran'.

"What?"

"Dad's had a heart attack."

Her eyes snapped open and she stumbled out of bed. "Oh my God. Is he okay?"

"I don't know."

"Where is he?"

"Manchester Royal Infirmary."

"I'll be there right away," she promised.

She rushed into the bathroom and splashed cold water over her face. Her heart was beating at a thousand miles per hour. She was still wiping the tears when she got into her car. It was bitterly cold and her teeth rattled as she spun the car around. She jumped the red lights and ignored the one way signs. She arrived at the hospital within ten minutes. She parked and ran into a room full of walk-in casualties. Then she was standing in a corridor. It was a mirror of the one Yasmeen had been in only a few months ago.

She found Imran in the corridor. Ammi was there with Shazia. She hugged them. She spoke in Punjabi. "What happened?"

"All I know is that he was at the restaurant," Imran informed her.

"What? At this time?"

"Yeah, don't ask me. They phoned home and woke Mum up. I had to bring her."

"My Ajmal, he's dying," their mother said, tears

streaking her face.

Sorayah put her arm around her mum. "It's okay. Don't worry, the doctors will look after him."

Then to Imran, "How come we can't go in?"

"He's had a heart attack. They won't let anyone visit him for at least twenty-four hours, not even close family. Just in case."

A door opened and a nurse appeared.

"Miss…" Sorayah began.

The nurse smiled sadly. "I've already told your…"

"Brother."

"Yes, I've already told him that your father is okay for now, but he's unstable and can't be allowed any visitors."

"But we're his family."

"Then you'll understand that you don't want him to have another heart attack."

Sorayah was silent. "Can we stay here?"

"You can stay as long as you like, but you won't get to see him. We'll contact you when he's allowed visitors."

Sorayah nodded. She was about to give her contact details when the nurse interrupted, "Don't worry, your brother has already given us all the telephone numbers."

Sorayah returned to her parents' home, following Imran in his Mini Cooper. She parked the car and followed her mother, Baji Shazia and Imran into the house. Their mother forced them to have breakfast. They ate in a heavy silence. After breakfast, Sorayah phoned Shabnam and told her what had happened.

"Oh no! What are you going to do?"

"Can you cover for me today?"

"Yes, of course. Anything. Do you need flowers? Lucozade? Let me know."

The day passed agonizingly slowly and the night was a long one. Imran phoned the hospital several times. Their father had improved and they'd be allowed to visit the next day.

"How did this happen?" Sorayah asked Shokat. They were in the Kohinoor. Shokat looked haggard.

"I dunno. Saleem rang for the ambulance. I don't know how he found abbaji. If he hadn't, abba would be dead now."

"We've got a lot to thank him for. Where is he?"

"He hasn't come in today. I rang him a few times, but he didn't answer."

"Has he taken the day off?"

"I don't know."

"Did he come in early? What time did it all happen?"

"Before five."

"You mean Saleem was here in the morning when abbu was? Did they have a private meeting in the early hours of the night?"

"I don't know."

She insisted on helping out at the Kohinoor. Shokat didn't seem to be in the mood to talk and the day dragged. She spent a lot of time in her father's office. Shokat was silent. "Don't worry Paijaan, he'll be okay."

Her brother shook his head.

"Are you alright?" she asked him.

"It's your pabhi. She's so happy. She thinks I'm going to inherit the business. I swear she's praying that abbaji dies."

Sorayah cursed.

"She keeps saying I deserve to take over, that it was mine all along. I don't want abba to die. You know that."

"Yes, I know," Sorayah whispered.

"I can't manage the business on my own. I'm not ready. I don't want him to go."

She put her arm around her brother. They sat down. "Where's abbu's secretary?"

"Who? Oh, she's left. Gone to Bradford, I think."

"So both Sameena and Saleem have gone?"

"Yeah. Both of them."

"Strange place, the Kohinoor."

Her father had recovered enough by the next day to receive visitors. He looked pale, sickly and glum. Sorayah's heart went out to him, but she kept her distance. She was just glad that he'd woken up.

Everyone was there except Basharat. Abbu mumbled words of welcome. Mumtaz wept. Ajmal admonished her. "I'll be home in no time," he said in a weak voice. Then he asked Shokat for a business update. Imran told abbu not to talk too much about business. Ajmal welcomed Shazia and asked her to bring the children next time. He admonished Shokat for not bringing his: "I only get to see all my children when I'm lying in a hospital bed. The Lord teaches us lessons," he said.

They sat for hours. There were long silences and they took turns to sit near him.

Her father murmured something to her mother and moments later Sorayah found herself alone with her father.

"Sorayah," he croaked. Sorayah slowly moved next to his bedside. They hadn't shared a word since he'd awoken.

"Are you okay?" was the question she was dying to ask, but she couldn't.

"Why did you leave me?" he asked in a hoarse voice.

"I didn't leave you," she whispered. "I've been here all along." She didn't want to talk about business. She knew it would inevitably lead to an argument and she wanted to avoid that. She felt none of this would have happened if she'd stayed in the capital.

"Why did you go and work for Jafar? Why?"

"He offered me something I couldn't refuse."

"What, puttar? What?"

"He offered me freedom." She was crying, because it was true. "He offered me a fifty-fifty partnership and he put a lot of money on the table. You didn't do that for me."

"It was all yours for the taking. Didn't you understand? You never needed to ask. You could have just taken it."

Sorayah looked away, a lump in her throat. She handed her father a glass of water. He drank. "Abbu, don't talk about the business," she whispered, afraid it might bring on another heart attack.

"Your Jafar did this to me."

"Come on abbu, let it go."

"No, listen to me. I came back to the restaurant in the early hours of the morning. I saw a light in my office and I went to find out what it was. It was Saleem, the restaurant manager. I got the truth out of him. He's been working for Jafar Ali's cousin all this time."

Sorayah frowned. She wasn't sure if this was one of her abbu's games. "Are you sure about this?"

"As much as I know that you're my daughter."

He told her about the David Mirza incident, how he'd borrowed a huge amount of money and when the rascal had come to collect he'd been left penniless. Sorayah was shocked into silence. *Uncle Jafar couldn't sink this low. Not this low. And I went into business with him?*

"I'll find out if it's true."

"Don't you believe me? You prefer to believe that harami instead of me, your father?"

"I believe you, abbu. I just want him to say it to my face."

"Well, if my word isn't good enough then leave."

She left.

She walked along the corridor feeling dejected. She'd worked so hard over the last few months and tasted the sweetness of victory. She'd built her own restaurant. Now the taste was tainted with the bitterness of betrayal. If her father was telling the truth, then the partnership that had been a lifeline to her would have to be severed. *How could I have been so easily manipulated? Because I wanted to be. Because he said the right things. Because of a million things. A million choices that I made, all the wrong ones.*

Imran followed her. "What did he say to you?" he asked.

"I need to speak to Jafar Ali," was all she told him.

She drove to the Shandaar. She knew her business partner would be there. It was early and quiet and she made her way to Jafar Ali's office. He was in the middle of a phone call. She knocked on the door and strode in without waiting for him to ask her to enter. He finished the call quickly.

"Sorayah daughter, did you want to discuss something?" he asked in Urdu.

"My abbu told me it was Mohammed Qureshi," she began, "your cousin."

Jafar laughed. "Your father was always the fast one."

"My father's lying in hospital, possibly dying and

you're shrugging this off."

"Your father's been unhealthy for a while. I didn't cause the heart attack, he did."

"You set my father up."

"Not me, my cousin. You can't blame me for that."

"But you put a few ideas into his head?"

"One or two, but listen, daughter, it was always business. Just business."

"I should end our partnership now. It wasn't worth it for this."

"You don't want to make a rash decision. You're a big girl, you've entered a man's world. I'm sure you too had to break a few eggs along the way."

"Your daughter is my best friend, you've known me all your life, and yet you still did this to my father?"

"You're being melodramatic. In the morning your father will be better and you'll forget this ever happened."

"And what if he isn't?"

"God gives and takes all life."

"Don't take God's name after what you've done."

"Grow up. This is how the game is played. Not with dolls and make-believe castles. This is real life. I'm sorry it had to be this way, but it is. Anyway, you've got work to do back at the restaurant and you should get going."

She felt degraded. All this time she'd just been a pawn. Jafar gave her the freedom to do things her way, because he was sure she could deliver – and that it would damage her father.

"Our partnership is over," she said, the words somehow sounding unreal.

"Sorayah," he snapped, "think carefully. You'll have nothing. Not a single penny. If you walk out of here, don't expect me to bend over for you. We're partners today and that's how we remain."

"No. You did something no partner would do to another. You harmed my family. I won't forgive you for that."

"Your father would have done the same to me."

"No, this was never my father's style. He can do things in a nasty way, but not this. You're not the man you pretend to be. We're no longer partners."

"Sorayah, if you walk away, I swear– "

"Swear what? That you'll stop me? If only you were half the man my father is then perhaps I'd believe you, but I don't."

She walked away with all the courage she could muster. She'd put her soul into Maharani, it was the dearest thing in her universe and she was letting it go.

"Sorayah," Jafar called. She heard a crash behind her. "Sorayah, you can't do this, all that work – your father tried to stop you, don't you remember? He didn't want you to succeed."

Jafar Ali continued to shout, but she ignored him, her footsteps leading her inexorably away from Jafar Ali and the Curry Mile.

23

Ajmal was looking at the ceiling of the hospital room, his eyes unblinking. *Why does the ceiling look so strange? Where have the stars gone?* His throat felt dry enough to ignite a forest fire. His chest was sore. Pain throbbed in his right side: a sharp pain in his head and hip. He opened his eyes to another blurred roundness that gradually became a brown haze, hovering over him; he heard the distant notes of a voice, words he could not quite capture and then he slept.

He was awake. A headache raged oblivious to painkillers. *I'm going to die. This is it.* He looked down at his body. It looked shrivelled to his eyes. He felt the sting of self-pity diffusing through him and with a mental lurch he broke free. *I'm a fighter, I have the Killer Instinct...Damn you weakness!* He sighed audibly. He struggled to birth a smile. He was losing the fight. *How long do I have left? What if I die now? What will I leave behind? Who's going to remember me?* The silent whimpering self-pity returned. Diazepam slipped him into sleep.

He surveyed the hospital room. Mumtaz had dozed, her exhaustion overtaking her anxiety. The doctors had restricted the family's visiting time to three hours each morning. The children informed him that his wife had slept little since his heart attack. She looked so serene in sleep. It had been many years since he'd watched his wife like this. He felt a tenderness for her he'd forgotten. *My good wife. What did she do to deserve a gunda like me?*

His children visited him daily. The doctors were strict, allowing only closest family relatives. Queues of well-wishers came and most were turned away. The astute claimed they were brothers and sisters or part of the extended family and Ajmal welcomed them all. Cards and tokens covered one wall of the hospital room. Now all the visitors had gone except for Mumtaz.

He closed his eyes, but he was tired of sleeping. His soul was restless. He heard the business calling to him and he was imprisoned. He sensed his business shudder with anger. He yearned to shake his head and tell her, convince her that he was dying. *I've left Shokat in charge, but can he manage without me?* He knew the answer and despaired. *All my work gone, finished, khalaas, all to be taken away.*

The Angel of Death was on its way. *Khuda forgive my sins.*

He had a good memory of all the things he'd done, all the lewdness and rudeness and the dirty deals, the actions he'd taken to win his rightful position as Curry King. *But have I done enough to make sure Shokat's ready to take over if I'm not there to change his nappies? I should have prepared him a long time ago, but I wasted too much time doing unimportant things.* He knew without doubt or equivocation that Shokat was unready, unprepared to negotiate, to twist and manipulate, to fight and win. *If I were a real lion, I would have killed him and found someone stronger, but he's my eldest, what else can I do?*

The only other son who might have been helped was hopelessly lost to him. Basharat came to visit him the day after the heart attack. The earrings were gone, the *gunda* had grown a beard and gone religious. *That khanzir was useless beginning to end. Basharat had the makings of the Killer Instinct in him, but never for me, never for the business. He could have made millions selling curries with me!*

267

Ajmal imagined his honour fading into dust with his passing. *My children never did my izzat.*

Tiredness overtook him and he plunged into a dark sleep.

He turned his head sideways. Mumtaz's eyes were damp. *My good wife, always there to save me and what did I do for her?* Shokat looked drained. On the other side of Mumtaz was Sorayah. *Shokat should be in the restaurant.* Ajmal's anger was a distant rumbling cloud. He blinked and it was gone.

"Sorayah?" he croaked in his native tongue.

"Take it easy abbu, you've got to rest," she replied in Punjabi.

"I've got the heart of a lion."

Sorayah smiled. "Yes, I know, Dad, but even lions have to rest sometimes."

He vaguely recalled telling her about Jafar Ali and Saleem and telling her to leave, but he wasn't sure if it was a dream. He lapsed off and awoke with a raging thirst. He groped blindly, saying, "Pani, pani," and Mumtaz handed him a plastic cup filled with water. He gulped down the water, but the thirst remained. He looked round the room seeing the concern in his wife's eyes. He couldn't bear for her to see him so weak. He closed his eyes and feigned sleep.

Have I done enough? he wondered as day spilled into night. The family had left. Mumtaz insisted on staying, but the doctors wouldn't let her. Ajmal wanted her to stay. He'd been briefed by the doctors that his health was delicate and that they needed to monitor his heart without interference. He looked over bottles of Lucozade and piles of grapes and fruit that family had left behind. *I need a cigarette.* He almost laughed at the thought.

His secret wish was to return to the Kohinoor and check the takings for the four days he'd been away from the restaurant. *I need to know if everything is okay.* He'd demanded a verbal report from Shokat earlier, but his son was reluctant to tell him and Sorayah wouldn't have any of it.

"Abbu! You know you should be recovering. Shall I call the doctor and get him to sedate you?"

He had looked away. *She was right. Why tempt fate? But I still have to know!* He wanted to shake them to make them understand how important it was for him to return. *Sorayah of all people should know what it means to me.*

He recalled a memory of Sorayah when she was four years old. He used to take her with him to the restaurant every day during the summer. That September he'd enrolled her in a local nursery. The first day he'd taken her to the school, she'd cried so much it had broken his heart. "But I don't want the nursery, I want to go to Zeez!" 'Zeez' was what the little Sorayah called the 'Lazeez' restaurant. The school nurse had phoned him daily that week. "I've never seen a child cry so much. Who's Zeez? Is it a teddy bear?" the nurse asked him. *What was her name? Abigail, yes, Abigail.* "I never thought a child had so many tears." Ajmal promised Sorayah he'd take her to Lazeez after school and he had. From then on, he had to drop her off and collect her from her school and then bring her to the restaurant. Eventually she'd made new friends at school and wanted to be with them. He remembered the day she'd refused Zeez for her new friends. It had broken his heart again. He still brought her in on special occasions – weekends and the

Eid parties he once used to have, they were his way of bringing Sorayah back to him. *But I lost her to London and that harami.*

Ajmal looked at Sorayah sitting beside his hospital bed and smiled. She smiled back and patted him on his hand. He wanted to tell her how much it meant to him for her to be in Manchester with him, but he couldn't. "Of course puttar, no reports from the restaurant," he told Sorayah, "I won't ask any more questions about the business until I'm better."

"Good. You better not. The business is fine without you." Ajmal didn't believe it for a moment, but he swallowed his automatic response.

He was absolutely one hundred and one per cent sure Shokat would fail without him. His eldest needed several years before he was ready. *But who could help him?* Basharat was a loafer, Imran was out of the equation. He rummaged through his mind and tried to think of any male relative or friend. There was nobody.

His mind wandered, half asleep, until it finally came to rest. *What about Sorayah?* But that was impossible. She'd gone over to the enemy. He hadn't mentioned Jafar again to her or the family. *Sometimes I wish she'd been born a son, but she's Jafar's now.*

It was during this morose thinking that his wife asked him: "What are you thinking about, Ajmal? You'll be home soon, God willing."

"It's a shame our daughter has gone over to that gunda, Jafar."

"She's left him," she told him simply.

"What?"

"Don't get excited, the doctor said you shouldn't get

270

excited." Her eyes were large, tearful and anxious. "She told us that what you told her was true. The partnership is finished. But she said she'll be going back to London after you're better."

Ajmal beamed. It was the best news he'd ever heard. *Sorayah will give Shokat the help he needs if I can talk her into it. She's already helped him out with what to say to customers and even I couldn't convince him he had it in him. But she won't listen to me.* He rolled the problem around in his head looking at it from every angle. *If I beg her to stay she'll help. How can she turn me down now that I'm lying in this hospital bed? And if what Mumtaz told me is true, then she'll hate Jafar so much she'll destroy him.* His old optimism reasserted itself. *And when I return to the restaurant I can train Shokat up some more, but at least Sorayah will be there to steady him in the meantime.*

He spent his waking moments running dialogues in his head. Like any prospective meeting with a difficult client, he rehearsed what he'd say, trying different types of attack, anticipating responses and answering them. *Killer Instinct, I'm going to need you to bring Sorayah round. Mere khuda, please change her mind.* He slept with a smile on his lips.

Ajmal felt the anger in his throat. It came so fast he saw scarlet. He wanted to punch the doctor.

"I have to go home, Dr. Freedman! I have work to do!" he insisted. He yearned to be out. Some of his strength had returned, but there was still a numbness in his chest, a general fatigue that occasionally overwhelmed him. *They'll never let me go home if they think I haven't recovered, but I have to return.* His unshakeable belief in his invincibility was back.

"You can't go home, Mr. Butt," the doctor repeated

for the sixth time. "With your heart in this condition I recommend you stay here at the Infirmary until you've finished the course – and most importantly you must remain calm. I cannot stress that enough."

"I have the heart of a… "

"Mr. Butt, I don't think you're taking this seriously. You must absolutely stay," the doctor repeated.

Ajmal glanced at Imran. He didn't trust doctors, but he trusted Imran. He looked at Imran hoping for moral support.

"He's right, Dad," Imran said in English, "you have to rest and finish your course of treatment. You've had a heart attack and you need to stay in for at least seven days. That's just standard procedure, Dad. They've promised you'll be cleared for surgery within the next two months. There's nothing to worry about," Imran said, "Shokat will look after the business."

Will he? Shokat will destroy my business. All those years of hard work ruined.

The doctor left Ajmal with Mumtaz and Imran.

"Imran, you're my cleverest child," Ajmal said in Punjabi. Imran tried to interrupt, but Ajmal carried on like a jawan. "No, you are. You got top marks at school and you got ten GCCCs. I'm very proud of you. But you are a little naïve about Shokat. Do you think he's even half of me? Do you think that he can run the entire business by himself? Do you know what the competition is like out there? He'll be eaten alive in a single afternoon. Can't you see how useless your brother is?"

"Abbu, I can't answer that," Imran said, replying in Punjabi.

"Yes, you're a good boy. Not like your dad shouting

at everyone – probably caused my heart attack. But you didn't answer my question. Do you think that donkey, Shokat, can take the reigns of my empire? Do you?"

"Abbu, I don't know much about business. I'm just a doctor."

"I know you're a doctor and you're the best too, but do you think he's going to be able to do it? No, in a year he'll have lost it to that bastard Jafar."

"Abbu, take it easy, you need to rest."

"How can I rest, puttar? How can I rest while my future's about to be destroyed?"

Imran was silent. Ajmal looked around the room, at the machines monitoring his heart, at his wife looking worried. *I have to leave here soon or I'll go pagal.*

Ajmal was expecting another group of well-wishers to arrive when he heard a commotion, lots of talking and movement outside the door. Out of curiosity he tried to raise himself onto his pillows, but was too weak to move. A moment later Imran opened the door and moved to Ajmal's side to whisper in his ear.

"Abbu, it's Uncle Jafar. He wants to see you. I've told him it's not a good idea, but he said he just wants to see how you are." Imran's Punjabi was agitated, broken.

Ajmal was surprised at the arrival of Jafar, so surprised he was speechless. Then, it was all clear to him. *The haramzada wants to see my dying, eh? Well, I'm not going to give him the pleasure.*

"Send him in, yes, send the kutta in. Let's see what he has to say."

Jafar Ali stepped into the room. Ajmal kept a cool disdainful look on his face. Imran was hovering behind Jafar, probably to make sure nothing went amiss. Mumtaz looked afraid, her hands trembling. Ajmal guessed she hadn't seen Jafar face to face for over ten years.

"Ajmal, assalamualaikum, I have come to see if you are well," opened Jafar in Punjabi.

"Uncle, you shouldn't be here. Abbu isn't well," Imran interrupted in the native tongue. *Good boy.*

"It's okay, Imran. I can take care of myself even if I am lying in a hospital bed. Salam, Jafar. So you've been waiting for the old lion to be weakened before you chose to come and see him, eh?"

Ali shook his head. "We were good friends once. Perhaps the best."

It was only then Ajmal noticed the walking stick in Jafar's hand. *An old man just like me.* "That was a long time ago," Ajmal replied smoothly.

"Maybe it was, but I still remember we were friends."

Ajmal's bravado suddenly dissipated and he felt weak and defenceless. He had nothing he wanted to say to Jafar Ali.

"Leave me in peace. I'm close to death. I want to be close to those who are my friends and family not with those people who are my enemies who've worked tirelessly to bring me down. You stole my daughter away from me. Imran, take him out of here."

"Wait, Ajmal," Jafar said. He held up a hand to stop Imran. "I didn't work tirelessly to bring you down – you worked tirelessly to bring me down. Who stole the Manchester City Council contract from under my feet?"

Ajmal grinned. "That was just luck," he said and felt energy surge through him. He managed to prop himself onto his pillows. Imran rushed to help, but Ajmal shooed him away.

"No, Ajmal, you took that away from me when it was

in the bag. But I'm not here to argue with you about that. I'm here to find out how you are."

"Why are you interested in my health all of a sudden? What has taken you ten years to come and ask me how I am, eh? You send your spies to find out what I'm doing, you buy out my closest workers? And now you expect me to shake your hand?"

Jafar Ali nodded as though acknowledging a deep and troubling question. He looked across and said to Mumtaz, "Salam sister, I didn't see you," and then turned back to Ajmal. "Your daughter helped mine when she was in greatest need. Without your daughter I would surely have lost mine. Ajmal, I tell you, we've been enemies a long time and I know what it takes to make business successful, but there are things beyond us both. Even I recognise the friendship our children have. It's the friendship that we used to have, but we lost."

"What are you saying? That you want to be my friend again? Don't be a fool."

"No, not at all. I'm not saying that. You misunderstand." Jafar took a deep breath, "I'm not talking about us. I'm talking about our children. How can I to stop them from being friends with each another? Do you think I haven't tried? I'm getting old, just like you, I'm going to die one day, perhaps sooner, perhaps later, but if I know anything it's this: when I'm gone and I'm dust, do you think our children will ever stop being friends even for one day, do you think that our goray children will stop and say 'He was the enemy of my father and I'm therefore his enemy'? Do you think they'll ever say, 'We went to their house but they never came to ours'? Do you think they'll ever care? Tell me, Ajmal, tell me, because I really want to know if you think they ever will keep our izzat like they ought to?"

Ajmal considered Jafar's words in silence.

Finally he replied, "No, I guess they won't." It was the starkest darkest truth he'd heard in a long time. *Yes, our goray children will disown their heritage the moment we touch the earth of our graves. They'll pile the earth over us and keep the memories of us locked away so they can do whatever they want without sharam stopping them. It's true, our children have no understanding of izzat and they never will.*

"Ajmal, look outside. It's raining. When it rains do you shout at the heavens and say to Allah, 'Why's it raining?' No, you get your umbrella and you open it."

"And your meaning?"

"It's quite simple. The friendship of our children is inevitable. I can't stop it even if I wanted to stop it. We can stop each other, but we can't stop our children, so I want to finish all the bad blood we have spilled between us. I want you to know that I don't see you as my enemy any longer. I see you as the father of my daughter's best friend. And that's that."

Ajmal considered this for a long moment. *He's not asking to be my friend, just to not be enemies. But, isn't that the same thing?* Ajmal decided that perhaps it wasn't. *A truce, he wants a truce. Why not? What have I got to lose now? And Sorayah's left him.*

He nodded slowly. "I've spent long years, working hard to secure my future on the Curry Mile. The road hasn't been easy. If I'd probably looked at the future instead of the past I may have been in a better position to… " Ajmal's mind wandered to his immediate problem. He saw Shokat in his mind, a hovering worry. *I have no true successor. What do I do?* Then, "Why don't you sit down? Would you like something to drink? Imran, get your uncle something, he must be tired, he's come all the way from Cheadle Hulme."

"Wilmslow Road," Jafar informed him.

"Yes, yes, Wilmslow Road."

Imran poured Jafar Ali a glass of water and left the room with his mother in tow.

The two men sat and talked about their families and their businesses. Through the door's glass porthole, Ajmal saw Imran outside, chatting amiably with Javed. For once he wasn't surprised.

Jafar Ali had left and the room felt empty. He felt strangely relieved. He didn't fully understand why Jafar had come. Something gnawed at him.

Imran entered with Mumtaz. Ajmal was anxious to see his other children too. He missed Shazia and his grandchildren. He missed Shokat's children. He suddenly wanted to see them all, he wanted a thousand children around him calling him granddad.

"Is everything okay?" Imran asked and Ajmal nodded. Imran sat down. There was no idle chatter. He lay back and contemplated the ceiling.

As the visiting time drew to a close, Imran got up to leave. Ajmal told his son, "I want you to tell Shokat to come and see me tomorrow with Sorayah. I want them together. Don't forget." Imran nodded and left Ajmal with Mumtaz.

A sound awoke Ajmal. His wife was pouring a glass of water. "Do you want some water?" she asked.

"Yes." She handed him the plastic container. His hands were shaking slightly. "Where are Sorayah and

Shokat?" he asked.

"They're outside with Imran."

"What are they doing there? Why aren't they in here?"

"They were talking and I didn't want them to disturb you. They might have woken you up."

Ajmal grunted. "Call them in. I need to speak to them two. I don't want anyone else to come in – tell Imran to make sure."

Mumtaz called in Shokat and Sorayah. They entered looking anxious. Mumtaz sat down on the chair near Ajmal.

Shokat and Sorayah asked how he was, but Ajmal raised his hands impatiently, "Sit down and listen." He paused. "I created my business from scratch," he began, looking each of them straight in the eye. "I made it what it is today. I have a dozen restaurants and I'm a multi-millionaire, there aren't many Pakistanis who can say that! I get personal calls from the General Musharaf, do you know that?"

They watched him in silence.

"Shokat, I've chosen you to take over the business." He let his words hang in the air for a moment, letting them sink in. "I may not live for much longer," he raised his hand to stop his two children from interrupting. "And I need to be sure the business is safe." He looked at Sorayah. "So I'm asking you, my daughter, to help your brother in this venture."

Sorayah remained silent. Ajmal was surprised at her coolness, her distance. *How can she turn me down?*

"I want Shokat to take over, but he can't do it alone, he needs you Sorayah. It's the most competitive market in the world. Shokat's going to need people he can trust."

Sorayah shook her head, "I can't, Dad, I'm going back to London."

Damn her! How can she be so selfish! Why can't she see that I need her?

Ajmal raised his finger and waved it at her, "No, Sorayah, you know where your life is. It's here in Manchester. Promise me, you'll look after the business with your brother after I'm gone."

"Abbu, don't talk like that. You're not going anywhere. You've got the heart of a lion, remember?"

"Promise me you'll stay. How can you say no to me? I'm dying."

"I can't."

"Then I'll die with a broken heart." He closed his eyes for a moment, and frowned, feigning pain. He opened his eyes and saw the concern in her eyes. *Excellent.*

"Abbu!" Sorayah looked away. Shokat was looking even more anxious than before.

"You'd walk away from your family and leave the Kohinoor and all the other restaurants to disappear? You know, without you, Sorayah, the Kohinoor would never have existed. It would be just a dream. You thought it up, and now you're going to go away again? You've really broken my heart."

Sorayah was looking out of the window.

"Sorayah, listen to your father," Mumtaz interrupted. "Your father wouldn't ask if he didn't really need you."

Ajmal smiled inwardly. He couldn't have wished for a better champion than his wife at this moment. He'd observed the growing closeness between Sorayah and her mother. He calculated it was something Sorayah wouldn't want to lose. Not in a million saal.

Shokat hadn't spoken once.

Ajmal sensed Sorayah sliding into his trap. *She can't get out of this without turning her back on us again. And she won't do that.* He felt as though dice were being thrown, the endgame of a long and drawn-out kaid. He started coughing again and Mumtaz handed him a glass of water.

Sorayah finally spoke. "Okay, abbu."

Ajmal was exultant. He felt peace descend on him.

"But only on one condition."

Ajmal smiled indulgently, "Of course puttar, what is it?"

"That I'm in charge."

Ajmal was shocked. For a moment his vision blurred and he didn't see Sorayah. Sorayah coolly looked back at him.

"Well?" she pressed.

He tried to stop himself from smiling, but couldn't. "Okay, puttar, you're in charge." *At last, one of my children actually has the Killer Instinct.* He beamed at her in pride. Then to Shokat, "I know she's younger than you, but did you hear what I just said to your sister?"

Shokat nodded once.

Then to his wife, "Mumtaz, you are my witness, I'm handing over my business to Sorayah, and listen, just as there's only one sun in the sky there can only be one person in charge, but you, Sorayah, you have to work with Shokat. You must be like a pair of hands. One hand must always let the other hand know what it's doing. Do you understand?"

"Of course abbu," Sorayah said. She was trying to hide her glee, but Ajmal could tell she was delighted. *Oh, how heartless she is. What a fine daughter I have!*

"Shokat?"

"Yes, abbaji," Ajmal heard Shokat say. He looked relieved.

It was evening and darkness had descended on a cold and wet Manchester. It was the seventh day of Ajmal's stay in the hospital. Sorayah had already installed herself in his office and reported to him daily allaying all Ajmal's fears. She behaved as if she'd done it all her life and he realised that she had. Shokat had happily accepted the new status quo. He couldn't imagine him contesting the title with Sorayah. *Perhaps it's better that only one of my children has the Killer Instinct. This way they won't tear each other to pieces.*

Later that evening, Ajmal awoke out of a storm of a dream, opened his eyes and saw Mumtaz and Sorayah watching him. They seemed to be standing on a beach and he was lazily drifting further and further away. He looked at his daughter for a long moment and smiled.

He closed his eyes and never opened them again.

"Abbu? Abbu?" Sorayah was shaking her father, but he wasn't moving.

"I'm sorry, miss," a nurse said, "he's gone. I'm really sorry."

And then the tears started, sliding down her face, surprising her in their suddenness, in their completeness, as if the whole world had died and she was the last person on earth, witnessing the end of everything. Her tears turned to sobs and she was racked by a pain so fierce it burned all her memories away and left only her and her father, before a long, wet inhale brought her out of the darkness and into the light.

She felt the arms of her mother and of Imran. Even through her tears, she could see her abbu, his eyes closed. He looked so calm, so peaceful. She refused to believe he was gone.

"No, he can't be gone. He can't be."

Then the rest of the family was there, hugging and weeping. She held her father's hand tight, as if trying to bring him back. His hand was already cooling in hers. She sobbed his name.

"Sorayah," she heard Imran say.

"How could he leave us?" she asked, guilt coursing inside her.

"Don't, Sorayah," Imran begged her.

She felt Shokat's presence and then the doctors and nurses were coming in, bustling around, edging the family away.

She knew she had to let him go or she'd go insane. And then somehow she knew that her abbu had died content. She finally understood that at the end her father had found tranquillity. Despite all the arguments they'd had she'd loved him more than anyone else in the world and then the peace he'd felt at the end found a place in her heart and she let go of him and let the hands of her family pull her away.

24

It was old and the sun was a speck of saffron in the sky. Sorayah watched the men throwing earth into her father's grave. She was sitting in the warmth of the Mercedes with Shazia and Yasmeen. They didn't speak. Sorayah felt numb.

"I think we should get back," Baji Shazia said.

Sorayah nodded. They'd have to return home soon. The Butt household was filled with mourners and she had a duty to welcome them in.

Shazia drove.

Sorayah looked back. She saw the distant figures of Shokat, Imran, Basharat and Javed among the others at the graveside. Then Southern Cemetery disappeared behind them.

At home, Sorayah helped out in the kitchen. They were preparing for the khattam. It was the first such meal to take place in the Butt household. But everything felt wrong. She crept into her father's room. It had been left untouched, his suits left hanging. She sat down on his bed. *Abbu's gone.* She still couldn't believe it.

He'd contained so much life inside him, so much energy and passion. Jafar Ali's plot tasted like ashes in her mouth. *But he extended the hand of friendship at the end, didn't he?* She despised what Jafar had done in tricking her and her father, but she forced herself to let go, she didn't want to spend the rest of her life chasing the shadow of vengeance.

Early next morning, she went to the graveyard with her family. Ammi, Shokat, Shazia, Imran, Bushra and all the children made the journey. Only Basharat wasn't there: he'd left the previous night on a trip with friends.

There was no tombstone to mark her father's grave. She placed the bunch of flowers at the head of the mound of earth. They stood around the grave, cupping their hands and praying in the sighing wind. Sorayah stood for a long time after everyone had returned to the cars. She wished her father could hear her. *Don't worry abbu, the business will be safe with me. Kasam.*